GOODBYE

Other Books by the Same Author

Novels
THE LAST HOURS OF SANDRA LEE
THE CAUTIOUS HEART
THE LOVING EYE
A BED OF ROSES
THE FACE OF INNOCENCE
THE BODY

Collected Short Stories
AMONG THE DAHLIAS
A CONTEST OF LADIES
LORD LOVE US
A TOUCH OF THE SUN
THE PASSIONATE NORTH
SOUTH
SOMETHING TERRIBLE, SOMETHING LOVELY
FIREMAN FLOWER
THE STORIES OF WILLIAM SANSOM

Short Novels
THREE
THE EQUILIBRIAD

Essays
AWAY TO IT ALL
BLUE SKIES, BROWN STUDIES
PLEASURES STRANGE AND SIMPLE
THE ICICLE AND THE SUN

Miscellaneous
WESTMINSTER IN WAR

Children's Stories
IT WAS REALLY CHARLIE'S CASTLE
THE LIGHT THAT WENT OUT

GOODBYE

William
Sansom

 THE NEW AMERICAN LIBRARY

GOODBYE

I

'So my wife is leaving me.'

On a grey mid-morning in late September Anthony Richard Merrydew Lyle stepped from the verandah to the lawn of his London garden, muttered these words with a bitter little whistle, and winked at a robin perched on the wall.

'And not for the first time,' he told this bird, adding: 'You're early this year?'

It was evidence of a slight unease that he addressed the bird at all. Usually he frowned on this orange-chested follower, with its sharp sergeant's eye, who used him simply as a worm-turner. Wherever he worked up and down the garden the robin would follow and perch staring at him, head to one side, at a time when he liked to be alone. If he dug his fork into the earth and left it for a moment, there the bird would be, sat on the handle. If he shooed at it, or disgraced himself with a wild flapping of the arms, it would fly in a sarcastic half-circle and come to rest again on, say, a hollyhock, in the belief that this was a tree. The bird even hurried him, in his capacity of jobbing earth-turner, expressing impatience simply by the constancy of a morose, knowing, beady eye. Expletives died unheard. A rendering of *Who Killed Cock Robin* had not moved it. But now here was Lyle talking to it as if he had no other friend in the world, even trying to draw its attention to sounds thumping out from a window above their heads.

'You'd think she was really packing up, wouldn't you? Bonk goes a suitcase! Clickety-click-click—those are

7

her venomous heels! But I'd say she was really taking it out on the cleaning, the old doing-round, eh?'

No answer. The bird was plainly deaf. He moved out along the path to where a chestnut showed a few spiked fruit fat and green among the first yellowing leaves. 'Only four years ago I'd be helping young Tom throw sticks at them,' he said, 'and now he's probably having it off with a tart in Macao or some place. I trust I'm not addressing a lady?' he added to the robin.

Conkers to charlies, in four easy years. How short those years from thirteen to seventeen—but how long for those in them! Next thing he'll be second mate and married, the bloody fool.

How had last night's row started, how on earth? How formless such quarrels were, hour-long bickerings, long strings of words unremembered, sudden snapshots of a sneer, a stamping exit; the closing in of a cold, outraged stomach.

A new sound struck the air. A voice singing. A baritone on a gramophone, from a window over the wall.

> '*The days themselves are dying fast,*
> *Summer and love are past,*
> *Farewell, my love, farewell.*'

Old, scratched, echoing to a muffled outmoded orchestra, sad out over the September garden, out and fading to nothing somewhere by the first falling leaves at the garden's end. He looked upwards, a warm southerly wind was blowing a low grey cloud blanket across the sky.

> '*Already as in a golden dream*
> *I see two others standing there*
> *Among the roses:*
> *How can my lonely heart descry*

8

GOODBYE

That they were you and I,
Were you and I?'

Heavens alive, bird, where on earth did they dredge that one up from? Haven't heard it since I was so high—where? Pier? Summer, seaside, sad evening?

'See how the wind begins to blow—
Summertime was long ago,
Already long ago.'

They could scarcely have chosen a more suitable accompaniment to dear Zoë thumping her temper out upstairs. He looked round the garden and thought: How desolate, all ending, all going, the wreck of summer and the echo in this old song of all summers past, all life wasted and gone.

Particularly now in watery late September, a time perhaps remembered from childhood as marking the awful empty end of summer holidays. Not yet the blaze of autumn, no drama, but the remnant of all green things shrinking and tired, dying stalks, dead flowers. Tall hollyhocks stripped and leaning, Michaelmas daisies pale and white-leaved, a few chrysanthemums straggling overblown, the Virginia creeper on the turn, greenish red like a messed-up metal, verdigris and rust. How desolate, and the sky so grey! None of the deep black sleep of winter, no buried pause. Such was the hour of the stacked deckchair, the wet windblown shingle, the hour even in this seedblown metropolis when the swallow is off and the sun declining, warmth gone. And he in his paunchy grey trousers, his old pullover and his thinning hair—was he gone to seed yet?

No. Presentable when polished and a bit tanned, lean enough man of forty-five, plenty of go, executive in bond

9

department of active merchant bank, holding down a good screw and making a bit extra on the side when in the know. But thinning on top, and wouldn't it have been better to be manager? A broad brow and brown hair, grey eyes blank and snaky, either sad or dangerous, lips long and thin and pressed together, which again you could take two ways, determined or ascetic.

> *'The time has come, the ship must sail*
> *I clasp the rail, my heart beholds*
> *Our summer island sink away*
> *Into a sea of grey.'*

Not bad really? Summer island . . . sea of grey . . . and not the first time those words had balladed forth from such a very window. What of all the Edwardian years in that brown Victorian house? Surely many had sat just there, at a rosewood piano smelling of mice, and soulfully moaned? And where were they now? Gone, gone with the mice.

> *'Farewell, my love, farewell.*
> *Farewell forever.'*

No doubt, thought Lyle, he would shoot himself before the morning drifted into lunch. Damn September, damn Zoë, damn all rows and the time they wasted. It would be Savory-next-door's gramophone, it was like Savory to collect such frayed and passé music. The other windows next door were shut—it could only come from Savory's basement hidden behind the garden wall.

But must get *on*! And with what? Too green still to clear the garden, too late to plant anything—but why not set about what all the summer had been postponed, straighten the end trellis and crop these lime-branches, slash the saplings? He took the easy way out and wandered over to have a look at the compost heap.

The row had started with the Leamingtons, the Leamingtons had been in for a sherry and on their withdrawal he had allowed himself that most perilous luxury, a sanguine and clinical comment. When asked by Zoë how he thought Sarah Leamington had looked, 'Empty,' he had said. In another mood Zoë might have leered or laughed. But she had been thinking deeply about Sarah Leamington, and his remark had insulted not so much Sarah as the depths of her reflection. 'Empty?' she had said, abruptly cold. And then, *then* he should have denied himself, but he had not, he had felt an awful strength of sherried calm come swelling through him and he had said:

'A recital of how your good Sarah Leamington managed the appalling journey from Great Missenden to London, with the full schedule of trains and buses and the eventual price of a taxi-cab, together with the itinerary of the cab, followed at a considerable tangent by her expedient views on apartheid taken straight from a daily rag well known to be lucratively invested in South Africa—'

'She's been there. She should know.'

'Oh, my God.'

So it had begun, he should have seen that Zoë was concerned about the 'something' which Sarah had brought in with her, the dress and the hat and the far-flung air of one who has crossed seas and continents. But he had not. And so a bitter argument had not so much developed as spun round in giddying ellipses, they had in turn shouted and kept deadly silent, she returning again and again to one early point as if for the first time, he struggling for logic with badly bruised bitterness, and so on for hours and in the end she managed to get him raving and repeating himself while she relapsed into studied coolness, deftly turning him into the woman and assuming a male air herself, until finally she slammed down his supper (cold) and went upstairs only to come blinding down again with the time-honoured words, 'I'm going to leave you. I'm fed to the teeth.'

Said before. Not often, once, twice, three times over the years—but a phrase which would take a night and half a day to get over, a phrase that lifted it all from tiff to row. Indeed, he felt uneasy this morning—real meaning always rang ominous within the meaninglessness, as with the difference between one swear word and another, both simple words, one not so simple.

When he got to the compost heap there was nothing much to do, he looked it over and then turned again towards the house, remembering to limp a little as he got near. A sizeable square white mid-Victorian house, four bedrooms, the property of Him, man of solvent means, and with a Her inside it. So he went very quietly in and through to the front.

Along the street he saw George Chalcott-Bentinck washing his car, and limped towards him. Saturday was Daddies' Washday, there were daddies out all over the place washing their cars and wearing the odd sporting clothes that went with Washday. On other mornings the street seemed to be full of milk vans. A nice broad street, planted with unusually old cherry trees. Wonderful white blossom in spring. The houses were mostly square Victorian houses, detached or joined, some built of brown brick, some plastered cream or white, two painted grey and blue, and at one point a russet burst of three new-built Georgian houselets, each, it seemed, more garage than house. The grey sky flew past the upright chimneys of all these immobile homes like a false sky back-projected in a film.

'Morning, George. My wife's leaving me.'

Chalcott-Bentinck straightened up and smiled.

'Oh? Good show.'

'Suppose it'll be the South Seas for me now—Tahiti and all that hula.'

'Did you have words then?'

'A few. But they're said to cement the long years of matrimonial togetherness, are they not? Where would we be without the stimulation of a few words now and then?'

'Passion's policemen, old man.'

'Ha, but in pretty plain clothes? I say, you'll have to shine those hubs a bit.'

They stood back to survey the silver hubs. Then Lyle added, rather to himself: 'Turned me into a woman while she was at it.'

Chalcott-Bentinck's chin dropped. This was outside the usual round of wedded wit. He turned his face stonily away, pretending not to have heard—and fortunately saw an intense spare figure in blue tweeds bouncing athletically far along the pavement.

'Hello, isn't that your friend Powsey?'

Lyle looked. 'We're a close-knit little community.'

'He's turned off.'

'Not so close then. By the way, I'm going back to the office on Monday.'

'How well did they stomach sick leave for a ski-ing accident in late summer?'

'My dear fellow—it was very near the truth. The ankle really was weakened by that fortunate Swiss smash-up back in February. Better to say I resprained a Swiss-sprained ankle—to say "tripped over rogue colander in kitchen and strained ligament" hardly sounds dignified, if even male. It's a clever man who takes his annual holiday in the snow and extends it with a week or two in bandages: I've simply extended the extension. It's better now, though, dammit.'

They chatted on for a few minutes. Bentinck went on rubbing at his car. Watching him, Lyle felt guilty about his gardening—but again he felt anxious as he turned back towards the house. It was so free and friendly in the road. Zoë was as yet this morning an unknown quantity. They had breakfasted separately, he had been 'sleeping on' for a few days while his ankle was repairing. He had his own small bedroom, a result of Zoë's periodic sleeplessness and night-reading: they had first tried twin beds, then developed this sensibly into separate rooms when Tom at seventeen had gone to sea. Still, there had been no 'good morning' this morning, no lathered pecks in the bathroom.

Sulking is stuff for children; it must be surmounted. But as he mounted the stairs to see her and brazen it all cheerfully out, his steps slowed, he paused uneasily to pick at the corner of a picture frame. Gold paint needed, but what colour gold? Whenever anything in the house needed mending, there was always this kind of complication, always a choice and a decision. He went on pausing and picking, though he knew quite well it was an excuse —the little bit of white plaster had showed for a good two years. He even managed a little argument with himself that this was not really an excuse, that *sometime* something had to be done about the frame, and perhaps this was the time—and, as guilt so often serves sin, the argument itself served to further his delay. Then with delight he heard the door bell ring.

He went downstairs at a trot—but on light feet, mustn't be caught by Zoë halfway up—and opened the door to see whom but Hodgson the long-awaited plumber! This doubled his relief—it is a standing household rule that nothing, whatever it is, must stand in the way of a plumber. So he hurried Hodgson round to the leaking kitchen tap and Hodgson took one short appraising look and told Lyle he must turn his water off— much as a sea-captain might take in tide-race and wind velocity before barking some casual decision to the discomfited landsman. Together they went down into a cellar hung with cobwebs like a fishnetted nightclub, and found the dew-beaded tap sitting on its long lead snake. 'I'll have to go upstairs and tell her,' Lyle thought. 'She'll turn a tap on, and then it'll be my fault.'

So he crossed the hall again to the stairs, rehearsing how to break the ice. Perhaps a disarmingly humble touch?

'Really am so sorry about last night. The water's off.'

Not quite right. Perhaps, then, a breezy:

'Pax, eh? *That's* right. Everything in the garden lovely? By the way, there's no water.'

No, some sort of bridge was necessary, a certain hum-ing and ha-ing, even an embrace and perhaps even her last word, which must be swallowed—Hodgson perhaps needing him. Or why not just ignore the trivial little tiff altogether, rise above it, sweep in as if nothing at all has happened? Simply a bold:

'The water's off!'

But that sounded too much like the arrival of the fire

brigade—he would have to say it with a real big smile. Could he smile? And wouldn't it sound like something he had cooked up? You simply don't smile with such news. Damn the woman, she'd just have to find out for herself if she wanted to be so difficult. He turned back from the stairs feeling he had won a point.

When he got to the kitchen, Hodgson looked him straight in the eye and shook his head with professional wonder:

'My, you've got lovely water,' he said.

It was no more than a plumber's simple tribute to the flow—but Lyle felt cheered. It suggested a smooth-run, Arcadian establishment. It was Lyle's house, it was Lyle who paid the mortgage interest, and it had lovely water! He nearly turned back to the stairs, automatically propelled to announce this ridiculous piece of good news—when the doorbell rang again.

This time he was clever, he cleverly stopped himself going to answer it—the bell should pull *her* downstairs! Down she would come and together in the hall they would knock into each other, and in the very abruptness of so casual a meeting all would be made easy. It might even be the fish, he could offer to take in the fish—'I've got Hodgson in the kitchen'—and in the general flurry, with the fishmonger as a genial third party, he might even *drop* the fish. How about that?

The bell rang again. He could still hear her banging things about upstairs. Was she making too much noise to hear it? He waited, then put his head through the dining-room hatch and saw through the hall and front windows the back of a man in painter's overalls leaving. It was Jenks! He ran for the front door:

'Jenks, Jenks!' he called to a white leg already disappearing into a little red van—how quickly they moved!—and had to yell once more before the leg began to extend again and drag out Jenk's shoulders and curly red face.

'I thought you wasn't in, I rang and rang.'

'I was!' Lyle called. It came out with an odd ring of pride. Jenks was as important as the plumber, more so in fact, since he was an itinerant odd-jobs man and had at last come to erect a lean-to for Zoë's bicycle. Zoë, in defiance of the all-consuming petrol engine, had suddenly in middle years taken to the bicycle.

Jenks measured up a space by the side wall with a deftness which brought admiration from the master standing by. How much they knew, with what decision they went to work! 'Frame you with two-b'-two and your roof bitumoid, eh?' the man asked.

Lyle could only nod gravely.

Then he was called in by Hodgson, then out again to Jenks, then in again to have the water on (all clear!) . . . and so the morning went by, helped on with a routine search for pipe-cleaners, glasses, matches, and long consideration of a door knob which had been wobbling for eighteen months—would Jenks have time, was it advisable to draw him off one operation to another? Jenks had by now sold him on a concrete floor and cedar walls—the damned bicycle had doubled its cost already.

So that it soon came to be lunchtime and he found himself standing in the dining-room with some sense of virtue, of works accomplished, as he listened to Zoë's movements now in the kitchen. He could not remember what he usually did at such a time. Probably nothing: but the charged air—was he charging it?—made him feel that some sort of action was needed. However, it was somehow impossible today to yell into the hatch through which for years they had shouted at each other.

The trouble was that Zoë usually made up a quarrel first. Her woman's practicality had no patience with long hours of sulking resentment. Besides, silence was against her nature. Yet now she put down two plates of kedgeree, already laded with vegetables, came round from the kitchen to place these on the table, and sat down without a word.

He took a quick look at her. Her lips were not pursed. There was no sign of a too straight neck. Her ease made him the more uneasy. Something had to be said.

'Kedgeree,' he said.

'Yes, kedgeree,' she answered.

Silence again.

He put down his fork. A sacrifice had to be made, defeat accepted. He put forward his head and said with a naughty facetious little smile:

'Good morning, darling.'

She looked up blankly, smiled casually:

'Is it?' she said.

Better! Battle to be lightly joined? Light banter of lovers reuniting?

'You seemed,' he said brightly, 'to be having quite a time upstairs.'

'I was just getting a few things together.'

'Oh.'

'It's of course quite a business to figure out what I'll need—indeed what is yours and what's mine, after all this time.'

'You have the advantage of me?'

18

She looked at him calmly.

'I told you last night my mind was made up.'

His stomach fell. What great confection was this?

'About what?'

'I said I was going to leave you, dear. And so I am.'

So this was to be a full-scale upset . . . hours of complicated argument lay ahead. It would be comparable in its way to earlier upheavals—like the time she had decided to buy a caravan for holidays, followed by a postbox full of prospectuses, hours and days even spent inspecting the terrible egg-shaped machines themselves, and all after a while subsiding into delay, stalemate, dismissal. Perhaps such eruptions were necessary. Life's keel too even? Dreams to be given the material test?

But she had said 'dear'. It was a tenderness that terrified him.

'Oh, come off it, Zoë.'

She raised her dark eyes and stared through him, only looking at the thoughts inside her.

'My mind's made up,' she said. And went on placidly after a pause: 'Eat your kedgeree.'

He attacked the white mass with a violent dredging of his fork: 'I certainly will.'

And went on with his mouth full: 'You're just cooking up a great scene. The day'll be wasted. Tomorrow too no doubt. I hope you remember the Bucketts are coming to Sunday supper? You'll just exhaust yourself shifting whatever you're shifting. It'll all have to be put back.' He pretended then to yawn. 'Or is there a secondary reason—you've probably wanted to get at those cupboards for years.'

She was very quiet. 'The cupboards were turned out this spring. No, our things are extricably mixed. I'm just extricating what is absolutely personal, mine, and one or two things you may have bought but which I've a claim to after all these years. Suitcases, for instance. The books'll be a bother.'

'Suitcases?' he said, seeing the landing piled with old cases with their locks broken.

'Naturally the man of the house supplies such things. I'm not asking you to return all the food I've cooked for the last seventeen years, am I?'

'Eighteen.'

'So you're conscious of it too?'

'What?'

'Oh, nothing. Why talk? Though I suppose we'll have to. Later, though, later . . . I must get an hour, I didn't sleep. . . . Cheese? Fruit? You know where.'

She was so restrained that for a moment he almost believed it—and went through a series of selfpity, fury, loneliness and even an abrupt rise of love for her, a lump in his throat. But the daylight, the plates with their knives and forks, the gleam of furniture, the long dark yellow hang of curtains reassured him—people simply did not act like this. Why, she would be talking fast and endless, pacing even . . . and there she stood now waiting a moment lost in thought, picking at nail varnish.

He watched her with curiosity. Funny cow. Attractive still. Why her, not others? Had her particular make-up some unanalysable, inbred influence over him? Dark hair growing in such a way that she always seemed to be 'shingled', whatever her hairdress—something to do with a long straight neck? A skin slightly yellow or brownish, that would in some be called sallow, yet with her more 'oriental'. A planter's wife touched with years of the sun and perhaps a slight osmosis with the natives? A bit chalky on the arms, perhaps. Eyes with a glint of blue to the whites: gipsy? Humorous mouth, wide smile,

teeth very straight and long, regular as piano keys.
Strong devil in her way. But delicately boned, elegantly
slim, looked wrong carrying a suitcase.

Still, such appearances are not unique—what about
character? Phew! You could tick the points off on your
million fingers. Take a simple instance, take her heart, it
would look on close observation something like a fly's
eye, a mass of facets—one minute throwing beams of
sunshine, the next dark bloody murder. But you could
never call her temperamental, not in the operatic sense.
Here was more a gentle sway, an incessant to and fro,
an infernal hammock, a dangerous ocean. Garrulous?
Yes. Taciturn? Yes. Considerate? Yes. Thoughtless?
Yes. So it could go on.

How can you define a fairly normal soul? Only by
exaggeration. Pick on her obsessions? Pick on her
periodic outbursts to change the house round, make the
dining-room the sitting-room? But you must place
against this the long months of quiet. Pounce on the fact
that she worked once a year wrapping parcels for the
undernourished? Deduce from this a fundamental guilt:
tie it in cleverly with that avid scrabbling at nail varnish?
With the adulteration of clocks—keeping them five
minutes fast to save last-minute rushes—and with the
watering of drinks? No, no. It gets out of balance. You
are more truly faced with a variable human being, made
up of capacities rather than characteristics, and even these
are slowly changing all the time.

He finished his cheese and took an apple out into the
garden. But one characteristic wouldn't change—she had
studied at a university and done well there, or been well
done, for out of her mouth forever after could come blasts
of sudden logic sounding creepily from a wool of womanly
light-talk. Baffling illuminations of the awful complexities

within, her tongue's a red light, he munched to himself, then threw the core into a clump of chrysanthemums. It knocked a head off. Damn, can't waste it—now I'll have to pick a vase full.

Past the remains of a herbaceous border, sad detritus overblown with grass, September stalks at all angles, white mildew shrivelling and ill growth of Michaelmas daisies, willow-herb casting scythed beards about everywhere. He turned his face away. Depressing to be reminded of a summer when everything had been green and strong, irritating to see the result of sloth, too little weeding, too little squirting. He coupled the two together and felt himself to blame for the decline of summer. Why had he not planted dahlias—bright dahlias for September? He walked past it and through a rustic trellis which cut off the bottom of the garden (ramblers with grizzled brown heads uncut, hips like green apples), through into bush and compostland, undemanding land, of its nature derelict. It was a safe place. You could light a bonfire here without a second thought. Might as well pitch a tent and stay till it all blows over.

The trouble, if you got down to it, was inconsistency. What a man likes more than anything in the world is consistency—it can be seen in every phase of life, from political conviction to a toothbrush propped back in its proper glass, from a neatly concluded cigarette (something attempted, something done) to the soul-salving arrival of a train on time. But the need for a consistent framework has one even greater importance—it forms a point from which to deviate, with which to play and laugh. Without it, void. Yet the only consistent thing about a woman is inconsistency. Do I mean 'a woman' or do I mean 'her'? Or is hers a different kind of consistency, regular but on a different frequency, something men cannot understand, like those high sounds only certain animals hear?

The problem was interrupted by a voice sounding from over the wall.

'Basement-alias-studio-garden-flat-30A calling Number 32. Pippip pip. Over.'

'Lyle here, L London y yellow l lousy e enteritis,' Lyle intoned over-distinctly, 'I am receiving you clearly. Over.'

'Reporting weather closing in this side. Wind S.S.W. Low cloud. How's things?'

'Oh, marvellous. Don't you just love September? The slanting sunlight, leaves all poised to turn to gold? By the way, got my robin?'

'Hello Lyle L London. Cannot make out your robin.'

'Damn, you're right, she's lurking here behind me all the time.'

'Whose bird's dad worked at Pinkerton's?'

'I say, Savory, if you don't mind a personal question, and I know you don't, what does my wife look like?'

Eight foot of brown brick wall separated them. In earlier days, long after they had met socially, these neighbours, two men strolling alone in their gardens, had heard the crunch of a footfall, a cough, the dead ring of a spade, and not known quite how to communicate. Once Lyle had queried, 'Is that you?' And a female voice, not sure whether it had been addressed or whether Lyle was talking to someone in his own garden, had burst into nervous song. It would not do to risk that kind of thing. So they had evolved a little game of radio-calls. It helped them, in any case, to talk. It was un-nerving to communicate through a wall, without holding, say, a telephone in one hand. Though sometimes they did even telephone each other through the wall, ringing the changes.

But now there was, for once, a perplexed silence. Then from Savory:

'Not receiving you very well. Over?'

'I mean, I know Zoë so well I can't see her any more. Know what I mean?'

'No.'

'The image is blurred. It's called love. But a stranger carries one or two clear photographs in his mind. If you saw Zoë coming down the street—what would you say?'

'Excuse me am I right for Hammersmith my flat's round the next corner.'

'Seriously.'

'Don't you think she looks that good? She's a fine grown-up girl, man.'

'Girl. That's something. Over.'

A short pause. Both men stared suspiciously at their piece of wall, at bricks, at mortar tunnelled with the holes of grey spiders webs, holes within holes where the monsters stood waiting to spring. Both men held their separate breaths. A picture of Zoë had indeed asserted itself to Savory. Dark woman, yellow as old sunburn, handsome but eyes a shade too close together, as if she was staring at you through binoculars. Wonderful teeth. When she had bent over to pick up that awful dog of hers, Mange, there had been shown a memorable buttock, suspender-belt outlined like a Palladian pilaster, reticent chiselling bursting with pure form.

'Lyle L lover-boy? Pip-pip, didn't mean she was a girl. She's a woman, she's intelligent too, you're a lucky man. Signing off now, repeat, signing off.'

'No, don't go old man!'

Savory was thinking, Zoë's amused mouth slightly opening and a dark glint of delight in her eyes at some abstruse pleasantry of his which normally might have needed explanation. On several occasions. Over-intelligent. And then the time he had made a thumping error, enough to make his remark quite pointless—yet received the same amused reaction from Mrs Lyle. Her timing, at least, was perfect. Now why didn't this limping husband stuff his embarrassing questions?

'Hear Schuler—the *Farewell*—out the window this morning?' he asked to change the subject.

'I certainly did. Happy little piece.'

'Curious song. Generations of musicians refused to play it.'

'I can see why.'

'No you can't. There's some good odd reason. Either it's connected with some forgotten disaster, or latent in the ballad itself. Like Gloomy Sunday and the suicide epidemic.'

'Starting one of your collections? Lethal music?'

'Thinking of it.'

'God help us.'

They chatted on. Overhead, trees stretched rurally. Ample gardens lay to either side. As everyone said, it's just like being in the country. Yet only ten minutes from Oxford Street! Owls boomed their way throughout the nights, traffic hooted quietly from a muffled main road. There spread above the two men, at that point in the wall, a large old prunus with long yellow leaves like fingers of gold against the grey sky, delicate long fingers in golden doe-skin gloves. Or crispy gold French fried potatoes, as you wished. It was easy to romanticize in such gardens. So Victorian, they all said. Yet in the Victorian time of their building those same trees had been prim and newly planted, and the walls staring with bright unweathered yellow brick as in any new suburb today.

Lyle crept closer to the wall.

'Father, I have sinned,' he whispered.

'How come, my child?'

'I need sanctuary. What are you doing tonight?'

'Glueing myself to the telly, child.'

'May I join you?'

'You speak in mysteries. But any time after eight.'

'I'll be there, Dad.'

Turning back to the house, Lyle stopped, as he always stopped, by his best bed, a riot of thick green geraniums whose big-leaved co-operation encouraged him to weed and trim with fervent success. The immaculacy of this one bed both excused and exposed certain delinquency in the others. It was always thus a pause of love-hate, congratulation and guilt. But today his attention moved elsewhere, his ears were still trained on the upstairs windows. And sure enough there came that thumping again. She was up and at it. It was to be a long, exhausting campaign. Conclusion: I shall have to keep myself scarce. I cannot stand a brooding house. I shall be reading books upside down, my un-nerved fingers will knock little ornaments off tables.

Thus he did more gardening and clearing that afternoon than would normally be done in a whole weekend— hoping that from time to time she might see him bent on these virtuous equable tasks. Furthermore, he took his string bag out to the nearby shops and returned with a blight resistant, a spray for thripps, and various new stocks—cigarettes, even rock-salt, for winter with its ice lay ahead. He derived pleasure from constructing for the future, while Zoë wasted her time dismantling.

GOODBYE

When at last at seven o'clock he re-entered the house, the dog Mange was standing in the hall with bowed head, his ears hanging lower than usual. Soon be ice-balls on those lugs, Lyle thought. 'How-do, Mange-boy? Feeling hangdog? O-o-oh—luggage, eh? *They* know when mistress go travelling *they* know. Was his mum-bum going out of her mind den,' he whispered, 'you miserable beast?'

The dog wagged, morosely, its whole long behind. Lyle glanced up the stairway to the landing banisters— a furtive look, a boyhood's night-glance reversed. A leather strap hung down from between white posts. From a trunk? My father's old black thing? What *is* going on? Better go up and face the music. This can't go on forever—or, of course, it largely could?

He placed blight resistant and rock-salt on the floor by the disconsolate dog, and mounted the stairs at a run. Leaving me to make it up, making me into the woman, eh? Well, here's Warmheart on his way.

But at the top he stopped stock still amazed. It was beyond a joke. The entire landing, was blocked with suitcases, trunks, boxes, packages, piles of clothes and linen, and many a separate item, like her sunlamp, their electric kettle. A small pile of books stood by itself. He went at these savagely—as might be believed, *his* Byron, *his* Life of Jane Digby, both long discarded by him but her passion, all rights assumed by default. For a moment he forgot his errand in a fury of injustice done: but then heard her in their bedroom and stepped forward, paused, took a further step, paused pretending to himself a suitcase had stopped him, stepped over it and with a deep breath found her.

Her sleeves rolled up, a grime of dust up her arms, one hand up to brush back a tousling of hair as she turned and said evenly, as though nothing much were happening:

27

'I was looking for you. Your bedroom's straight enough. I've put some cold food out downstairs. Open a tin if you want some veg. I'm not eating.' And went on to place a painted ivory fan on a mahogany writing-box, and these on the bed.

He looked round the room again amazed. Pictures off the walls, white squares already like ghosts of the past. 'I—I—' he stuttered. 'You're going too far!'

She shrugged, smiled a little. 'Far enough,' she said, and carefully laid two vases on the bed. They rolled together.

Suddenly sorry for her: 'Zoë, darling, you really mustn't—let's make it up, look'—and he could hardly help a grunt of a sigh—'I'll help you, we'll get it all back in no time—'

But now she did stop moving. And she was looking sorrowfully at him. Or sorry for him?

'Tony, I'm *serious*. Can't you see?'

'But then why—why ever?'

She shrugged, looked from one window to another, curtains undrawn, glass black with new night.

'It's all over. We're not what we were. We just go bumbling on with our separate lives side by side. What's the use? There must be something more to living than this. Now Tom's off there's time to think, really think about things. Well, I've thought. I'm thirty-eight.'

'Bumbling? Some people would call it companionship.'

'And love?'

'It is. Proper love, the backbone.'

She shook her head. 'No, Tony, no. It's all dead.'

'What's dead? We kiss, we joke, we see people together, we sometimes sleep together.'

'The latter's changed its character. The former—what else can you do?'

'My God, we have *rows*.'

'Too many.'

'They show we care. They stimulate, you used to say.'

'Used to. It's the quality of all these things. Ours has become a marking time.'

His warmth went, he felt she was turning it all at him.

'You marked time pretty well last night,' he grunted.

She looked at the ground; put a hand on her hip, making an elegant slim figure, good broad shoulders bearing thoughtful downcast head. Then slowly, like a lesson to a child:

'I'm leaving you. I'm young enough to get a job. Others have. And I have my little income.'

'So we're the victims of solvency? And what about Tom?'

'He's a sailor. He'll have two ports to come home to.'

'Don't joke.'

'You know as well as I do he's out-grown us. He's affectionate, that's as far as it goes.'

'Even if you're in China, a home's a home.'

'You know perfectly well how much I love the boy. And the most important thing—suppose we *are* considering him—is to show a properly happy face. Not a half-face.'

He slammed out of the room.

She could just stew in her own mad juice. He wasn't going to play.

He spun round and shouted back:

'I suppose you expect me to pack a suitcase and go to a hotel?'

Again the even, almost tired tones:

'I've already told you your bed's all right. It's I who am packing.'

He nearly yelled, 'You'll be sorry when you pack it all

back'—but stopped himself, it would put her on the defensive and only delay things: already she was going to absurd lengths. He almost believed she meant to leave.

At least—she might go through the process of leaving, go off simply to frighten him? He would have to plead in the agony column, become a heartrending initial. Only, it had all started from such an ordinary run-of-the-mill row; if she were in earnest surely this was too trivial an occasion? Yet there was always the spark that sets off a long brooding of gunpowder?

Downstairs he pretended a kick at Mange, and made for the drink cabinet. And my God I deserve one. But stopped, and poured orange juice and soda, and tossed this back like a beaker of rum. The sprained ankle had suggested a good chance for a fortnight's diet. He would keep to it. Nothing would affect him. Resolution fortified him like a drink; but then, as if alcohol indeed possessed him, he lurched into the sitting-room and knocked over a small table. Damn her, damn her, damn her!

Bless her heart, she might be having a pretty dull time of it after all? Tom gone? Don't suppose I'm all that much of an inspiration nowadays? Suppose I've declined into set ways. Take too much for granted. It's in line with a most humiliating phenomenon of marriage, its awful way of reproducing, there in your own home, all those husband-and-wife jokes in the funny papers, one after another—sickly smile at new dress (cost?), spring-cleaning, deckchair versus lawnmower, male head buried in newspaper, the lot. Once he had found himself coming in late after a business dinner and taking his shoes off in the hall. He had quickly slipped them on again—it was going too far. But then had tripped on the untied laces in the bedroom, retrieving himself only by grasping a swing-ing cupboard door as if indeed this were a lamp-post.

All right then, pep up things in future? Theatre seats, week-end in country, umpteenth honeymoon?

At the word future he felt for the first time a question.

Her words were still there. Marking time, dead between us, half-face. Said with such—what, exhaustion? Resignation? He looked round him startled. She couldn't really mean . . .?

When was it they had the Change?

All certitude dropped away, he stood there alone looking round the room, which had suddenly died. Dead chairs and a dead sofa, no fire in the grate, no sound at all and the windows glassy dark. One lamp too heavily shaded. What could ever happen again in such a room?

Even the sounds from above were stopped.

Mange strolled slowly in, scraping his long nails on the parquet. He stopped at Lyle's feet, squatted down and put his chin on the floor.

Nothing more.

Alone there, with only the dog, he felt the colour leaving his face.

II

HE sat in a yellow-lit room facing Savory's blue television screen. They sat side by side, the two chairs placed terribly buswise.

From half-past eight until now, nearly ten, they had watched forgettable things and not a word said about Zoë. He kept stealing a sideways glance at Savory, rolling his eyeballs till they hurt. Could he ask the man to turn it off and have a talk? And would this fellow, whom he did not know too well, be a useful, even a wise confidant?

Savory was in advertising, a copy-writer with dabblings in the film and television branches. To Lyle he represented the Arts. Certain mild eccentricities underlined this peculiarity. For instance, who else would have brought home that Schuler record? And he collected drainpipes. Not indeed the pipes themselves, but photographs of unusual pipe infestations on the sides of houses he encountered on his way about. He had unusual views. He was a Thinking Man. His job, broadly, was to influence people. Psychology! And he was a bachelor.

Unfortunately this evening he was in a too spirited mood. He kept jumping up and playing with the instrument. During a short play photographed dully in a pale office, he turned on a flickering dazzle with one of the side knobs. *Much* more dramatic! With a comedian telling a long story, he turned off the sound altogether. You see? The man's a natural clown! An operatic singer was allowed to sing dumb—a kind of pneumatic medical chart, Savory said. And when a Minister came on for a political speech, he dubbed in a song in Dutch from the radio. It seemed to fit.

So Lyle had to sit dispirited and confused, ashamed that he had run away from his own house, writhing with forced laughter, yearning to tell. It had been beyond him to say: 'Look, I'm in trouble.' When suddenly Savory turned the set right off, and said casually:

'Well, what's on your mind?'

'What?'

'You don't often come here humouring me. And you don't seem to be finding me very humerous.'

Lyle felt naked without the television. Chairs, bookcases, tables sprang up all round him—private apparatus making this man so much more a stranger. For the first time he realized that what he had to say might sound pathetic. And this stranger, a tall man looking suddenly much taller, was looking straight at him, waiting like a doctor: he saw him very plainly, as indeed one sees a doctor—the outline of a tweed suit, a jagged collar with one end sticking up, long legs with big shambling feet turned inwards. Black-grey hair with a forelock tousling a hard white face. Small dark eyes under a boxer's brow. A mouth full of short discoloured teeth. Into all this Lyle took the plunge, shutting his eyes and going in sideways.

'You're a bachelor,' he said.

'I am.'

'It may be difficult to—'

'Don't say you've got a ripe old daughter up your sleeve? All for me?'

'Men don't for some reason talk about it.'

'What?'

Savory was plucking away at a loose cuff-button. He, too, was uneasy. This made it so much the easier.

33

'Know anything about the Change?' Lyle asked, over-casually.

'You mean . . .?'

Lyle nodded darkly.

A pause. Savory snapped the button right off. He looked at it with suspicion.

'No,' he said.

'I think my wife's having it. She says she's leaving me only she's only thirty-eight.'

'That's—that's awful.' Savory put the button in his mouth and bit it.

'It's too early.'

'Is it?' Savory said.

'They have hot flushes and feel very queer and of course the curse goes on and on and they know they can't have any more children and it's psychologically upsetting.'

'Mmm.' The man was frowning hard and tossing the button from hand to hand.

'Some of them go a bit mad,' Lyle said.

'Yes. One hears vaguely—'

'That's just it! Vaguely! What do we *know* about it?'

'It's sort of very seldom talked of, I mean.'

'One can see the whole thing. A great physical change leading to a desire for other kinds of change. A new life.'

Savory nodded. Lyle spread himself more easily in his chair. Savory was really most helpful.

'But surely you'd *know*? With the—I mean?' Savory said.

'The psychological symptoms may precede the physical. Anyhow, she just can't leave me. Just like *that*? People simply don't do it.'

'People can do anything,' Savory said firmly, spoiling it all.

He held the button between forefinger and thumb, quizzing it. 'But *can* she do it? Private income? Relatives?'

'A very few hundreds a year. They didn't leave much. Except a damned great old barn of a place near Gosport. Sold it at a fine profit. Police training college. I suppose she could get a job too.'

'Police Training College?' Savory said with interest. He put the button firmly down on a sidetable, and said: 'Change is out, you know. Far too early. Could be, but disregard it.' He looked up from the button, suddenly sly, his eyes looking very small, and said: '*Cherchez l'homme* if you ask me. Not that I mean to suggest anything—but, any suspects?'

'Zoë?'

Lyle smiled. He shook his head.

'Quite sure?'

'Oh, no.'

'No she wouldn't or no she would?'

'You don't know Zoë. Quite out of the question.'

He laughed easily, and found in mid-laugh his lips were stretched wide and dead as a dummy's lips. Savory squirmed in his chair, making a large angular pattern of legs, slumping down in pretended ease as he tossed the button high with nonchalance to mutter:

'It's been said before and we all know it yet it's hard to speak openly—but what woman isn't a woman to herself? I mean, we don't know our own selves, do we, let alone the woman in a woman, even wife. I don't want to disparage—'

'No, no. Of course not.'

'But there must be a *reason* behind all this. Let's say you don't suspect anyone. Right—but think round it—something might occur to you later, some suspect you

35

don't suspect—otherwise, what alternatives? Any madness in the family?'

'Ha!' Again a laugh that ended too quick. 'No more than any other,' he muttered.

What was all this? Adultery? Madness? One moment he had been living an ordinary life, picking squashed greenfly out of his thumbnails, catching a morning tube and coming home again to a well-known female figure settled in ripe love and liking, a pillar, a sort of wife-sister —and now all those big words, black as headlines, grey as a judge's wig! Absurd. Yet how else do they come to anyone? Heralded by trumpets?

He was being tapped at by the button. Savory's eyes were doctoring at him, policing him.

'Oh, madness—I mean neurotic symptoms. To me, you see, you seem like any contented couple. Never known either of you go off the deep end about anything. But what goes on inside? What don't I know that you must know? I mean, has she strange ways? You know her.'

Know her? Indeed. Or do I only half-know her? Attribute my own motives to her actions? Have I ever, or lately, bothered to discover the *real* Zoë? My God, screen blurbs following close on headlines—stop the drama! And who is this apparently real fellow here come to that? Not a friend—an acquaintance. Close neighbour. To whom I've run, as being the easiest port from the storm in my own tea-cup, tea-urn.

First met Savory when we banged fenders. Squeak-bang-crunch in the night, under May lamplight through cherry-leaves starring the avenue. Gracious tarmac, I'm safe! Nose on dashboard, wet sniffle of blood, wipe blood no let it stay looks dramatic—and then in the lonely night-avenue, no witnesses, temper risen to address whomsoever had done this to me, get my word in first, strike hard, and then this tall figure swaying to the window and holding up his hand, No no don't say a word, my fault absolutely, absolutely my fault, terribly sorry, and *smiling* with it. Took my breath away, took to him from then on.

Found we were neighbours, not unreasonably since it all happened slap outside our front gardens, and both of of us had already slowed down averting what might have been worse—and slap away he asked me in for a drink here in this very room smelling of bachelor and yellow with light from chrome parchment shades, dry with oatmeal folkweave and dirty deal and dusty with books and African masks and all his other things. Photographs of drainpipes, dressmaker's dummy with glaucous doll's head, lamp of Greek marble, old bicycle wheel inset over round mirror on wall, see yourself through bars he said. But I liked him instantly, honest and generous. Bit of a character, of course. Yet now what do I really know of him? What's inside this biscuity-tweedy smell of man, windows shut?

'Take another matter,' the button tapped. 'There's your boy gone to sea, gone away a good six months. Do you think she'd perhaps been waiting for this? Six months being a reasonable period to make the break-up look less abrupt?'

Could he be enjoying this? Me sitting here relieved only to be talking to someone—and is he making me enjoy it too? All this button-tapping motive-finding makes it clinically interesting—but in its way less hurtful? The very detail puts it all at arm's length. He'll be asking me for symptoms of antimony poisoning next.

'How's your own health been recently?' Savory said.

'For God's sake she's no Borgia, she's just a lower upper-class housewife—'

37

'You mistake me. I mean, have you been up to her?'

'Oh . . . people at our time of life—it comes in smaller bursts—'

'No, I mean the old night out? Do you take enough trouble over her? Posies? Questions about her inner self? They like that. It's called understanding.'

'We've been—as usual.'

'But is as usual enough?'

Had he been letting things go? Must one strive on through middle years on bended knee, bouqueted, the eternal suitor? Hadn't marriage settled that? Was there never to be any relief?

'Excuse me.' he said, getting up and going to where curtains hung across French windows, 'mind if I look out?'

Savory half rose, still cross-legged in the knot he had tied of himself.

'At your own risk. There's a mob of very large spiders pressing against the glass to get in. They come wobbling across like coffee tables.'

'Dumb waiters.'

'And they're all speckled.'

'We've got black ones in the coal cellar. Camouflage.'

'Clever devils. But in every cellar and cupboard you find their webs, all with the bones of a male hanging on the fringe. Who'd be married to a spider? Er, that is—'

The green balloon of a tree halfway down the garden was floodlit by bedroom lights from his own house. Across this now summery-looking backcloth of leaves a giant figure crossed like the shadow of an aircraft.

'One of ours,' Lyle said to himself. He walked outside. A pink neonlit sky proclaimed all the vast rumbling bright energy of the West End: but close to hand was the old garden mystery smelling of home. Two worlds—home and away. He felt the return of all those forebodings which an hour with Savory had alleviated.

As he stepped back, he spoke aloud to himself: 'I'm powerless.'

Two men alone, a dry place where nothing could grow. He caught for a moment the whole barren atmosphere of bachelors, the sordid company of books.

'I can't do anything,' he said.

'But aren't we just trying to find out a reason . . .?'

'And if we find it? She's like a wall. What am I supposed to do? Change suddenly—go berserk with rapier if it's a man—flood her with flowers if it isn't? Life isn't like that today.'

'Come, there are subtler shades of persuasion.'

'Not with someone who knows you so well.'

He suddenly banged his fist on the arm of the chair: 'Put yourself in my place!'

Then looked round the room and added quietly: 'But of course, how could you?' Again that room with its thirties functional furniture, its piled papers and its cheese-plate left balanced on two books, its smell of man and dust—again this brought the vision of a dry lifetime lonely for the colour of another voice. Yet when he had been here before he had thought: How snug and cosy, how free and comfortably male!

'Never been married, but I've had my associations,' Savory said. 'They all fell through one way or another.'

'Oh?'

'Either the girl left me, or—'

'But why? Why did she—they leave you?'

'Almost unexceptionally a simple switch to another man. They like to keep a reserve handy.'

'Oh.'

'Funny thing is—when it was me, I can never remember quite why. Not for another woman. Usually a simple falling away. Loss of interest. You know the moment of sludge after the old sex-act? Multiply that moment by hours and days—something like that. We're animals.'

'The girls don't feel that?'

'Expect so. That's when they call up the reserve.'

'You wouldn't put it any—er deeper than this?'

'Superficially deeper. It's all worked out on the surface as something else very deep. That's when the Human Relationships Department comes into play. You're found to have lack of understanding and so on: horrible habits, coldness, hardness, no sympathy, no *feeling*. Horrible habits are never so much as noticed until sex goes off the boil. Its the biological move that really moves. No case is alike, though all are bloody similar.'

'You're talking of affairs.'

'Some quite long-lasting. There's been, let's see, a three-yearer—she went off with a Pole in the end, fellow played the cello at her. Lovely girl too. Always reminded me of a seagull. Selfish as a seagull too. Still we all say that about each other. Then there was a two-yearer, I'm afraid I faded out on that one—too acquiescent, if I must be cruelly frank with myself. One likes a bit of a battle, I don't know why. Though you're relieved when there isn't, aren't you?'

Lyle again found himself sitting on the edge of his chair, too attentive. He forced himself into an easier position. 'It all seems suddenly so complicated.'

Savory gave him a smart tap with the button.

'Marriage. It has its complications, but it simplifies a lot. Live with someone and there's never that deeply settled once-and-for-allness. There's a deep and ancient sanctity in marriage. Tradition, mutual bond, patriarchal approval—you get something like it in a nutshell when you stand for the National Anthem. Out of date, the intellect says. But no—there's a satisfaction in it deeper than ordinary sentiment. Solidarity. Reverence. Okayness.'

'Why haven't you then?'

'A long story,' Savory said, and proceeded to tell it. For a good hour girls called Peggy, Sheila, even Oriana, came and went on the quiet air. No need to egg the man on. It was part confessional, part contemplation.

Lyle listened with growing interest. It fortified his male entrenchment. Here was the world of woman, mystifying, desirable, inconceivable. Soulful Peggy with the big generous mouth was a willing girl, all softness and love: but after a while it was like living with putty. She never demanded, always agreed—a spaniel of a girl. No, there must be conflict, Savory said. But not too much. Take dark and earnest Sheila. Profound opinions on everything, and a woman's tongue to state them: this organ would wag on far into the small hours but it was, of course, the wrong organ, the intellect dowses desire as efficiently as humour. One could only lower the earflaps and turn over.

And Ursula, butter-blonde and sweetly muscular, whose tirelessness on the tennis court was only matched by an inexhaustible rapacity in bed. Nothing could wear this good clean girl out. On the short term she definitely did you good—got the extra pounds of fat off. But for ever? Who marries his rowing machine? And then there was Spiritual Therapy, Therese indeed, whose cheerful-

ness and outright goodwill to all things bulldozed you
into a state of slaphappy kif. All's for the best always.
One got one's second wind and punch-drunk praised the
yellow daffodils with her, threw bread to well-filled
sparrows and of mortifying old age pensions took the
bright view, 'Well at least it's something, isn't it?' It was
relaxing for a time. To live affirmatively saves a lot of
trouble. But it couldn't last. Again no conflict, no
opposites. The minds of man and woman, Savory said,
are made differently and it is in the to and fro of these, just
like the to and fro of the physical act, that love best
prospers. 'Mind you, nowadays the conflict must be kept
mild, in tune with today's "reasonableness": and that
brings me to Liz and the question of companionship.'

The button gave a suddenly loud clack, it sounded big
as a roulette disc as Savory brought his hand down hard
on the table. He leaned forward and stared hard into
Lyle's eyes:

'Why don't I marry Liz?' he asked loud and mourn-
fully.

Lyle, confused by so many women, and in spite of his
interest by now a little soured that his own problems had
been put in the background, said rather shortly: 'How
should I know?' But quickly added, fearful of losing this
valuable new confident: 'You seem to have had a full
and varied love-life. How do you do it?'

Savory looked glum. 'Over the years, over the years.'
he said. 'Bunched together they sound a lot. But Liz . . .'
and he looked powerless and at a loss . . . 'we get on so
well together.'

'That's good, isn't it?'

'I can't find a thing against her.'

'Well then!'

'Of course, there are small things. She's too good at

wrapping up parcels. She can telephone two people at once. She's got a computer memory—names of about a million actors, how to cook a bloody Brazilian bean omelette, all the latest one-way streets. Gives me the deficient willies.' Now took the button up and bit it with his teeth. 'I say to myself—I'm the man of imagination. Why be worried by such practical trifles?'

'I know,' Lyle said. 'Zoë's rather the same there. But I rather like her efficiency.' Surely that would get them back to Zoë, their rightful subject?

But Savory went on, biting his words through clenched teeth on the button.

'No. It's because I'm a coward. I daren't say the word!'

Lyle rose. He had to go and look at that light again.

A sudden cry from Savory. He looked round. The man was staring up at him in amazement. 'God,' he said, 'I've done it!'

Lyle paused: 'You mean, you *have* proposed?'

'No you fool. Swallowed the bloody button. Damn the woman,' he swore. 'It's just like her. Now what'll I do? Ring the hospital?'

Lyle crossed to the French windows and saw that his house was now in darkness. He returned across the carpet on tiptoe. Why on tiptoe? Not to disturb her, in case she put the lights on again?

'What are they made of?' Savory was saying. 'Bone? Plastic? Might be anything.' He tugged another button off his sleeve and bit it. 'Bloody granite,' he said. 'Still, they're pretty small.'

Lyle wanted suddenly and desperately to get back to his safe darkened house.

'Well, old man, I think I'd better be getting along.'

Savory's voice was suddenly high-pitched:

'And leave me and my button?'

Lyle said hopefully: 'Expect it'll come out in the wash, you know.'

'How'll I know whether it's ever got through?' Savory piped. 'How'll I know it isn't wedged somewhere?'

'You might examine, you know—afterwards—'

'Don't be a fool. We're on to water closets here.'

'Take other measures.'

'The pancreas. It might even get into the pancreas,' Savory said thoughtfully. 'I wouldn't like that. No, better phone the hospital.'

And Lyle had to sit there while he dialled the casualty ward. The nurse the other end was Irish. There was long talk of buttons and stomachs. He was finally told to wait and see and report any later discomfort.

At last they said goodnight.

Lyle walked out into the night-deserted street. A cat moved swiftly along the pavement from lamplight to shadow, low on its belly like a large lizard. It was immensely lonely with this one cat and all the parked sleeping cars.

And what was he to do? The solution was no nearer. A difficult hour or two had been passed—that was all. He walked lonely towards his own gate. He tried to tell himself that he had only left his house for convenience, to avoid an unnecessary rising of tempers: but then admitted that really it had been fear of the whole situation. So frank an admission raised his spirits a little—he could face facts! And at the same time his mind found a further excuse—it was only common sense to sleep on such things. All would be better in the morning.

'Lyle! I say—Lyle!'

Savory's tall tweedy figure was gesticulating in the lamplight. It raised a hand to its mouth and bellowed a whisper across the few yards of night pavement.

'You haven't got a bedpan you could lend me?'

Lyle gritted his teeth.

'Sorry,' he called.

'Only for a few days?' the figure called.

'Haven't got one in the place,' Lyle said, and turned away seeing very clearly not one but two bedpans stored away in his loft. He put on his limp a bit and went in through the gate.

III

THE next morning was Sunday, a day distinguished by one or two small differences. They were accustomed to rise half an hour later; the newspapers were different; it was he who made the breakfast.

But when he went downstairs to boil the kettle, he smelled bacon frying already. He paused. The sense of doom to which he had awoken turned to one of danger. What was she up to now? And what did this break in the routine remind him of? Of course—expeditions, days out. When she cooked up an early breakfast while he carried things out to the car, rugs, baskets, golf-clubs. In fact, going away.

His eye caught the square of clouded sky showing through the landing window. Rotten day for a trip. 'Damn,' he said automatically, and aloud.

'Tony!' she called.

So she was speaking to him?

'Yes?' he said carefully.

Her voice called back with full ordinary morning energy. 'Your breakfast's ready!'

So she had relented? Relief made his whole body feel bigger. He had been cramped with nerves, like a man trying to hide away inside himself. Now possession bounced back. He decided to be cold, dignified. He descended the last flight of stairs at exaggerated ease.

He opened the kitchen door. She was busy at the stove. 'It's on the table,' she called.

He said casually: 'I thought Sunday breakfast was one of my small contributions?'

46

'I had to get on.'

'Oh?'

'I was up early anyhow. Slept badly too.'

'No doubt.'

Silence. She had not risen to bite. He sat down and knifed at a sausage whose end poured out like pink cauliflower. He would never have let that happen. Like any once-a-week cook, his own work at the stove was perfect, precise as a major surgical operation.

He looked up and saw she was wearing an old summer dress, presumably for work. Goose pimples greyed her sun-browned arms—the wind must have changed. He gave a little associate shiver. Her profile showed him she had not yet put on any make-up. Her hair was uncombed. Now she looked indeed sallow. Worthless, an unkind male streak said, all this trouble over a woman like that. But in the same second he was sorry for this.

The grey September light still coloured her morning disarray, and the thought came, more generous if equally overbearing, that this might be the answer. Poor dear, she felt she was finished. She must be miserable—she simply wanted to go away and hide! He felt now he could not ask her the questions he had in mind, those Savory had suggested the night before.

But just then she turned.

'Coffee,' she said and her eyes met his calmly and directly, not caring a jot whether he lived or died. She might have been wearing all the warpaint in the world.

He bowed his head and swallowed the sausage-end.

'I'm taking mine up,' she added, tray in hand.

He put down his fork.

'Are you going to enough theatres?' he said.

She stopped surprised. 'So you think I'm being theatrical?' And had got as far as the door, before he

stuttered: 'No. I mean, ought I to take you out more?
I feel I ought.'

'It'd be difficult. You'd have to commute to—hell, I
nearly said it.'

'So it's not that.'

'No.'

'Zoë, there's something else . . . I don't know how to
put it—but I don't suppose you've, to put it bluntly,
started the, well, the, you know, the—'

'Salt. I knew I'd forgotten something.'

'Change.'

'Zoë's soft brown eyes turned full on him, flickered,
brightened with amusement, as if a light had been turned
on behind them. She laughed the short laugh of women at
men's innocence.

'No, Doctor,' she said.

'I was only trying to help.'

'Salt. Help what?'

He looked at her astounded. 'Why this whole situation!
It can't go on. There must be a reason. There's a reason
for everything. Is there another man?'

Again a flicker of amusement. Her smile became playful.

'Well, now,' she said, 'that would be telling, wouldn't it?'

He looked at her hard. Could she really be playing at a
time like this? He could not be sure.

'You might as well say,' he said.

'But what would you do if you knew?'

He clenched his fists and muttered, suddenly angry:
'I'd . . . I'd . . .'

Beat her? Smash his fist straight into that man's
knowing face? Run the rapier through?

She was watching him closely. He unclenched his fists.

'I suppose the age is past for violent action,' he said.

He looked blankly at his bacon, the fat was white and cold. 'I suppose I'd be hurt. I suppose you'd become that much less valuable.'

The glint subsided, her eyes went vaguely to the grey morning outside the window.

'There you have it,' she said wearily. It sounded as if she was talking of something quite different; or of everything. She said no more and crossed to the door.

'Well *is* there a man?' he said sharp.

'Damn, I didn't break the top of this egg.'

'Is there?'

She went.

The kitchen subsided. Grey morning outside, cold bacon, cold toast: the luke feel of a stove turned off, cooling every moment. His own voice had almost convinced him that there might be a man in this affair. Alone now, he felt a hole in his stomach. Nonsense, he said, believing it the more.

He took a mouthful of bacon and toast, pushed the rest of the plate away from him—to impress whom that he had finished?—and stood up. Had there been signs? Who the devil could it be? That young Welsh window-cleaner, she's been a bit over-chatty with him? The Indian home-help, they'd both agreed how useless yet how beautiful he was—like a god: and wished he'd had eight arms like a god, four pairs of hands, ha ha ... Or the odd out-of-work actors they hired for weekly cleaning? But who could know with a woman her age? Or any woman, come to that? The stories one heard.

Standing there in a growing vacuum of ignorance, his mind tried to retrieve itself by ticking off their friends, no, no, no, it ticked, and this brought to mind the Bucketts who were due for dinner that night. He hurried out to the hall and called up the stairs.

'Zoë?'

Thump. Click-clack of heels. Same as yesterday. It was still going on.

'Zoë!'

'Yes, what is it now?'

'Will you ring the Bucketts or shall I?'

'Why?'

'To put them off, of course.'

Her face appeared over the banisters. She had made herself up, brushed up her hair. This appalled him. It seemed plainly to do with that other man.

'Why put them off?'

'With all this going on?' he spluttered. 'How can you imagine sitting with people . . .'

'Won't it be rather a relief?'

'Jill'll see all those trunks. Anyway, we can't just pretend nothing—'

'I'll say I'm having a turn out.'

'My God.'

'Oh, don't dramatize things so.'

'What? *What?*'

But he realized she was right, it would be a relief to have someone in. A lonely evening avoided. The very presence of these old friends might save the situation. Old friends, the lifeboat.

'Very well,' he muttered, and turned away to face the Sunday house. Already it had assumed an unlived-in look. Curtains hanging straight down, ashtrays clean, chairs sitting about as if no one had ever sat in them, even the carpets stretched waiting for no footsteps at all. Quieter on a Sunday, the sounds of traffic less. No workmen would call, nobody, no postman, nothing.

There was a sound of dull knocking, as if water had gone wrong in the pipes, an airlock. 'Something *else?*'

he thought. 'The long trail after that plumber again on Monday?' Then looked down at the quiet hall carpet and saw it was Mange sitting brown in shadow and thumping his tail on a piece of bare parquet. 'All right, you bugger,' he said aloud. 'Walkies. Do us both good.'

For after all it was Sunday morning and usually a time for energetic enterprise of some kind, if you weren't knocked out by the papers.

Joyously, in his way, the spaniel preceded him, weaving hairily to and fro with a centipede movement. Snatching up a lead, Lyle felt as always masterful: and this was a day when it would be no good kicking around the house, masterless there indeed.

Taking the dog for a walk proved a remarkably sufficient outlet for his energies. Action is relative, he even looked forward to dinner with the Bucketts, even saw the food itself with pleasure.

But then, as with the spaniel he faced the street, the brown houses, the grey sky, the tired green of the trees— it all looked as empty and purposeless as the house had done. There was Chalcott-Bentinck still washing his car. There was the red pillar-box, waiting as always. For years he had walked this same neighbourhood of streets. They now 'bored him to death': in fact, he was growing certain he would die here. More frustration. What about that golden stone house in Gloucestershire? What about the dream-villa on the Tuscan coast? Yet on a good day— liver, bowels, psyche in order—each house would blossom with astounding new interests, cornices, chimneys, windowed roomscapes he had never noticed before. He sighed and walked in the opposite direction from that man washing his car. No more jokes about South Sea freedom.

Yet were things really so serious? The whole situation was probably no more than vaguely restless—like the memory of a bad dream: life proper would resume itself later. Zoë was plainly having one of her crises. It was worse than usual, and this presaged an uneasy future, if from time to time such attacks should mount in force. He waited gloomily while Mange sniffed round the trunk of a plane tree rising magically from asphalt. He lowered his eyes away from the occasional passer-by; it would be intolerable to be asked the time, or a street direction. He was like a man full of his own illness, who thinks everyone else should be aware of this and not of their own daily lives.

Then a couple passed wheeling their hydrocephalic child: both the parent's faces were smooth and unlined with care, the legacy of years of gentle quiet devotion. He felt his own troubles shrink, and despised the smallness of the marital world.

Round a corner he ran straight into the flying figure, in his electric blue tweeds, of Eric Powsey.

Together for a few seconds they danced to and fro, blocking each other's pavement; but since they knew each other, smiling with all their teeth like joyful partners in that dance. When at last it stopped, greetings were exchanged. Like many oppressed or nervous people, who think beforehand that they cannot bear to talk to anyone, Lyle found instant relief in this new company, although it was only Powsey, and although Powsey immediately embarked on one of his obsessed theorizings:

'And how are we this fine grey Sunday?' he asked,

rimless octagonal glasses glinting against a skin gone dirty with a sunlamp. Behind the glasses lay small blue eyes of a three-cornered-looking shape, with pleading eyebrows above, as is fairly common in faces with prominent teeth. 'Her Majesty's prisons are full. Our welfare hospitals spilling over. There's plenty of war about. The exchequer blossoms on alcohol and tobacco, on keeping the nation poisoned. The man who gives up smoking drives a dagger into Britain's heart.'

'That's one way of putting it,' Lyle managed. 'Mange, stop eating that!'

'Many a gardener could do with such nutritious horse-do,' Powsey murmured. 'My kingdom for a pan-and-brush. You don't get much nowadays. Shall us sit?'

They were standing near an oak bench set back on the pavement. Lyle had never sat on such a thing before. It was meant for the aged, or for people without gardens. As a local householder he was superior to such benches. It had enscrolled on its back-rest: *Rest in Peace with Hislop James*. They sat down. 'It's also meant for people turned out of their homes,' he thought, 'those who know no other rest, Hislop.'

'Oh yes, we've all progressed all right,' Powsey went on, offering pink plastic gums against the tan. 'Look at sex. What you might call sex-in-the-open, overt-like, was meant to free, to *liberate*-like people's repressions, to get them thinking of something else. It's done the proper opposite. Nobody talks of nothing else—your paper, your book, your theatre, they're all full of it. The old animal comes out topside.'

Lyle caught at this, as a man itches to squeeze a spot. 'But how free are we sexually, really?' he asked.

Powsey glinted at him. 'Some are,' he said.

What on earth could this estate agent know? He

remembered that Powsey was forever scurrying round the local streets letting flats, selling houses. 'What exactly do you mean?' he asked sharp.

'I mean . . .' Powsey said, and then added with a playful shake of his head, 'I mean . . . no . . . no . . .' He smiled secretly at Lyle, wishing to be drawn on.

Could there then really be another man? Lyle was torn between fear of knowing and desire to be told. Even told by Powsey, who had always been a figure not to be taken very seriously. Powsey had effected the purchase of his house many years—fifteen—ago. And Powsey also had an intimate knowledge, like a doctor's, of a singular episode in Zoë's and his life together—when two years after settling in there had been a landslip in the garden, and a housewall had cracked to reveal many hundred pounds-worth of dryrot. Something had been wrong with the insurance: Zoë and he had had a tough storm to weather, and this had been a happy time, for, as with a war, adversity had brought the two of them closer together.

Yet Powsey himself was difficult to take seriously. Those bright blue tweeds, the tan, the rimless glasses, yellow shoes spongey with resilient thick rubber: it was a too precisely thought-out equipment. He ought to have looked like some offbeat sophisticate, say a xylophonist from the Argentine. But he ended up simply looking like Powsey, enthusiastic Powsey, with his peculiarly pleading eyes and five felt-tip pens in his outer breast pocket. A spry forty-year-old, a meat-eating vegetarian (allowance, one pound of meat a week to allow for nature's carnivorous teeth). Married to a jolly mouse. Full of patent learning and obsessive attractive theories. He was the victim of popular science, the digest, the idea-journalist. Not a flat-earther by any means, much nearer the knuckle than that—but usually half-baked, no leavening of horse-sense.

Yet now Lyle had to take him seriously, as he went on wagging a coy head: 'No . . . no . . .'

'What are you getting at?' Lyle repeated sharply, the emptiness growing in his stomach.

'That would be telling,' Powsey glittered.

Then abruptly he assumed an alert, efficient look. Licked his lips over a cleanly outlined jaw. Somebody had said that Powsey had a black plastic Aberdeen terrier on a little fringed mat on his television set during the day. At night, when the programmes were over, this dog and mat were exactly and ritualistically replaced over the set, in readiness for the next day.

'But since it's the Sabbath, and the taverns yet fermé—since we have nothing permitted us to do, partners in crime, but walk our feet off, why not make this the moment of confession? Why wait for the shades of night? Nothing against the hard light of day, is there? My wife's having a ding-dong.'

'Eh?'

Lyle was appalled, hit below the belt.

'In fact allowing for half an hour on the Greenline to Harrow-on-the-Hill,' Powsey added, looking at his wrist watch, which told the days and months too, 'and the traipse down the hill to Woodland Way, number fifteen A to be exact, they should be at it at this very moment. He'd hardly offer her a cupper first.'

'Good Lord!'

Powsey looked at him keenly. 'Why? I'm having one too.'

'A cup of tea?'

'No, the old one-two. Nearer in to London, though.'

'Oh.'

'Got her own flat. Fifteen-year lease. Nice and secure.'

Mange came up white-jawed and trembling, and sat down looking from one to the other of them, rolling blood-rimmed eyeballs upwards.

'Nor is it the first time,' Powsey went on enthusiastically. 'She's had affairs before, plenty of them. Mind you, she's no nymph. It's more like the healthy way to look at things, and not just look but *act*. A young plumber's mate, a feller in dry-cleaning—it's actually an electrical worker now who lives up in Harrow. See what I mean? No lah-di-dah—these fellers are men on the spot, right available, no introductions necessary. It started when we got Gillespie on Love-Play. Heavens, she said, how could I get up those antics with you, now, after all this time? I'd laugh my head off. Ah, I said, so you wouldn't if it was someone new? Then we had a very interesting discussion. Am I boring you?'

'No, no,' Lyle said.

'We took a decko at married life biologically rather than sociologically-like. She had to confess to unexpressed yearnings: after, say, a chance eye-up with some good-looking chap in a bus or shop. You're inhibited, I said. She said, But we're *married*! Look at it more clinically, I said. What you've got's no more nor less than a social tabu: and there's all your healthy animal instincts withering. You'll get cancer.'

'What?'

'Withering of creative cells. You go and try the next greengrocer, I said.'

'Greengrocer?'

'He'd like it, I said. Be careful though. There's the neighbours. As for me, you can trust me, I love you.'

Powsey paused for a moment, as if something had startled him. He put out a bright blue leg and pulled at a

sewn-in crease. 'A week or two after, she came to me and
said she'd done it! Some chap that sold encyclopaedias.
I'll say it now, I'll be frank with you, I was quite knocked
over! I'd never really thought. Yet now when I had to
think, I thought well it's my lifelong custom always
to put theory into practice—I don't go for hot air—
so I can't grumble. Good for you, I said. It was, she
said.

'And now promise me you'll have one too, she said.'

'And you did?' Lyle asked enthralled.

'Oh yes,' Powsey nodded. 'Though to be honest it
wasn't that easy. Our lady-wives have an unfair advantage
there. But I got my number one afternoon in Islington,'
he said, like a soldier with an old wound.

Our lady-wives! But it was impossible to listen to this
and think of Zoë in the same breath? And now people
were passing with prayer-books in hand and a church bell
had started tolling. Am I being sanctimonious? Lyle
wondered.

'Of course it isn't really the antics,' Powsey said. 'It's
the change that's beneficial.'

'But—' Lyle tried—'aren't you jealous?'

'We're careful. That's the whole point. Nobody
knows. So why be jealous?'

'But what about them together? I mean, she's yours,
your private love. They'd whisper together.'

'Oh, it's added to our happiness, no tie. This way
we're bound yet free. And you're not going to lower the
whole blessed state of matrimony to an animal act, are
you?'

'No. But—'

'What about the spiritual joys of companionship?
What about two minds that think as one?'

'For Heaven's sake, you don't believe that one?' Lyle

said rising. 'I thought the whole thing ran on the idea of contained conflict? Without which there is no stimulus?'

'Now that's very interesting, very interesting.' Powsey said, also rising, as for an extended discussion perhaps now on their feet.

Lyle found weird words coming from his mouth. 'Mange must go home,' he said severely, indicating the dog.

Powsey nodded, as if this were the most natural thing in the world.

'Well, it's been a grand jaw,' he said, smiling, his clean-cut chin stuck out. 'Though—' and a blind look came from behind the glasses—'I've never told anyone all that before. Mum's the word, Mr Lyle. I expect I *wanted* to be indiscreet!' he lightly laughed.

Lyle was already striding off, with Mange worming along behind, when Powsey shouted after him: 'Knew I had something to tell you! Don't smoke when you're employing one of those patent home cleaning-fluids. Fumes inhaled through a cigarette create phosgene. Pure phosgene . . . it's not right!'

Lyle waved and went on faster. Hounded out of home, hounded back to it. Hounded indeed, he swore at the wriggling rump now plodding on busily in front: but did people really act as Powsey had said? Was the orgy a way of life, as the press seemed to imply? The thought excited him. Freedom might have its compensations? He saw bachelor chambers; shaded lights, a Turkey carpet, a few brass and mahogany pieces and a valet, all at least forty years out of date.

GOODBYE

As he came to his own front-gate the pleasantly raffish picture faded. Gloom seemed to dowse his own real home in a special cloud. Dark windows shadowed an inner emptiness. Nothing good in there.

Framed between two trees, two limes that dripped a sooty honey-gum over the small front garden, making it a dead place of blackened privet and acuba—framed thus, the house itself stood stained as an old piano key by rain and fog. A few reticent decorations, cornices and a console or two, distinguished this squared-up façade from the hard affair a run-of-the-mill modern architect would have built. On good days, Lyle could survey his mansion with pride: It's mine and it's in pleasant mid-Victorian taste. But on bad days he saw it as just another dull example of early speculative building. And on very bad days, like today, it simply leered at him, a hulk of broken sashcords and venom, tattered and empty as his own wasted life: the same life upon which, on a fair summer's day, he would contentedly congratulate himself.

He tiptoed in, as into a ghost-house, sliding his key quietly, hurrying Mange in a whisper. Silent in the hall he listened upwards. Like the concierge of a small hotel, he had learned over the years to identify most of the sounds made in rooms above: now his head swivelled like an old stag sniffing scent, and placed her in the spare bedroom—on the linoleum by the window! A regular swish-swish meant cleaning—he heard her bracelet knocking against something. So cleaning was proceeding, too? This suggested permanence. Or was she only fulfilling some housewife's obligation, intent on leaving the place honourably shipshape? Upon which she could congratulate herself?

He hurried quickly through and out to the garden to

see if he could see from there whether it was cleaning. Sure enough the lowered plastic venetian blind was snaking about in an unusually horrid way. He stared at it a moment fascinated. It wriggled and swallowed and sloughed itself, like a roll-top desk gone mad, a rutting python—Zoë's unseen hand was hard at work. But unseen eyes behind it too? He nipped quickly back and under the verandah.

A spade crusted with dried earth, a burst bag of bonemeal, a large terra-cotta planting-pot stood round accusing him. He stopped thinking about cleaning. Instead he found an image of her upstairs, among luggage, dressed in that old summer dress, and remembered when it had been new and he had been packing for their holiday—three, four years ago? A striped dress, satisfactorily in the old sunblind tradition yet with smart up-to-date colours of toad and kingfisher, a dusky firefly dazzle. How smooth her dark skin, how polished her black hair! Gold at her ears, and that whole broad-shouldered slim figure moving about like a fashion model, elegantly sexless at this time of tickets and packing, yet soon to relapse alluring before a sparkling glass in an airplane seat. How touching she had looked as she counted things, inwardly absorbed, like a child with its first sums! How preciously in need of his protection, worrying about the flying weather!

How easily too the years used to drop away as they set forth together in new holiday clothes, ticket-happy, the mortared life of London left behind, the winey sun ahead! Where was it to—Rapallo, no, that year to Gardone? The cold lake water. Freezing stuff down from the mountains but fat lemons all about! And then that memorable Italian couple with rice on their heads—fat and rolling and loving, rolls of silkbound flesh and oil-black hair, middle-aged man and wife and bottles of silver-bucketed *spumante* in a rose-hung arbour, all teeth and laughter, pouring risotto over each other's heads and crying Rice, rice for the Love of God and Our Blessed Anniversary . . . what a wonderful mess, and the waiters all laughing and bringing more rice to bless the wedded bliss.

Lyle smiled to himself and thought: Must remember to remind Zoë of that. And then remembered how empty that arbour had looked for the next fourteen days, for the couple had motored away, and this was an odd thing often with holidays, you arrived at a weekend with things going on, and the next day the weekenders have left, leaving the place thenceforward uneasily empty, making the first night a dream of somewhere else. And then he remembered he could not of course now talk to Zoë about it, and made a dive for his secateurs.

He stamped down the garden and attacked a clump of mildewed Michaelmas daisies, withered, white as Mange's jaw. Damn her, they'd been so happy, what was different? He scattered long stalks behind him, swinging like a furious grey-bagged threshing machine. Nothing was different!

His mind grew clearer with physical action. Nothing was different—and adding it up, what was really happening now but nothing again? Of course she wasn't leaving. He was simply driven out of his mind by the frustration of not being able to do anything about it.

No one could manage such a situation. A blank wall. Only to be dealt with by waiting. Meanwhile the only people he had talked to had supplied no solution, but instead revealed their own absurdly inconsequential lives—Powsey, Savory—oddly enough, both love-lives. Or not so oddly, associatively induced by him. Well, it would be a refreshing change to talk this evening to his old friend Buckett.

He finished off the mauve daisies and carried the stubble to the end of the garden. Make a fire. Trapper Lyle searching for dry twigs, man of wide-open spaces. Then back to attack the slack green gloves of a fig-tree. Hack, hack, snip, snap—Big Bully Lyle went about savaging all over the garden. Quite a mound of burnable stuff grew on his pile. The exercise freed him, his chest grew stronger. He decided not to lunch, partly because now and then he had a recuperative fruit-day, partly as a punishment for Zoë. And sure enough, at some time well past the ordinary lunch hour, she appeared framed in the French windows and called: 'I've put the cold meats out. We'll be having hot tonight.'

'I don't want any.'

'You must eat something.'

Concern for him? No, habit. Habit learned in the nursery from some old nurse telling her that everyone must eat to make their teeth curl. She would have said it to anyone. He had once even caught her saying it to Mange, who scarcely needed such encouragement.

'Nothing, thanks.'

'But Tony, you *must*.'

'Too busy.'

That was good. Two birds with one stone. Showed he was off his food, starving. Showed he didn't care, other things on his mind. She stood for a moment more, undecided. He wanted to stay and taste his victory, but had to turn away to play it to the end. The end was a whole branch of buddleia. Bloody fool, he thought, seeing the cut branch in his hand—wanted to keep that one, she's got me rocking again. And then abruptly his inside gave a great gulp of loving towards her, still standing there at a loss, and in that dear striped dress. He turned again, but she was not there at all.

For a good hour he hacked on, the garden took on a satisfactory cropped look, and he went to get dried grass and leaves from under a bush to start a fire—only a soft townsman would have stooped to newspaper. Then he sat down to rest on the old garden seat, green paint faded to a dead nostalgic blue. The sky still raced grey overhead, as it had done all morning: yet there was little wind at garden level, and such a colossal flow above seemed to have little relation to reality, where was it coming from, whither going? Just a monstrous flying fuss about other worlds, like masses of migrating Chinese, nothing to do with here. He sat on for a few minutes more.

'Hello? Is that Mr Lyle's residence? One moment—I have a call for you.'

Lyle shrunk into himself. Surely he had been quiet in the last few minutes? He sat rigid, not daring even to turn his head, in spite of the eight-foot garden wall.

'Come on, I heard you—all about rubbing two Boy Scouts together to make fire.'

So he had been talking aloud to himself? Certain compulsory sentences repeated themselves when he went about manual movements—when he told himself to 'shut the door', he would always add, *Je t'adore*, making this sound like 'shut the etc.', and saying it over several times.

'Busy,' he said to the wall, and walked back to the big prepared wood-pile.

'Wrong number?' Savory's voice complained. Then: 'Seriously, Lyle—there's news! She's out!'

Lyle stopped in his tracks. Zoë out? A big single drop of wet fell on his forehead. He looked upwards for a bird.

'Out?' he croaked. And to make sure: 'Out, caller?'

As he stood there waiting, the first rain drops hastened into a patter, the bushes crowded with whispers, and so did his well-prepared bonfire.

'We need no longer fear the future! She came smilin' thru, old man—bright as a button, you might say.'

Lyle swore.

'I'm very glad to hear it,' he said, and then shouted: 'Must go now!' running towards the now sodden pile of stalks. 'Rub-two-Boy-Scouts—' he muttered, striking a match.

The sheltered dry tinder crackled richly, flames flickered, hot blue smoke went up. Lyle watched anxiously. It was more than an ordinary gamble, he wanted deeply to achieve something. But the flames sank away, died. From the sodden pile a thick white wet smoke lazed out like a fog. He turned on his heel and walked back towards the verandah, abruptly sick with hunger. It was three o'clock.

On the way he glanced up at the bedroom windows and saw Zoë's profile pass, then pass again. To and fro she went. People seen alone through the windows of their rooms take on a quicker motion: no sound, no known purpose to slow them. He thus had the impression she was hurrying. Her figure caught the grey September afternoon light, the darkness behind made her look like the subject of some long-ago photograph. Alone in the weathered white façade, this one domestic figure, absorbed in the present yet seeming to do with the past, saddened him. Like a little boy, he thought, put out in the garden . . . his own mother and the maids of those days had looked like that . . . and Tom, had he stood here and looked up at Zoë, his mother? How precious and how pathetic this continuity of the generations! He wondered where Tom was now. Somewhere off China, the Philippines perhaps. Those slow ships got about so.

He stole into the kitchen and popped a slice of cold beef into his mouth. For want of something to do he saw boiled lights on the stove, and began to cut these up for Mange. They had a sick, boiled, dishcloth smell. When they were hot on the stove, the steam inside them piped painfully, a last expiring cry of the castrato bull whose living lungs they once had been. How could one touch a dog which ate such things? Absently, he put a thick sliver into his mouth and chewed hard.

He leapt back, spitting it out, and at the same time trod on Mange's paw. Mange crashed back yelping against a rack of tomatoes, which rolled red all over the floor. Still spitting, he slithered on tomatoes. Ever to eat a mouthful of lights by mistake had been one of his nightmare apprehensions: now he had, and it marked the day with final horror.

Whatever he did would go wrong. He was rattled and accident prone. If he licked an envelope, it would cut his tongue; a cellophane packet would tear off half a finger-nail; an important letter would fix itself to a blob of marmalade on the bottom of a tray, and go kitchenwards for good; the lavatory chain would come away in his hand. He hurried from the dangerous kitchen. The slight shudder of his footsteps slid a sliver of lights off the draining-board down on to the plughole of the sink, covering this expertly, so that a dripping tap would later try to overflow: and the same footsteps trod tomato pulp and pips across the hall carpet to the cloakroom, where he wrestled with a macintosh whose sleeve was inside out. The belt slid unnoticed to the floor. He left the house billowing like a khaki bat.

This time he walked fast away from his immediate streets and across a traffic highway to where a small asphalted park lay. The rain had stopped. It had showered just enough to dampen everything: but the puddles at least washed the last tomato off his shoes.

Youths were playing football on one patch of grass, cricket on another: it was that sort of intermediate time, a shapeless time of change. Moodily he watched the football bounce on to the cricket pitch, where it was well-fielded by a batsman who whacked it back with a bad soggy sound. At another time he might have laughed: now it only seemed intolerably messy. Was nothing straight and clearcut in the world?

Certainly not a blue-uniformed military band, inferior musicians of an undistinguished regiment, who sat under their green-painted cast-iron canopy and ground out crippled waltzes from a long dead musical comedy. He walked away from this.

A Salvation Army cluster began a brassy hymn a street away—caught between, he heard both sounds horribly merged under the blowing, sodden clouds. Soon a church-bell would start its dustbin tolling, an Irish tenor come moaning along in midstreet—he made off back to his own district, among people walking stiff and Sundayly in light overcoats among shuttered shops.

Over most of Europe, he thought dismally, this was a time of laughter and food and finery. The Catholics order things better. Those old licentious popes had their point. He could not even buy anything—there was not even that simple means of self-assertion. At least Powsey was not abroad. It suddenly crossed his mind that the reason for Powsey being seen so often walking alone was not after all his estate-agent's duty but simply that his wife was absent with another, and so he had nothing better to do. 'I'm in the same boat,' he muttered, 'I'm like Powsey.'

So it was that when he returned home he decided to snap out of himself, bath, dress up in a clean shirt and his newest suit. This decision was hastened by sounds from the kitchen—Zoë was preparing supper. The field was clear upstairs. Also, those oven sounds had a comfortable ring of usuality. And when he got to the upstairs landing, he was astounded to see no trunks and suitcases about. So all had been stowed away again? The long march back to normal had begun?

He turned on the bath, and went to his room to put links in a shirt. He paused for a moment looking vaguely round the room. Something, he felt, was missing. Yet everything seemed to be in place—his bed-side table with pipes, aperients and bottles of phlegm-cutter; his ivory brushes, his framed photograph of Tom in uniform, his other pictures—those damned racing prints which had followed him all his remembered life from flat to house to house, disliked but part of an unbreakable tradition. Carpet, curtains —he even checked on these.

Then he suddenly saw—the long plush-framed photograph of Zoë's family house in Hampshire, since a police college, had disappeared! He had hung the photograph because it contained an intriguing example of the twenties scene, a garden group in cloche hats and Oxford bags, a gardener standing aside with his watering can, pogo-sticks lying about, and the ivy-clad red Victorian mansion behind to lend a feeling of light novels of that time. He had often complained, why go back to the Edwardians? They still had it pretty good in the twenties, it wasn't all jazz and pyjamas.

He hurried along the landing to her room. And with horror found it stacked with luggage, now all neatly packed—in fact, one stage further in the march away.

There was now no longer the note of a place disordered with breaking up, but the horrid calm of a room prepared for the next resident. A neutral hotel moment, all bags packed, drawers emptied, only the bill to settle.

She was certainly being pretty thorough this time. Gone too far now to lose face? Would she actually go—and only much later come back? Was she rigging this so that he would have to chase her, beg her to come back? He was appalled at the tedium this implied. Hours and hours of talk, even travelling somewhere or other to find her! Appalling the waste of time and effort—how could he *find* the time? Simultaneous with this discovery came a decision to return to his office the next day, the first time this had occurred to him.

He found the bath overflowing, the overflow blocked. More plumbers. He used the towels to mop up the water. In the linen cupboard, no fresh towels. She'd packed their towels! He hurried back to her room, attacked the first suitcase—then desisted. It would only look as if he were trying physically to stop her, and that would never do. He fetched a bath-robe out of his wardrobe.

Summer gone, he thought, carrying this bathing appliance. And through the open bathroom window came the strains of Savory's gramophone, again that dolorous song:

GOODBYE

'The days themselves are dying fast,
Summer and love are past,
Farewell, my life, my love, farewell.'

He banged the window shut, and watched the grey
clouds outside disappear behind a personal cosy cloud
of steam. 'Whatever happens, however much the marital
tantrums develop, I shall always have these private,
intimate comforts.' Yet—what a depressing defence! And
he defended himself against such defences by adding:
As one believes one will always have the pleasure of a
good book—and then the eyes go. As always the pleasure
of spring—till you're so old it becomes simply part of all
pain. And the future of a hot bath? Nervous eczema.

He was dressed too soon, but it made him feel a lot
better. Earlier that day he had caught in the mirror the
image of his depression—thinning hair, paunch, a
sagging grimness about the mouth, bags beneath the
accusing steel of his eyes—all emphasized by a slop of
grey trousers beneath messed-up working shirt and torn
cardigan. But now refreshed he saw a man well-kept
for his years, which were not after all so many—a man
with well-brushed hair, the good colour of steamed
blood behind old sunburn, the prop of a high white
collar, the gleam of a dark blue suit. His grey eyes
glittered with intelligence and approval.

He went down to set out a drink-tray. The gramophone had stopped. The evenings were drawing in, and
he was pleased to warm the sitting-room with a glitter

of light. The Bucketts were due at seven, and seven it nearly was when Zoë came down dressed and ready. And the telephone rang. The Bucketts were delayed on the road, they would be half an hour late.

So, polished and dressed up, the two of them found themselves alone in the evening preparedness of their sitting-room, with nothing to do. Zoë poured herself a drink and wandered over to the French windows. 'For once everything's ready,' she said, and the words dropped slowly and separately on to the clean silence.

He found it almost impossible to speak. The quiet raced as her words seemed to stand there, growing big and black: 'Good, yes, fine . . .' he said, and petered out.

'You've cut the mickies!' she cried abruptly. Not noticing the silence, as she had not noticed him hacking away during the afternoon?

'They were white with mildew,' he said. 'Rotten time of year, neither one thing nor the other.'

'It's quite warm still. Only looks chilly.'

'The wind's still in the south-west.'

A time of truce? She had plainly geared herself up to entertain the Bucketts, there was no relaxing now. So, coolly but with a kind of relief, they exchanged a few sentences between now quite restful silences. It was like being two other people, and this was a release.

She was still standing by the windows. He found himself admiring her broadly elegant shoulders, the brilliance of her dark hair, the slim lines of a kind of golden dress, her excellent ankles. She stood casually, but never slopping, never leaning on anything; all muscles trim. 'Thoroughbred,' he thought, 'why doesn't she shiver?' He knew well enough—she was too bloody well sure of herself. Yet ageing? Hardly a sign. Perhaps a slight squinting look about the eyes, but no lines unless you looked very hard for them. In any case he had to wear reading glasses, and without them most faces smoothed out. Reading between the lines, he tittered.

'What?'

'Oh, nothing. Oh yes, I was just thinking about those two at Gardone, d'you remember, the rice all over them?'

'Sticking in their hair.' She sighed. 'Seems a long time ago.'

'It was. Three years.'

'You saw my dress today,' she said.

She might have stuck a pin in him. It was intolerable for someone to be so perceptive.

But he said nothing; and then it suddenly came across him, as he envisaged the two of them isolated in this prepared room in their prepared clothes, that they must appear very much like figures in some drawing room play. In the play, they would be exchanging marked confidences about life: or steaming up to a battle: or brittlely witticizing above inner tensions. How different the reality, he thought, with its slow slough of ticking time, its reasonableness, its dull daily bread. Even Chekov wouldn't do. She could hardly walk over to the empty fireplace, and say, for instance: 'When I was a young woman . . . so to speak . . . at Vanuschka, and the Michaelmas daisies came to show us the summer had ended . . . how I loved them! . . . they showed that another year had passed . . . how I loved the future then!'

Oh no. Yet, on the other hand, did he not want to say something very similar to this? Would it not be better to put such things into words? How sad this lack of communication, this familiar disease of a mechanical age.

But she was saying: 'Down at Lessingham we used to

have great beds of the stuff. . . . Mickies. I was young, but even then I never liked them . . . it meant the summer's end . . . and school again, I suppose . . .'

Amazed, he could only say: 'They were all mildew.'

Here they were communicating after all! He stared at her wondering. There stood this completely different person—and as a woman completely different engine— to which he was indissolubly linked. Or, dissolubly linked. With whom he had passed through the various stages of the long thing absurdly called by one word, love. As younger animals, lyrical with passion, steamy with heat. As the years passed, lessening this into a routine much the same as eating, but finding beyond it a growing habitual companionship and trust. And bound all the time by tighter mutual possessions and daily needs, and unbreakable loyalty. Yet all this was born astoundingly of the conflict between entirely different engines—centripetal and centrifugal, hunter and nest-holder. My, what a grand totalling of give-and-take! Yet it hardly seemed so, it even seemed to work.

What would it be like to be a male tyrant, a rich Arab? A Victorian clubbing-and-whoring husband? What had happened to the sexes in the last decades? Had women become more like men or men more like women? Talk of a matriarchy was still plainly nonsense— it was still nonsense even in America—you could tear any newspaper apart and add up the male and female pieces. Yet the patriarchy had gone underground somewhere. Take an electronics engineer aproned at the sink—he certainly wasn't thinking of chintzes and bowls of begonias? Differences had subtly been sunk beneath appearances, women in pubs, men in aprons. It was something like the class system, which had ceased to be an unalterable hierarchy of rank and station—but continued simply on the basis of different interests. Class-conscious as a man of the working-class breeding pigeons might not have much to do with his working-class neighbour who studied in the public library: or a clerk who loved cricket having nothing much to say to the chess-player introvert next door.

Zoë said: 'I turned the chicken down, but . . .' when the door-bell rang.

'It's them!' she shouted.

Then clapped a hand across her mouth: 'Heavens, I forgot to tell you. Jenks rang when you were out. He said he had a spare Sunday today and could he go ahead on my bicycle shed. I told him we'd reconsidered the matter.'

'Reconsidered the matter?'

'I told him it was all off.'

'You said that to Jenks?'

'I'm sorry. He didn't sound too pleased.'

'*Jenks!*'

'There's the bell again, I must—'

He stood reddening. His stomach seemed to empty with fear and his face grow hot with rage. To have put out Jenks, the absolute necessity of his life, the last handyman on earth! But alongside this, as in a long second of slow realization, with the absorbed mind still trying to reject what all the surface senses already know, he tried not to see what her simple message really told him.

'I can't believe it,' he said, believing it at last. For he saw now that Zoë did mean what she was doing. She was leaving him all right.

'Hello! Tony! Long time no see!' Jack gruffed.

'Ciao, Antonio,' trilled Jill.

The Bucketts came larger than life into the room,

crowding it, blazing with colour and presence. He swallowed and drew himself up to attention. Jack Buckett's strong red face and soft black eyes, his country tweeds: Jill Buckett's ample flowered figure, her face painted white and red and blue, her big smell of powdery scent. Her name was really Susan. She was called Jill because of Jack and his surname, the nursery rhyme. Jesus, he thought, old friends. Three, four hours of them. Melon, chicken, vegetables of all bloody sorts. Wine, cheese, the lot. 'Let me get you a drink,' he said.

Without asking them what they wanted, he poured two glasses of the drink he himself was drinking. How possibly to endure it? He saw moreover the terrible adjustment always to be made to the Buckett's way of life, which was not theirs. The Bucketts were trend-beset. They were the living prey of glossy magazines. They affected every new cut of cloth, and since so many others did, managed though in middle age not to appear ridiculous. Their car they changed every year, their flat with its perennial alterations was a decorator's heaven, and they changed their dog too often too; it was an unspoken wonder where the old dogs went to. Had the Bucketts, the saying went, an unlimited supply of aunts in the country?

Jack had already caught him by the elbow and walked him a few paces aside as was his forceful way. 'We were just saying,' he said straight in, like a man of parts avoiding small talk and the ladies with the same expert gesture, 'that the future of a day out to the coast will have to involve the double-decker car-carrier—shove your mini on and stay there snug as a slug the whole damn day, no messy driving, lovely view of the channel, frozen snacks to hand—'

'Excuse me,' Lyle said, pointing confidentially at the

door, 'excuse . . . back in a moment,' and left Buckett in midsentence.

He only stopped when his back was safely against the closed door of the little cloakroom preceding the lavatory proper, among golf-bags and tennis rackets, macintoshes and umbrellas and gumboots. His hats hung blind as bats from pegs. He stood in the half-dark and his face screwed up with sudden pain. Zoë! All her coolness of the past days had frozen in one second to the cutting coldness of a woman with no further interest in a man: like cruel young girls of the far past who had left him for another boyfriend, gone off without even bothering to smile, eyes only on their new purpose. Coldness? It was worse. It was neither cold nor warm, it was nothing, it was absolute indifference.

He moved into the lavatory and sat down. Am I being dramatic? he wondered. But no. Zoë might indeed attack and re-order her own part of the household—but never would she interfere with his. There were unspoken laws—he would never interfere in the linen cupboard, she would never transplant a rose. And when it involved such a figure as Jenks, it was doubly unspeakably unspoken.

A renewed gust of rain struck the window. Bonfire, pile of mickies! But by all God's good in Heaven, how could she have permitted this dinner if she were serious? It seemed utterly heartless. Senseless, too—for if she went, everybody would soon know? He began to hope again... then saw that indeed it might be no more than a symptom of indifference, cruel perhaps, but not intentionally so. It could scarcely be intentional if she didn't care?

But—and only now could he realize this—announcements would surely in time have to be made? Could Zoë have chosen tonight to let the cat out of the bag? These the Bucketts were among their oldest friends, they had formed with them a kind of backbone relationship without much outer meaning; Jack Buckett he had known from early days as a young man trying to be about the town, and Jill had coincidentally lived near Zoë's parents in Hampshire, and the forces of propinquity and a few mutual acquaintances still worked.

It was too cruel. Suppose she had already telephoned them, suppose she was already in league with the Bucketts? He suddenly saw she would never have planned a new life without help or direction from someone or other. Who, then? There were indeed old friends of hers he never met, whose names he did not even know. But their very insubstantiality put them out of mind.

He rose abruptly—if there was going to be an announcement, if there was already a discussion, he must not miss it. But stopped, paused to pull the chain, and to make washing sounds afterwards, in case someone might be looking for him.

'Such a pet, and ever so intelligent,' Jill-Susan was cooing high, 'we left him with the porter for the day. The porter's crazy about him.'

Their damned dog. What colour was it this year? 'Sorry,' he said, 'something in the kitchen,' and he said it grimly, looking from face to face in suspicion.

Zoë gave a gay peal of laughter. 'No go,' she said,
'I've told them I upset you about Jenks. Forget it,
darling—a couple of beers'll put him right.'

'Jenks doesn't drink beer,' he said, 'he has an ulcer.
And I'll have one soon if I don't get a drink,' he added
brightly, baring his teeth.

His lips stayed terribly stretched as he poured gin.
But at least, he still felt armoured within his suit, his
fresh shirt.

'I say,' Buckett said, 'you're looking rather dressed up
for Sunday supper? Apologies for these rustic rags.'

Jack's animal eyes twinkled at him. The armour
collapsed.

'Spent the afternoon clearing the mickies,' he apologized. 'Had to change.' His mind searched wildly, he had
to say something more: 'And that reminds me, this man
Jenks told me once he saw a man clearing—'

'Another drink, Susan?' Zoë said.

'—clearing in one of the gardens round here, one just
like this, and when he looked a moment later the man
had vanished clean off the face of the earth—and in his
place there was a big buck negro doing some sort of
wild stomp! Bees. He'd spaded up a bee's hive. His face
was black with them—'

'Euch!'

'You could have slashed a wasp's nest this afternoon,'
Jack said. 'No joke.'

They talked for some minutes about bees and wasps.
Everybody had some story to tell. Here was a common
interest. He dared to glance at Zoë. Vital and unmoved,
she was describing a certain pest-destroyer's fanatical
love of wasp-nests, of their beautiful and careful engineer-
ing. Yet this man's job was to burn them out. Like men
who shoot birds, he thought, taken up against his will.

The loving hunter. Would a surgeon so love a cancerous growth, marvelling in its cellular ingenuity?

And Zoë was saying: 'Have a last nip, while I go and get the chicken out. Free-range!' she added, and went off on her heartless high heels, and bees petered out for want of further anecdote, and Jill suddenly cried: 'But you *must* both come to us soon! Next week! Surprise!' And she went on to describe some extraordinary new arrangement of greys and greens and reflected lighting, while he again breathed quietly. At least this meant that no announcement had been made.

They went in to dinner. There was the absurd rule of placing, which set Buckett to Zoë's right hand yet opposite a sideboard set with silver he was known to dislike.

More than this, though, the two husbands and wives were left facing each other, an obvious incompetence. And then there was the drawing of corks and the pouring of wine, while Zoë called through the hatch for help, and both Bucketts rose and wandered about with vegetable dishes, setting these down in out-of-the-way places.

Once settled, angling in and out the hidden table-legs, they ate melon and Parma ham. Sharp little cries of 'delicious' from the Bucketts. Like the words 'how pretty' for any piece of furniture, however beautiful, the food word never varied from 'delicious'.

Lyle sat there digesting this with the warming venom. They all went through the usual discussion as to ginger or not with melon. Sooner or later someone would say the Italians used salt—hence the ham. Jill obliged with this. And a few minutes later there was reiterated applause of the chicken in what sounded like one desperate word, freerangefowl. There was a mixed-up passing of vegetable dishes and salts and peppers and the filling of wine-glasses.

Guests and hosts, they all worked hard; and sat very upright round the glitter of cutlery and china. Not for long, he thought. They'll be sprawled all over soon, and putting ash on the bread plates. Animals! And when at last, still hungry from his lack of lunch, Lyle took a first bite into the chicken, his mouth was instantly torn with pain. He recognized a symptom of former rows—for many hours past he must have been gnashing his teeth, which were ill-fitting. Each mouthful was a little agony.

At least he didn't have to talk, with the three of them hard at it capping each other. His ears took in odd sentences, his head nodded yes or no. He sat slewed round at Jill and watched her large white face with its blue eyeshadow, its slash of red lip, making a redundancy of the old joke about 'put-a-flag-over-their-faces-they're-all-the-same,' the Union Jack being already there in Jill's case, custom-built.

Jill was a plump white-skinned woman whose fat was formed and muscular, not the kind you could poke your fingers into, no give: uncompromisingly tubular, there was the feeling of a well-filled white sausage broadly beribboned by a dress. Yet a highly fragrant sausage, for a love of flowered materials, much exposed flesh, and a huge use of deodorants, lacquers, powders, and scents gave her a predominantly fresh and blossomy look. It was unfortunate that a very short upper lip gave her also an expression of perceiving smells far less pleasant and far too near.

This face discussed at him a few of the latest plays, giving in each case a reviewer's view yessed into granite certainty over tea-cups all over the town: and then went on to that perennial problem, should one live in the country or in town?

Question and answer were supplied with litanical precision. Lyle, his ear-flaps lowered, found himself watching the play of her knife and fork. She never stopped patting the little piles of food on her plate. Round they went, a pat to the sprouts, a pat to the meat, a pat to a piece of skin put to one side as a specialty, a pat to the one potato. It was a ritual dance before the sacrifice—for suddenly snickerty-snack went the knife and fork fast as knitting needles, slicing and piling some of everything on to the fork, whose amazing rich burden was then ruthlessly swept up to vanish between prettily pouted lips. Moloch!

But through this, and through his growing apprehension about the blob of French mustard on the plate-rim, he was thinking over and over again: She's leaving me, she's leaving me all alone, I won't have her any more . . . and this unhappiness grew mixed up with Jill's foodplay, so that now, as Jill missed a pat on the potato, he found his finger raised and pointed at it in accusation. Jill stopped herself in mid-sacrifice.

'Why are you pointing at my potato?' she asked, laying down knife and fork.

'I—I—well—'

'There isn't an eye in it?'

'Oh no.'

'A maggot?'

'Good heavens no.'

'Then why point at it? He was pointing at my potato,' she informed Zoë, with a lightish laugh.

'I wasn't actually pointing—' Lyle began seriously.

Jack Buckett intoned judicially to Zoë; 'It seems your husband had been pointing at my wife's potato. Does he want the potato? Are there not enough potatoes? Not enough to go round perhaps?'

Zoë raised the potato-lid with a flourish. 'He's always pointing at people's potatoes,' she said.

Lyle got up a smile: 'It's the done thing,' he told Buckett.

'Not much privacy,' Buckett said, 'if you're a potato. People always pointing at you.' He went redder with pleasure. 'Origin of potato-and-point, I suppose?'

Lyle clenched his teeth. 'You were saying, Jill, about people with a weekend cottage having to have two of everything—I have to have two of everything as it is, living in this house with its stairs. Two lots of glasses, two pairs of slippers etcetera. So would I have to have four?'

'Come again?'

'Four potatoes?' Jack asked.

'With a cottage, I mean. What Jill was saying.'

'Oh,' she laughed, 'pre-potato-like?'

Another mention of that potato and he would burst.

He said sharply to Jack: 'And you two would have to have God knows how many of everything the way you change your furniture every couple of weeks. What do you do with the old stuff? Got a barrow or something?'

Silence.

'Ha, ha,' Lyle laughed.

A further embarrassed silence. Then all at once:

'Some more chicken?'

'My dream cottage—'

'My wife's peculiar potato—'

They all laughed with amusement and fear. Then,

to change the question, Buckett quizzically intoned: 'Can anyone give me his or her definition of a "gentleman"?'—as if this leaden old question were put for the very first time.

Lyle looked at him sharply. Could he be serious? Couldn't he hear the words echoing over past decanters everywhere, in clubrooms and schoolrooms and wherever else Britishers sat wrinkling their brows in pregnant play? Was it perhaps a backhander aimed at him? But no, contemporary Jack had not escaped the years. And listen! Jill! With a volley of giggles like the exclamation marks in a woman's magazine:

'A chap who takes the weight on his elbows . . .'

Buckett gave a hearty laugh, then shot his chin forward very gravely at Zoë, nodding an indication that it was now up to her.

But instead of an answer Zoë gave a great yawn. Lyle held his breath. Now what?

'Sorry,' Zoë said. 'Very sorry,' then looked hard at everyone in turn. 'But I must tell you all—I've done something quite, well, extraordinary.'

Lyle rose from his seat.

Zoë was shaking her head at herself: 'Yes. I've really gone and done it this time!'

He could not face it, mumbled an excuse and left the room.

How would she say it? It was agonizing not to know, but impossible to face. He stood in the hall. Outside, through the black window, his illuminated ghost stood, darkly gilded with yellow light, an Old Master of modern man. He shivered.

And then a gust of laughter brayed through the closed door of the dining-room. It was a concerted laugh. He felt a pepper of dry tears—then blazed with anger. This put paid to the Bucketts too, two more he would never again see in his life—he flung open the door, and said: 'What the bloody hell?'

They were still grinning, gripping themselves.

'I'll dine out on this for *weeks*!' carolled Jill.

'What exactly is the matter for laughter?' Lyle said cold.

Zoë gave another great yawn and ended it with a giggle. She looked up at Lyle with eyes of weariness. 'I swallowed a pill,' she said.

'What?'

'A sleeping pill.'

'Why?'

'I thought it was a tranquillizer. Look—here's the bottle,' and she brandished it. 'What *can* I do?'

'Swig the lot,' Jack gaily said. 'Hostess takes overdose, hostess of the dosedest—'

'Coffee,' Lyle said, 'I'll make some coffee.'

He felt no relief. Like that reflection through the window, it was humiliating at some sort of double remove—as if he had been made the fool of a contrived parlour game.

'I can wait,' Zoë said. 'I think. Let's get some cheese into us.'

Lyle still struggled about inside himself, lonely left out yet in, hating Zoë for her continued poise, longing for her with impossible love, cursing what seemed the imbecility of all dinner parties—while over the cheese the talk sped like a bolt to the target of marriage.

'Here we sit, four well-married folk,' Buckett said, smearing something off his fingers on to the side of the plate. 'I wonder how many of the generation twenty years younger will be doing the same?'

'Wiping camembert off their fingers?' Lyle said. 'Have another napkin.'

'Antonio, you got a liver or something? I recommend one of your wife's pills . . . no, like these here napkins of paper—for who can face a laundry bill today?—the essential purpose is unchanged, but the fabric cheapened. Modern marriages are made to be thrown away.'

Zoë said: 'They're not that cheap, thank you. You don't get snow-roses and small birds in two colours for nothing.'

Lyle demonstrated his napkin.

'Each snow-rose has enough poison in it to kill a platoon.'

But Buckett bulldozed on: 'No. *Seriously.* I'm sure the young vaguely wish for the old till-death-do-us and so on. But they're too conscious of the escape route there. They use phrases like "we'll make a go of it". And they're naturally not without the usual healthy drive to upset tradition.'

Jill agreed: 'It would be so interesting to sound an American mind on this. They seem to have divorce as the tradition. I often wonder how firm the American woman's famous pedestal is.'

Buckett intoned: 'All marriages are unique though in ways they look similar. Take Jill and I. We're childless. I know you well enough to say that flatly and not as if it was a dark disease. So what happens? For one thing, we have much more time for each other. That is to say, really, Jill has much more time for me. Her mother-love pours all over me.'

'For God's sake, Jack!' Jill laughed.

'But it's true! And the effect is to make me into a kind of elderly only child, selfish as the day is long. This thing handed to me, that stitched, this that and the other—my whole life has become a battle against egocentricity, I can feel it growing palpable, like a tumour.'

84

He turned to Lyle. 'You'll have to look out, you know. Now Tom's gone you'll be in for a real cosseting. I don't mean it's all fair sailing—we have our tiffs, expect you do too—where would we be without them? But believe me, old boy, your declining years'll be spent in cotton-wool. And you'll have to fight. Not her, but *yourself*!'

'Let's have pudding,' Zoë said.

'Pudding?' Jill trilled. 'I didn't think, what with cheese—'

Buckett frowned at her. 'We *are* drinking a claret, my dear,' he whispered.

Zoë brought in pears syruped in wine, and Jill again trilled: 'Oh, I thought you said pudding!'

Buckett pressed his lips together and said nothing.

Lyle stared at his pears.

Jill leaned towards him: 'You're not very communicative this evening, Tony. What's on that master mind?'

'Let's eat up and have that coffee quick,' Zoë said, 'I'm dropping off again.'

He raised his eyes to her in gratitude. For a passing moment her poise seemed to fall away, her whole face to soften in condolence. They were again together, they loved each other. This farce had somehow sealed the end of all differences.

Her momentary softening broke into what it was, a large unending yawn. 'Oh my dears, I'm sorry,' she mouthed in the middle of it. He filled his own mouth with pear, pushed the rest away.

They disentangled themselves from the table legs and went into the sitting-room. Jill trotted herself upstairs, saying she wished to see a man about a dog. 'Poor little brute,' Lyle muttered under his breath, and led Buckett to the cloakroom. 'My old father used to grip me by the arm and say: "Pumpship?"' he muttered, trying to be amiable.

'There's a pub in Soho,' Buckett said, 'with Drip-Dry and Shake-Dry on the two loo doors. I swear it.'

In the cloakroom, the two together, old friends among hats and golf-bags, he suddenly let it all out, he told Jack Zoë was leaving him.

'Oh, Heavens!' Buckett said, and made a sharp fuss of arranging himself. 'Oh, heavens it can't be true? You and Zoë?'

'This time it is.'

'This time? You've had trouble before? I'd never have believed . . .'

'Haven't you and Jill? During some worse row than usual?'

'Never,' Buckett said quick.

'Oh.'

'Well–I suppose I did think of it once. But we never said as much. Look here, can't we do something? I mean.'

'You mean?'

Buckett reddened again. A sense of order was disturbed. But even in a wrong situation, he had to do the right thing?

'D'you think I ought to have a word with her?' he said. 'Why is it, anyhow? What have you been up to?'

'Nothing. And she won't even give me a reason. Ridiculous.'

'Quite.'

86

Both men nodded.

'I'll put it to Susan,' Buckett said. 'She'll have a word.'

'Tonight?' He said it with fear. The only thing he wanted in the world was to know. But as with a doctor's verdict, not now.

'I don't think tonight,' Buckett said, thinking not so much of a spoiled evening as of trouble itself, which had better be kept at arm's length. 'I'll get her to ring Zoë tomorrow. Sleep on it, you know.' And he shook his head, 'Dreadful, dreadful thing,' he said.

'She's all packed.'

'Packed?'

His old friend looked really shocked. 'But when then? When does she think she's—well, off?'

'I don't think yet. She'd have said.'

Lyle wondered: Would she have said? Still there, and impossibly going, she seemed already gone. 'I'm utterly in the dark,' he said. 'I—I can't really say more. Let's go in.'

In the sitting-room Jack gave a little yelp at a Lalique sphinx squatted on a writing desk across the room. It was an unexceptional sphinx, just too valuable to throw away. But he got Jill over to it, picked it up with loud exclamations of approval, and between strokings and further exclamations, whispered the news to Jill.

Their heads moved close together. The sphinx revolved. Lyle stationed himself in between them and Zoë and thought wildly for something to say. 'Should we have the fire on?' he said. 'It's time we started the fire regularly—' and then cut himself short.

Zoë said nothing, only leaned across and switched on the electric heater, a small grey box which showed no fire but whirred like a little engine room. The room, with its dull yellow curtains and quietly gleaming furniture, its chrysanthemums and its occasional glitter of china and silver, throbbed like a ship.

Jill returned to her chair with an expression of quiet serenity. 'I do think,' she said, 'that the chrysanthemums are better and earlier this year than I can remember.'

Clicks and tuts of approval as Lyle and Buckett seconded her. Zoë looked startled, and glanced down at the fire, as though this machine might somehow be involved.

Then, with the wine and food easing their stomachs, they began an uneasy hour, three of them knowing they knew an unspoken secret and Zoë supposed not to know they knew, but knowing they did in the first few minutes.

Sudden silences, brightnesses. The room took on a doomed personality, the folds of the curtains loomed with life, empty chairs filled with presence, pictures and flowers and objects all murmured that they were part of a home and household, and chosen by two people, two together.

Buckett sprawled over-easily in his chair, taking out an empty pipe and sucking it; letting it hang from a slackened lower jaw, which then he slowly revolved. His brow was furrowed in horizontal lines of non-thought. From time to time he wiped these into a single vertical frown of thought. But topics were difficult, the esoteric seemed heartless, the everyday pointed too closely to an everyday life soon to be broken up. So he attempted the kind of safe, fraternal frivolity he used with business clients: 'There was this chap,' he said, 'anti-nuclear wallah who went off his nut, spent the entire summer nipping up and down the beaches sticking notices on the sleeping bottoms of all the larger bikini-ed ladies, BAN THE BUM'.

The room tinned loud with laughter. But it was gone

sudden as sound lost round a corner. Jill smiled at her husband oversweetly. Help Zoë, indeed, said the smile. But were not her sympathies automatically more attached to this soon-to-be unattached male—even though her efforts must now be to re-attach him?

And Mange came plodding in, and was received with cries of delight, like a princess arriving among peasants in musical comedy. The old spaniel knew his stuff, going straight to Buckett and resting his whole jowl on a tweedy knee, rolling his eyes upwards, while from side to side his whole behind swayed in that slow and separate hipdance.

But Zoë seemed hardly to notice, though it was her dog. Lyle was suddenly terrified that she had decided to herself to bring the matter into the open. By announcing it himself, he had forgotten this danger. He thought wildly for some more solid topic in which they could lose themselves, found his eyes on the French windows, remembered, and spoke in a low voice the one word: 'Suicide!'

The Bucketts looked startled, Zoë raised her eyebrow.

He quickly went on: 'Chap next door's got a new record, I mean an old one, Schuler's *Farewell*.'

'That wailing old ballad we've been hearing most of the afternoon?' Zoë asked.

He nodded. 'And a very odd history it's got—so odd that musicians refuse to play it. It's got a jinx on it.'

'Like Macbeth? I've always heard actors don't—' Jill began.

'Exactly. But the chap Schuler, I believe, killed himself. It might date from that.'

'Or some concert hall caught fire.' Buckett said. 'Much is forgotten.' And added with a quick look at Lyle: 'Needn't dwell on suicide.'

So that Lyle saw he had a means to disturb them. Let

them indeed think a germ was hatched: 'Another song,' he went on quickly, 'was said to be the cause of mass suicide in Budapest one year. It was a sad song, the sadness was infectious. The Danube was full of the drowned.' He laughed, but with a bitter ring, as if he were trying hard to make light of it. 'There must be a whole history of such potent music.'

'I could have thrown myself out of the window this afternoon,' Zoë laughed. 'But seriously,' she went on, 'there are these outbreaks of infectious suicide. Even without music. I've heard of whole villages somewhere in Southern Russia—was it Bessarabia?—in the last century—they wiped themselves out to a man! The cause was religious. A general immolation.'

She had plainly decided to outplay him. He was to be allowed no bathos, no desperate message to his allies. Still, he'd got her going—the diversion was a success.

'And the most curious, and not unusual reason for suicide seems to be happiness,' said this well known stranger of a wife, with a pill inside her, in a gold dress, digging herself in, 'or what we search for in the name of happiness—'

'Good God,' he blurted, 'what about all the desperate cases? The prisoner and his braces? The leaping love-sick?'

'They may each have got what they wanted. They may have had suicide inside them, waiting to blossom. But what I'm talking about is, for instance, a case history like that almost lotus-living tribe in India—what's it called?—whose beautiful young people in beautiful weather grow tired of plucking the fruit from the trees and wander off deeper into the wood and hang themselves. They do it not because of disaster but for lack of it.'

'Good old Mange,' Buckett said uneasily, giving the dog a good scratch.

'The mind lost in a vacuum,' Zoë said.

'I don't believe it,' Jill said. 'Anyway, it's a morbid subject.'

'The mind screaming for something to grasp on,' Zoë said. 'And only fruit and good weather and health and limitless sex all about you.'

'What's the address?' Buckett tried, wagging a jovial pipe.

But Zoë went on: 'It's the same with the Welfare State—'

'Tell that to the taxpayer,' Buckett snorted.

'—raised and dulled to a Scandinavian pattern, where statistics show the highest European rate—'

'Nonsense,' Lyle said sharply, 'suicide statistics are notably suspect.'

'What else have you got to go on?'

'Too much goes unrecorded. Too many are covered up, many are prevented—depending on social habits, close communities, poke-nose neighbours . . .' his voice was rising.

'Then why do the authorities bother?'

'They're mad on bits of paper!' he cried.

'And some people are just mad on bits, they get them between their yellow teeth,' Zoë shouted.

Jack Buckett looked openly embarrassed. Jill's serenity had frozen all over her, she sat tense as a plump snow-queen.

Lyle lowered his voice and said slowly and carefully:

'And so many do it by accident. Simply because for a day, a week, things become too much. The end of a tether—as accidental as a fever germ.'

Zoë had raised her eyes to the ceiling, they could all hear her drawing in a deep breath for quite a tirade—when Buckett shot out his wrist-watch as if on manœuvres, and let impressive words fall in the air:

'We've got tomorrow, you know.'

Jill gave a big sigh, and began gathering herself together.

'Susan?' Jack said, rising. And to Zoë: 'Anno domini, you know. Must get our eight hours.'

'Yes, we've got tomorrow,' Jill echoed. As if it were a disease, Lyle thought. 'Darling, it was *lovely*,' Jill went on emphatically to Zoë. 'And I do hope,' she paused and repeated it, 'I do *hope* you'll *both* come to us very, *very* soon.'

Zoë looked her straight in the eyes. 'We'd *love* to.'

Lyle saw his guests to their car. However strained the evening had been, he saw that the tight-lipped lonely house would now be worse.

Zoë stood in the lighted doorway, a dark figure, a few details of the hall behind her—the curve of his white staircase, a picture glinting gold, a patch of red wallpaper. Yellow-lit, theatrical, the little framed scene looked to him like part of a stranger's house, with a strange woman beckoning from a lighted doorway.

Buckett poked his head out of the car-window and muttered in a low, ashamed voice: 'I hope you're not going to do anything silly, Tonio.'

'I hope so too.'

'I mean, it's a morbid subject. Stop even thinking about it. No good to dwell on such things.'

'You're right.'

But irresistible to put a slight darkness into his tone. Keep them on the boil. The windows slid up and the car went off grunting its up-to-the-minute power. He was left alone with Zoë's figure turning to go inside.

Then he saw the short dark blob of Mange silhouetted on the threshold. Good dog, rescue dog.

'I'll just take the dog up the street for a bit,' he shouted.

The dog? Strangely formal. But he could not manage old Mange's name, a privately shared affair.

'Come on, you!' he called, and down the steps the old beast lumbered. The door closed.

Along the lamp-lit street he walked, and stopped, and walked, as he had done now for years. But it was different. There had always before been the thought of a companionable house behind him. Now he saw the difference between loneliness and being alone. He could happily potter for hours in a different part of the house from Zoë, still feeling her company. But now he was bitterly lonely, lost. And the evening was cold.

Daytime had been neither warm nor cool, these were moist September days: but the evenings brought a drop in the temperature as on a cold spring night—yet still characterless, no brisk smell of winter yet. He turned his coat collar up, and this small action made him instantly into a furtive outsider. He felt himself slink as another man passed. It was a man he often saw around these streets, a well-fed clipped-moustached man who bounced along with his chest out very pleased with himself and his slippery-looking black labrador.

A little further on this man stopped. Then for a long minute the two humans stood there apart, while the dogs exchanged a friendly greeting, wagging and circling like women admiring each other's dresses. Lyle stole a glance at his fellow human. Of such proud dog-walking chaps he had only one thought: A race of lavatory attendants. But no such pleasantry came to him tonight: he was only struck by the silence between them, two anonymous townsmen. But now the man spoke, very loud on the quiet night, unembarrassed, as if Lyle were not there at all:

'Squire! Heel, Squire-boy!'

The labrador reluctantly followed, looking over his shoulder at Mange.

'Got all night, sir?' asked the man chattily. Lyle looked round pleased. But the man was only talking to the dog.

A car drew up. Its lights went on inside. Out came voices, laughter: then two girls, two men, who walked quickly, borne along by their own excitement with each other into a nearby house. They were young. They gave out a sense of evening beginning. September faded, it was for a few seconds a mid-summer's night, nothing to do with there and then, certainly nothing to do with a middle aged man walking his dog, his coat collar turned up, his wife gone. He sighed: Don't romanticize. They're just a couple of married couples going back to their flats, goodnight and Monday morning.

But they must have come from the south, where the lights of inner London lay, where the sky was pink. He stood looking at it. Strange how the pink stayed absolutely still, *la vie en rose* indeed calling a halt to the clouds. He glanced above at his own sky, a purpling plum against the billowing black of trees, and watched the clouds passing high above like a wide and silent tide-race.

'Come on, old chap,' he said to Mange, 'good old chap. Home.' It was a long time since he had spoken so tenderly to the dog.

Downstairs was dark. He stowed Mange away in his basket—the dog slept like a rich bedouin on a pile of exotic old eiderdowns and towels—and climbed the stairs apprehensive of what more must now be said.

Again he moved over-quietly. There was no doubt about it—he felt guilty. Why? Surely it was Zoë who was in the wrong? But her very sureness had put him at a loss—which just felt like guilt. He was put in the position of intruder, apologetic for his presence.

Or did he feel guilty to himself, for not doing something about it all? But what *could* he do? There seemed no means of discussion: and when discussion fails, there remains only violence or the police. The latter was absurd: the former—well, suppose he blacked her eye, wouldn't she just fall down and later rise to begin again, and now with a kind of right on her side? In any case, one did not black the eyes of middle-aged women. Though it would be a pleasure to get into a towering rage and let fly. But where was the towering rage? It could erupt on a small occasion, a row about nothing—but the more serious a situation, the less the rage: the impulse was more to move cautiously, like the captain of a large and ponderous ship.

Her light was still on. He had to go and speak to her. Even ask those practical questions which disbelief had previously precluded—where she was going, and when. He must at least let her know he knew she was in earnest.

She lay fast asleep in her underclothes. The pill, of course. Such a deep sleep, such a look of absolute departure from life, life struck down half-undressed and with the light going on and on. Bottles of various pills stood by the bedside lamp, and the thought again occurred: suicide. This was just how it would look?

He stood looking down at her. She scarcely seemed to

breathe: her mouth hung open, but in the innocence of
sleep she looked prettier and younger. He felt that it was
years since he had looked at her, at such a time of relaxa-
tion it was in fact the face he had known years before,
and his heart beat hard for the past and love of her. He
knew every inch of that skin, every small hair about her
temples, every eyelash, eyebrow, nostril, softness of ear.
One hand lay palm upwards, empty, doing nothing:
again innocent, in need of protection, like a child's. He
turned away and went quietly from the room, turning
off the light from the door.

In his own room he undressed. Then remembered she
would get cold without the coverlet. He must have felt
the look of her was too valuable to cover. He went back
to the room, and in the dark put out a hand for the
bedclothes but touched her hand, which closed warmly
on his. In her sleep, he thought. And what dreams? . . .
and quietly, not wishing to wake her, he lay down at her
side. Gently, gently he began to stroke. She groaned and
shifted. As, at first most tenderly, he began to make love,
he could still feel her sleepiness, and a hotness about her
breath. But a little later, from small tensions and from one
sudden movement, he knew she had awoken, he could see
in mind the bluish whites of her eyes staring upwards
in the dark. Then one, only one arm came round his
gently moving back: the other arm stretched wide and
away, dispassionate.

For a moment the thought of this arm, those eyes
widely staring, emasculated him—such half-love, such
distant obeisance made him feel again the unwanted
intruder and this angered him, rage grew and he lost
all gentleness and acted only to impress himself hard into
this far-off near body. Yet the arm on his back pressed
him closer.

Afterwards, still in the dark, he said bitterly: 'Why did you let me do that?'

Her voice, for the first time wide awake, isolated and loud in the blackness: 'I like it.'

It pushed him further away than ever. He was a nothing. But he could still touch her—he felt her hand. It gave no answering grasp. He lay there empty. He thought of the old saying about marriage being legalized prostitution. But at least a whore was professional, she made some attempt to act her job?

He sat up. If she was going away she should have refused him. This don't-care-either-way dispassion made the whole situation either unreal or too real, who could say? Too real. The warm pressure of that one arm had been like an awful form of politeness.

'I wonder who you were thinking of,' he suddenly said, then thought, no, she would not have moved so coldly to an imagined lover.

'I was asleep,' she said, 'at first,' and gave a yawn he could hear in the dark, a dreadfully final sound.

'Goodnight,' he said.

'Wait—get me a hanky, will you?'

He took a step in the dark and stubbed a toe on one of the suitcases.

'Get it your bloody self,' he said. 'Put the light on and get undressed. I can't stand this.' And bumping about on things in the dark he left her.

IV

THE first hour at the bank was endurable. It was a world where he was received without question. Routine received him, his colleagues nodded affirmity, the commissionaire in his uniform and the marble of the big hall pillars and the low chatter of machines showed a solid bone of life continuing as it had always done.

Up in his own bond-dealing office the morning was fairly slack, a mild to-and-fro of dollar bonds and the weekend's post made for little pressure. This was what he had come in for. He had come for the cover of the ordinary, and to resume his place as a husband providing for a balanced household. It was unreal, but it felt and looked real. It was also a means of avoiding a further talk with Zoë, and the dreaded news of when she intended to go.

Today was not like yesterday: no more hoping it would all blow over—now he had somehow to force it to blow over.

Yet she still simply presented a blank wall; and all the blanker for her neutral acceptance of him in the dark nothingness of the bedroom. See his solicitor? See his doctor? His mind roved round impossibilities: and the most absurd was the natural need to seek out an old friend—for marriage itself had removed all his old friends, their marriages and his marriage. Add the various other removals of middle age, what kind of help could he get from a telephone call to Scotland and Banff, where his oldest but now hardly closest friend had long ago gone?

He should rely best on Jill. A woman might indeed be

the one to make a woman speak. And Jill with no children might well have all the more time for it: but then he went into a daydream about Jill's commitments, he saw an ample vista of boutiques and wallpaper shops and special showings of this and that, and knew that any such life was over-filled, children were only the heaviest sparklers in a necklace of millstones round a wife's life.

Well then—he would perhaps try to get in touch with Jill, and in any case face up to Zoë herself when he returned that evening at the proper time, in the proper bowler hat, with the properly strained look of a man who has had a busy day. He sold several thousand Tokyo Electric and then telephoned Jenks. Apologies for the bicycle-shed affair: but he had other work to offer, would Jenks call round tomorrow? In the afternoon?

Only when he had put the telephone down did he see that he had made this appointment because he wanted an excuse to stay at home again tomorrow.

For it was indeed farcical to sit here with one's home breaking up. All these well-known people round him telephoning and bouncing up and down corridors with papers in their hands, all the little conferences and all the rest of the official façade. However many days of the year these people were together, no one had any real view of anyone's inner life. Plenty of jokes, friendliness, affection; but all distinct from their lives after office hours. In fact, the usual stream of life going on, and he the man about to suffer a major operation, his stomach hollow with condemned fear, and no one else caring a practical jot.

GOODBYE

He rang to see if he could see Varley. As he walked along to this superior's office, he began to limp again.

Varley said he was glad to see him back and then waited. Lyle told him that he did not quite know how to tell him, but he wanted to apply for more leave: there was, he said, making his strained face look helpless and urgent, a most serious domestic upset at home.

Varley instantly said: 'Of course, of course,' looking as though he had swallowed something unpleasant. The darkly general nature of the phrase 'domestic upset' precluded any detailed enquiry. Yet he had to say something, and tried affability:

'I always thought,' he laughed wryly, 'that a skiing accident in September was a rather too diplomatic event. No offence, of course. You have all my sympathies.'

'But it was true! This is, I'm afraid, coincidental.' Lyle meant this, he had convinced himself of his own story, quite forgetting he had tripped over that colander.

Varley rose. 'Oh, sorry.'

Going to the window he must have thought that as a director some paternal words were necessary, even to a toppish executive such as Lyle, for he stroked his grey hair thoughtfully and sighed:

'I expect you're somewhere in the middle forties, Lyle? I can give you ten years. I'm fifty-five. And without wanting to interfere, or indeed sound avuncular'—as he said it, he put his thumb in waistcoat armhole, a distinctly avuncular stance—'I'd like to say, keep that home of yours sweet at all costs. I don't know what your particular trouble is, but I do know some of the troubles we meet in upper middle age. Lyle, later on you're going to need all the companionship you can get. I'll put it in simple physical terms. No one properly explains what happens to a man in his fifties. The advertisements use words like "tired" and "depressed" and so on. But none of them gives you the real crux of the matter, which is that you lose *bounce*. You can still run up the stairs—but you don't always want to. You can still have a real old night out—but you can't be bothered. Tell you there's an egg to your tea? You're quite pleased. But you don't care either way, egg or no egg.'

Varley looked at him suspiciously.

'Yes, Mr Varley,' Lyle said.

'You've been having eggs to your tea, off and on, for just too many years. You're not tired of eggs. You haven't lost your appetite. You *like* eggs. What you've lost is simply the ability to get *excited* about eggs. And that's where the wife comes in.'

'Eh?'

'She'll be *there*, with the egg. You'll feel—how shall I say?—more settled about that egg in her company. No need to get excited. *She'll* be there. The substantiation of time, that's her. Your rejection of the egg and its fly-by-night excitement won't hurt so much. D'you follow me?'

Lyle was carried away despite himself: 'But wouldn't it be she, exactly her, who would come in brightly saying: "Here's an egg to your tea?" And you'd feel you had to respond?'

This seemed to confirm something in Varley's mind:

'Yes and no. She'd quite likely say it in a comforting, quiet voice: "Here's ... an ... egg ... to ... your ..." and so on. But the vital thing is, Lyle—*don't* cut away! You're going to need her. Don't think you can run off and get the better of time! Keep to her, Lyle!'

'What?'

Varley was staring out of the window, smiling and shaking his head at some personal memory.

'I know how it is at your age. I never went the whole

hog—cut a bit loose but never adrift. A passing, none the less touching, affair in Pimlico—as I remember, her alias at home, for business entertainment purposes, was Ivanhoe Investments Ltd. One can afford to smile. Be that as it may—I never once thought of *leaving* my wife. What you leave you'll never get back. And now the feverish forties are over, home's best—it's the only place to pass the long hours when you've lost the appetite for life.'

Lyle rose.

'I'm not actually thinking of leaving my wife,' he said.

Varley looked offended. 'Oh?'

'No. But thank you for your most helpful words.'

'Say no more, say no more,' Varley mumbled, and added, as if it might mollify the matter, 'Of course, most of us carry too much weight about on us nowadays. Fat's a killer.'

'Yes.'

'I expect things will right themselves.'

Lyle left, dazed and feeling a little mad. 'Ass,' he thought savagely, 'with his eggs.' But he already felt many years older, and fearful of the years ahead. He limped slowly back to his office, told his assistant that he was not after all up to it yet, put on his coat and walked down the stairs which became marble as soon as they came within view of the quietly chattering public hall. 'It's not exactly loss of appetite,' he thought. 'It's more— you don't know where to put your hunger any more', and looked down at the hall where so many were bent over smooth grey machines, or counting and annotating bills and bonds, or standing at the counter dealing with cash itself. All these people filled eight hours of their day doing this: they might resent it, but at least it made the leisure hours of greater value. But when even these free hours lose their value? When freedom plays its trump trick of becoming the ultimate limitless prison?

He remembered his training days down there when he served behind those same oxydized bronze bars counting certificates, and when people coming into the banking hall had looked so celestially free. They wore hats! Coats! They brought in the air of the streets! How he had envied them their little extra liberty, though it might simply have been stepping along from other offices to this bank. Well then—here he was about to step out onto the streets of beloved liberty, while across London his statutory gaoler packed up to leave.

He left the Underground half-way home to get some lunch. There would be none at home, Zoë lived her days on lettuce. But the place he went to, an old favourite, proved to be an unfortunate choice; he had not been there for some time, and now it had changed management and decoration and clientèle. He had a bad, uncomfortable, lonely lunch, feeling foreign among foreigners. When he left, he found the bus route home had been changed: he had to walk several streets to find how it went nowadays. This London he had known for so many years did not know him any more, he felt the more aged and cast out.

At home Zoë was in the kitchen dressed to go out and eating a large plateful of chicken left over from the night before.

'Hello.'

'Hello.'

She swallowed and looked up at the clock: 'I thought you were at the office?'

'I couldn't stand it. Zoë, look—I know by now you're serious about all this. I do see that now. But surely we ought to have a talk?'

'What about? I've said all there is to say.'

'Can't you see how I feel?'

She looked down at the chicken and said uncertainly: 'Of course I sympathize with you. And I know I ought to feel guilty. But I don't .There's a lot in making up one's mind. There doesn't seem room for anything else.'

'You're being very hard.'

'Sensible, purposeful.'

'And an utter bitch,' he said.

'Thanks.'

'Where are you going?'

She looked up surprised: 'Didn't I tell you? Friday.'

'I said *where* are you—what? Friday? You can't.'

'No?'

'But that's only three days! You can't just—'

'What you can't get into your head, Tony, is that I can. And nothing on earth can stop me. There's only one thing you can do and that's divorce me for desertion, eventually. The oddest fact about the marriage tie is that it's not binding.'

'So you're not marrying your fancy man?'

'There is no man.'

'Oh?'

'You can believe that.'

'Where are you going now all painted up?'

'Lipstick? I *say*! And eye-shadow!'

'Well where?'

'Around those diabolical shops, if you want to know. I shan't be in London again for some time.'

'Sure you can afford it? Saved up?'

She laughed. 'Certainly. Part of the payment for some

of the best years of my life. But not all of them. There lies the point. Now I really must dash—'

'I can't hit you,' he said quietly.

'No,' she smiled, 'that would hardly be it.'

'But I can be allowed to say that the marriage tie was once binding and it was binding not because of the law but because of the loyalty of the two people concerned.'

'And because of religious pressure. And money, money, money.'

'They were simply reinforcements.'

'Loyalty not very strong on its own?'

'You're a low bitch and you're trying to slide out because you haven't the guts to face some situation you won't even tell me about. You haven't even *explained* yourself! What do you expect me to do, stand here—' his voice was rising—'and smile? Doesn't all the time we've had together mean anything? What in the devil have I said or done to make you—'

He stopped. She had reached for her bag, taken out a half-crown, and thrown it on the floor. It rolled on the linoleum and whirred to a stop at his feet.

'—to make you take a step like this? Without any decent bloody warning at all, you announce your departure to nowhere—'

A penny followed the half-crown to his feet. Then a shilling. She was watching him carefully.

He paused again. It was a trick he had played on her during one or other of their rows, an attempt to make her stop talking. When in the male-female word-battle he had become exhausted, and she would still be in rising flight, the same words spinning out over and over again, until his ears ached and his mind whirled . . . he had taken up a pocketful of loose change and thrown it about the floor. As expected, she went about stooping and picking the coins up. And it did stop her. But not for long. With marvellous efficient adaptation, she learned to stoop and speak at full pitch at the same time.

And did she even feel foolish doing this? She had never shown it.

'Is it because of that?' he asked pointing to the coins. 'Have I upset you doing that kind of thing?'

She threw back her head and laughed. 'Good God, you're an ass.'

He had no wish to pick up the coins. But another instinct rose up instantly—because she had made a physical move against him, throwing things and laughing outright. 'I can't hit you,' he repeated. And then picked up a large bowl of what looked like dirty water and jerked it straight at her breast. The whole length of her dress changed colour and dripped.

'But mad bitches need a bucket of water!' he shouted.

She went white. She got up looking down at her dress.

'Chicken jelly,' she said. 'You bloody fool!' she shouted. 'You've ruined my dress, I'll miss Jill.'

'The hell with—who? Jill?'

'I had a date.'

She unhooked the dress, stepped out of it, held it up to look at the stain. 'Lovely,' she said.

'Jill?' he said, quieter.

'Yes Jill, Jill, Jill. She telephoned she was in a jam and wanted to talk, which meant she wanted to discuss us because you told her, didn't you? Last night? Christ, what a mess.'

'I had a word with Jack,' he said carefully.

She tore off her soaked brassière. 'I thought by talking to her I could get her to get some message through to your bone of a brain. I needn't have bothered.'

Standing there breathing hard, chicken jelly glistening

on her breasts, her words last night flashed back to him, 'I like it', and he was for the first time physically jealous.

If she liked just 'it', then she might take just anyone in the future? With an upset mind, especially going away, in new surroundings? 'I'll telephone Jill if you like,' he muttered, 'say you'll be late—'

'Telephone my bottom!' she said, strutting out of the door on high steps of anger. He gave a hopeless laugh like a little dead cough: then went quietly to telephone Jill to telephone Zoë that she was late and could Zoë fix a rather later time?

It worked. In a minute, Zoë answered the telephone upstairs. He went back to the kitchen—it seemed to be the proper place for some kind of ritual privacy—and a little later heard her leave the house. He looked down at all the money mixed up with running blobs of jelly. 'Foolish,' he said to himself, but felt not at all absurd as he went round picking up the coins, but instead neat and virtuous. He put them all in a bowl and washed them. It even occurred to him that this must be the first time in his forty-five years that he had washed money. And this reminded him of his age, and he tried to think back on what 'it' had felt like with other women long ago. Apart from a blur of youthfully smiling lips and a quickening of mental excitement, his mind remained a blank on most of this that had been so important in its time. It was like trying to remember the warmth of summer in a corridor cold with winter draughts. What a waste, he thought, pocketing the money.

GOODBYE

The house was empty for the first time since Zoë had said she was leaving.

It began to echo with the mouse-sounds that make up silence, creakings and rustlings of wind, the echo of a road-drill from the world outside—and he was made to feel what the future would be like.

It seemed inexplicable that such a silence is robbed of all its strength by the presence of someone else in the house: and it explained completely the force of companionship.

He glanced out of the hall window. Rows of chimneys against the travelling sky stood up stiller than ever. He opened the front door—certain evidence of loneliness, just to see the outside world—and looked up and down the street. Very little movement. The afternoon pause. Chalcott-Bentinck's car stood alone, no master home yet to tend it.

He stood uncertain, feeling a desperate loneliness fall on him: then, though even this empty street represented a better companionship than what lay inside, turned in again. 'Mange!' he called, 'Mango-boy!' with hope. But either Mange was deep in sleep, when he became morose and immovable as a cat, or out somewhere in the garden.

He started to go upstairs to take a look round Zoë's room, to bathe himself in the atmosphere of disaster. But he stopped, saving it up as a delicacy for later, and went to look for Mange instead.

He kept getting glimpses of her, memorial snapshots, as if she had already gone. Moments of strange girlishness, darting down a dab of nail varnish onto a laddered stocking, quick, quick, and a little skip afterwards. Trying to light a cigarette in the wind—no hope, eyes helpless at him. Strange, because most of the time you couldn't find the girl in her: she was poised, you couldn't see the

girl for the woman. Self-contained. Always laughed,
never giggled.

Amazing how she resumed a kind of perfect virginity
after they had made love: done, all over, intacta again,
her distant eyes declared. Like a self-sealing tube of
lighter fuel. It was infuriating, a man's nasty old need is
to make his mark. He quite relished the oven-burns on
her wrists—there at least was an evidence of affinity.

Mange sat in the middle of the lawn licking his old
parts. To the left, as you looked from the verandah, a
couple of limes, a darker sycamore, a silver aspen: to the
right, the dusky witchcraft of a may tree, again against
bright green limes with their blackened bushes beneath.
One odd and gracious ilex.

The leaves of all these trees were tired by the summer
but not yet turned. Yet a straggle of fallen leaves littered
the lawn, blown it seemed from nowhere. And in the
middle of this browning grass sat that russet shape of hair
drawing an old pleasure from the autumn of his member.

'Bad boy! Tchk!'

The dog, thinking this to be encouragement from the
master, went harder at his task.

Lyle walked on to the lawn, saw his wet bonfire
standing up like a little green hut at the end, and turned
away his eyes.

He looked down at the grass with its dark daisy-
leaves and wild moss, and there he saw a miniature red
plastic sword hilted by a kind of eagle-bird. He remembered that this bird's miniscule beak had once held a
paper pennant with some such words as Egg-anchovy,
possibly Sardette: hidden until now by the midsummer
overgrowth, it was a relic of a party back in beautiful
June.

Standing there in his bagging grey trousers, his grey

eyes under the grey skies saw the lawn smoothly mowed and women in their pale-coloured dresses stumbling to and fro on high heels, sometimes losing a shoe as it sank wedged in the bog of turf; and the men standing about like spruced-up undertakers in dark suits and white collars, a drink and a sausage and a cigarette in their three hands.

Flowers beamed rich with colour, golden June sunlight warmed the fresh evening scene, green trees billowed high above the chimneys. Those men also looked like warders in charge of the laughing, chattering women, who were intent upon exhibiting themselves, circling and flowing and over-animated. Half-filled glasses were left in secret corners of the grass itself; when he found them in the morning they looked private and sensual, as if things had been going on.

He walked a little further, feeling that as the summer grasses were dying away he might yet find one of those glasses, and if he did he would break into tears. He tried to steady himself: Don't be like everyone else, don't wallow in it. Get out of the house.

Then he found among the weeds under a tree the metal shaft of a pipe, and a blue tobacco tin. Tom's first pipe. Tom had come out and smoked quietly here, deep in growing-up thoughts. Why had he forgotten this prized equipment? Had he been suddenly called in to the house? Had Zoë's face appeared waving at the window? What had happened to all these little episodes, to time itself? No use consoling oneself with any continuum stuff—it did not feel so, the time was lost and gone, and that was that.

So the garden had secretly become a mosaic of small discarded objects—dog-collars, cocktail sticks, bits of toys, buttons, tools and anything else which dropped and hid itself as the vegetation lushly rose. Each winter bright little bits of plastic winked up at him from the cold. You could go about like a park-keeper picking things up for hours.

He bent down and reached for the pipe. A large red centipede, a long Chinese dragon in miniature, ran squirming out of it. Poor great armoured thing—better leave the pipe there, pipe and centipede's home, and a hundred bedroom slippers to go with it.

So his mind wandered as he wandered about this garden so full of various life. Soon a memory from that party in June came back—some woman in a green and black dress just laughing, simply that, nothing more. Why so fixed a picture of such a non-episode? Because something he had never even been conscious of had happened at the same time? . . . just as Zoë perhaps did not really know why she was going, or at most attributed the wrong reasons to her decision. A messy business— like this shrivelling, seeding garden which at other times managed to look so orderly and reasonable.

He kicked at a piece of broken plastic—God knows where it had come from. Plastic breaks easily enough but thereafter the pieces go on for ever . . . like all the damn past broken to a thousand unconnected, unusable facets . . . and he went on to think of Tom, how they had worried so much about him (at every age kind friends had said, 'He's at a difficult age,' no age was not difficult) and yet Tom had turned out suddenly so well. And had gone off. As he should do, bless him.

What if now a telegram came saying that Tom had yellow fever, was in danger? A truce with Zoë, a plane to the East, and all would be shelved and later solved. 'Please, Tom, *please*,' he said aloud.

At the sound of his voice Mange came padding up, his duty either completed or too tiresome to continue, and sat looking up with his spaniel eyes and white beard. 'Even Mange? Could Mange help?' Lyle's mind said. It was mostly her dog. If only it would fall ill, if somebody poisoned it . . . when a telephone rang distantly. Next door's? His? Jill? He bolted for the house. When he lifted the receiver, a man's voice with a pronounced Oxford accent said: 'Good afternoon, here is Ernst Popper. I am coming with my Hock wine for tasting in my car. I am in your district, please.'

'I am afraid it is inconvenient. Good day to you!'

Blasted intrusion. And now he was back in the empty house not knowing whether or not to go back to the troublesome garden—or where to go at all. The bell rang again. It still might be Jill?

'I thank you for wishing me a Good Day. We were just now cut off. I would like now the time to call on you—'

'Get the hell off my telephone!' he shouted. 'Donnerwetter—ficken Sie off.' He slammed down the receiver. Better try Jill, come to think of it. He dialled the Buckett's number. No answer. And also come to think of it, who was this Popper? Was it a cover for someone else? Zoë's illicit lover of the afternoons? He now found himself standing alert by the telephone, hoping almost lasciviously for Popper to ring again. But Popper never did.

At half-past five he marched from the house, concerned only with getting away from it and its garden and all its associations, and from himself also.

He had tried to ring Jill several times, but no answer.

No one else had telephoned him. Earlier he had found a note from Zoë about being back about nine and would he find his own dinner? He felt cut off from the whole world; so deeply that when he walked out of his front door and saw Chalcott-Bentinck already with his car, still with his bowler hat on and rubbing a wing with a little rag, his heart rose to see that life was resuming itself.

But—to think he was relying on C-B, even that Popper, for sustenance! Self-pity welled up again—self-pity seemed to act like a kind of chain-letter—and he passed Chalcott-Bentinck at an ostensibly fast pace, as if on some urgent errand. Once round the corner, facing another street of brown and cream houses, he slowed down.

It was, though, a slightly lively time of day, with the first people returning home from their work, with an extra flash of glass from passing cars. Savory was among those returning home, not bowlered but loosely flapping his tweeds and corduroy, artist-official of the advertising world. They stopped. Savory suggested a drink in his flat. 'Got something to show you,' he said, 'something special.'

But Lyle could not face going back near home. 'Look,' he said, 'why don't we go to a pub? I'm not very popular round about the house just now.'

Savory said, as if it were nothing: 'Of course—you were having a spot of bother with the missus?' And jovially added: 'Knew a chap once who put a notice BEWARE OF THE WIFE on his gate—two birds with one stone—maddened her and scared the burglars at the same time—'

'Savory, it's serious. She *is* leaving me. Look, do come and have a drink . . .'

Savory took a quick glance homewards before his good

nature said: 'Sure. There's a terrible place just a street away.'

Lyle was not used to the local pubs. Nowadays it was more restful to do any necessary drinking at home. But he did remember the old place, a bit broken down and quiet, which Savory indicated, and they went there. It now had highly-patterned fitted carpets, a number of different wallpapers, a black plastic bar, towering bowls of artificial flowers and other marks of affluence.

Upset again by the feeling of the passing years these changes brought, and wondering at the same time how the brewers could afford it all with people lurching all over such carpets—or didn't people lurch any more?—he heard Savory say: 'Look—I'm damned sorry about this. But above all, you know, you mustn't take the whole thing too personally.'

'Eh?'

'Just that it's happening a lot nowadays. What I mean is, don't feel *debased* by it.'

'But I do.'

'I know—but keep your dignity going. Have another? Remember, you're not the guilty party.'

'But that's exactly what I *do* feel I am. And I don't want to get drunk—not that old way out, thank you.'

'One or two won't hurt you.'

Then for a while he told Savory all about it. And Savory listened with quiet attention, giving him what at that time was the best consolation of all, an ear.

When, two or three drinks later, he excused himself to ring the Bucketts, there was at last an answer. But it was Jack. And Jack was oddly evasive about Jill speaking directly to him. There was a message from her, though. Not the kind of message for the telephone, though— could he drive over? Lyle gave him the name of the pub.

On the way back from the phone a hand gripped his arm. 'Meet the better half!' a voice said.

'Eric, you know I must fly,' another voice cut in, a woman's, before he was spun round to see Powsey's furrowed eyebrows and little three-cornered eyes, and standing by him a woman with brownish hair. Powsey drew himself up and saluted. 'My wife, Patsy,' he said. 'Mr Lyle.'

She was quite a big mouse of a woman. Colourless, undistinguished, nice-looking enough. Lyle was disturbed to think that herein lay the sexual vortex of which Powsey had spoken. If these things were possible with her, what hidden propensities had the more personable Zoë?

Then he remembered what was commonly said about the genus mouse-woman. And certainly Patsy now made off at speed, remarkably sure of herself. 'There goes my little bag of tricks,' Powsey laughed as she went, baring his teeth as if he were in pain. Bewildered by so much happening at once, Lyle blurted out: 'Mine's leaving me!'

'Who? What?'

A chance to cover it up. But he found he did not want to. Powsey, part of his near neighbourhood, appeared like another port in his storm. With a sudden rise of amiability he said: 'My wife is leaving me. I'm going to be all alone.' And the last words increased his feeling of trust for the blue tweeds in front of him.

'Good heavenly sakes alive!' Powsey said, plainly shocked.

'Come and have a drink.'

Lyle led him over to where Savory sat frowning darkly at a bright print of Regency hussars helping bonneted ladies out of a carriage. He introduced them. Powsey wondered whether Savory was a regular here too, for he himself dropped in most nights. Savory growled that he made it a principle to be irregular. Powsey laughed and said, Didn't he think that picture very kind of colourful? No, Savory said. Powsey said Savory was not one for Art, then? Christ! Savory said.

But when Lyle whispered, 'I've told him, he knows,' Savory instantly became polite and, on the surface, even friendly. He might have been told that Powsey was a member of some underground movement, or suffered from an incurable disease. Much was forgiven.

While they waited for Buckett to drive over from the modish working-class suburb where his brightly painted house stood surrounded by soot and sneers, Lyle felt the drinks loosening in him. The bar was slowly filling up. Savory sat back and shook his head, so that his forelock wagged in a serious-looking way:

'Now *what*, gentlemen, can we do *practically?*'

Silence as they considered this.

A man's voice nearby said: 'I say, that dog looks awfully like old Tiny Cartwright, doesn't it?'

A woman complained: 'Well, we've got to enjoy ourselves sometimes, haven't we?'

Powsey suddenly said: 'Will you be moving?'

It seemed a professionally ruthless question, though the man's face beamed genuine consideration. Also it was the first time that anyone from outside had declared the situation so finally wrapped and sealed. Lyle said loudly:

'I love my house!'

Savory intervened, kindly, but as if the question were

all decided: 'One of the ghastly things is the cleaning up afterwards. Legalities. Documents. Splitting up furniture, where to live—'

'Look, you know the way slates blow off in the winter gales?' Lyle said.

They nodded.

'And ceilings leak? And other things—the smell of gas? And pipes knocking? Will the boiler burst?'

They nodded again, in sympathy.

'And dry rot? And iced-up drainstacks? Frozen hoppers? Worm? Beetle? God, even a landslide?'

They nodded again—now a little nervously.

'Well—I can tell you I've had all those and I'd welcome them all back! I'd love living in that house whatever happened—if only my love was back there with me!'

Savory bowed his head and bit at a fingernail, Powsey looked, as usual, startled. Lyle went on:

'Every night for years I've gone round locking up at night, shooting bolts, turning keys, longing to get to bed—and I've cursed ... but God, wouldn't I love it now? The marks of old pictures on the walls, they're *our* marks, *our* shades of old sun and *our* draughts of dust! . . .' He felt he was going on a bit and tried a bleak manly smile: 'Why, I'd even welcome the attentions of that damned robin.'

Savory cut in sharply: 'You seem more married to the house than anything else.'

So they were going to stiffen him with hard words? Good. Anything welcome.

'Isn't everyone' he said, 'married to both house and wife inextricably? I remember old Mange on a lawn-mowing day, following the mower, green with flung grass, a dog gone green all over, a green dog. 'Who's an

Irish wolfhound now?' she said. Who else knows about that, who else has the picture? Only Zoë. When the lilies come up in June, shaggy as green Maltese terriers, we see them that way, we're reminded of what to others sounds a trifling episode. But not to us. And there's nobody else.'

Savory bit at him: 'You seem to be the only person who's had a past.'

'Without somebody to share it, it disappears. And I'm not only talking about the past. The present, every living day the present's making more of the past. But more slowly, I admit, as time goes faster. Why's that?'

Powsey began in a wandering tone: 'Time's a very wonderful thing. I was reading the other day how everything's really happening at once—'

'Balls,' Savory said. 'Time goes faster when you're older simply because your day's decided, you don't extend it by hesitating and choosing, as youth does.'

'Like space,' Lyle joined in. 'As middle age spreads and you grow solider, you seem to disappear, you don't feel *there* so much any more. Because you don't move so much. The perceptiveness of youth seems to come from movement—hell, what are we talking about?'

'But it's very interesting,' Powsey said eagerly, glasses glinting. 'There's a man, Dunne's his name, who says—'

'So you're feeling your age?' Savory said dully to Lyle. 'For instance you're writing off the things you thought one day you would do? Ticking off ambitions? Closing the regret-book? No time left? Sealing up the future? You ought to go out on the town, man! Go and get a girl!'

'I don't want to mess about with that kind of thing.'

A part of him wanted to add, 'Where?'

'Why not?' Savory asked.

'I never did that sort of thing. Zoë and I always kept—'

'Sure?'

Lyle looked up at the bad teeth and dark, hairy eyes: then at the interested glinting blue gimlets sitting beside them. 'They've already lost interest,' he thought. 'First the continuum and now promiscuity. Sympathy tires quick.'

Once he had suspected something of Zoë, and had purposely not followed up his suspicions in case they were confirmed. From cowardice, or from a depth of love? He found himself saying, for honesty's sake, or to stop being asked about Zoë: 'Once after a dinner I had to drive somebody's wife back to—to Sevenoaks. Her husband was away. Nothing happened, but it could have, it could have—there was a flare-up between, from both of us, she and I, we both knew it. I suppose habit stopped me. But it was so disappointing when we just said good-night. So very *sad*, you know.'

'But no you don't know—you never know,' Savory said.

'You've got to consider your biology,' Powsey droned. 'Perhaps it was only a woman's natural need to prove her attraction.'

Savory yawned: 'If a woman doesn't deceive her husband, she deceives herself.'

Lyle got up. 'Excuse me,' he said, and made for a moment's relief in the lavatory. Damn them and damn their generalities. All show of consideration had died, they were just talking. Where was old Jack Buckett? He pressed the pedal of a hot-air dryer and felt his hands go clammy. He waited, but his hands only seemed to get wetter: he gave it up and went into the bar again, wiping secret fingers on his suit.

GOODBYE

The bar was filling and gleamed with weird affluence. Glass of pictures winked through blue smoke, soft music clung to the walls like a warm draught, chromium shone and the wallpapers raged with flock and gilt. The brewers had skimped nothing except their customers, who looked shoddy and worn against such luxury, members of a beanfeast plodding through the rooms of a palace. Pipes, newspapers, beer—here and there slashed by the brightness of a woman's coat. The women looked like bits of coloured wallpaper. And no Jack Buckett.

When he got to the table it was as he imagined, his sympathizers were talking about something extraneous to the problem they were to solve: women still, but not *his* woman.

'In Tierra del Fuego,' Powsey relayed from some digest or other, 'they send the older women up to the hills to die. And I read that the Lhopa of Sikkim ate the bride's mother at the wedding feast.'

Savory replied, without listening:

'Suppose a really expensive modern painter, say Picasso, tattooed his wife all over? What happens later on? Does the nation stuff her? Ah—here's Lyle—'

But thankfully then Jack appeared in the doorway, peering about with open jaw. As happens with people entering unknown rooms, his defence system made him look as if he had just received appalling bad news.

Lyle's heart dropped. But he quickly got him a drink and introduced the others, saying that they knew all about the present trouble. He watched Jack closely. Had he noticed a newly worn lined look about the man's face last night? He really looked years older. Lyle swallowed, and said:

'You're not looking all that fit, Jack. Anything up?'

Jack looked at him surprised.

'Never felt better in my life.'

'Then it's—?'

'Didn't we say? We went away to a kind of hydro-place—colonic irrigaggers, starvation diet.'

'I see.' Lyle looked at the rugged new lines with relief.

'Feel ten years younger in fact.'

Jack paused. Cleared his throat. Looked at Lyle apologetically. 'I'm afraid my news is not good. Jill says Zoë's quite fixed on this business.'

'But why? *Why?* Did she say why?'

'Not exactly. Susan says its roughly a general wish to get away.'

'But what's the *reason?*'

Powsey put in: 'Things in general usually have a particular cause.'

Jack shrugged, looked sternly down at his sleeve as if counting the buttons and finding them insufficient. 'What women say together on these occasions—you can't ever know. Sometimes I think Susan's got her tongue in her cheek. But alas it's not. It's there in her mouth all the time. Bang centre and full of go.'

'Didn't she say anything more?'

'Said they were hours together. I suppose—talking round and round and round. Doesn't matter what she says, she's simply got to say it, thousand blasted words a minute.'

'Who?'

'Susan.'

Jack spoke her name darkly. It was unusual. He must be hiding something.

'But didn't she say *anything*—I mean, about where Zoë was going or anything?'

Jack still spoke sourly: 'Nothing definite. I did gather it has something to do with Hampshire—old family friends I think—but that's not where she's going. That's about all Susan said. The rest was hot air.'

'When I was a boy,' Savory said vaguely, 'I thought those two lumps they have on their chests were full of extra breath. Superchargers, as it were.'

Jack gave a tired laugh. Then: 'I'm afraid there's nothing I can do but confirm it all. I'm very sorry, old man.'

Lyle said slowly: 'Something's up. You're keeping something from me.'

'Me?'

'You're upset.'

Jack looked shifty, reached for a toothpick.

'May be. Something personal though. Rather not talk about it.' He made a brave attempt to smile. 'But then I'm upset about you, too. Now what practically are you going to do?'

A long silence.

'Drink up,' Savory at last said. 'Let's have another.'

Jack said: 'Plenty of water with it. I'm driving.'

They all laughed. Lyle felt hopeless. He wanted to be careful not to drink much, to keep a clear mind: but the alternative of the night outside faced him with blank indifference—there was simply nowhere for him to go. He thought of taking Mange for a walk: then saw the image of himself, pitiful lonely plodder with an aged, flat-footed hound, and called for another round of drinks.

So they sat on, drinking and talking. Again Lyle's problem drifted off course. Powsey had got hold of the word 'dichotomy': 'Those who consider us superior to the beast must be bonkers,' he said. 'We're split up the middle from the word go. We're one of the few species that both goes with the herd yet plays the lone wolf. Nearer to wolves than monkeys.'

'Like our best friend's the dog,' Savory chewed at him through yellow canines.

Lyle thought back on Mange. In a panic he suddenly wondered: Would she leave him with that damned dog? Or take the dog away? She'd even take the dog—she'd leave him absolutely alone.

'We spend our lives wanting different things at the same time. Peace and quiet and company and stimulation. The elegance of the past and the speed of the future. And so on,' Powsey piped high.

Savory intoned: 'Good luck to the Dignity of Doubt, but choice is wearing us all out.'

And Lyle, whose life had abruptly become one without choice, muzzily agreed.

The clock wheeled electrically on, the pub seemed to grow denser, though nobody new came in. Apart from Jack Buckett, still deep in his private problem, they grew animated, louder, capping each other, talking at absurd odds.

'After a certain age,' Savory yelled at Powsey, 'people become sexy at different times. There's many a healthy and even youthful-looking married couple living practically celibate, but for a formal bunk-up once a month.'

Powsey shouted back at him: 'The Ice-cap! One day we're told it's melting, the next advancing!'

Lyle found himself chuckling. Not the perfect answer, but not too far out. Then like a novice mute he remembered he ought to look sad. He bit his lip and let the load fall back again. And everything said seemed to be pertinent to, or symbolic of, his problem.

'Osmosis!' Powsey raved. 'Put an egg near a mushroom, put a melon with a bottle of milk! *And it's happening to us ourselves all the time!*'

'Real trouble about getting lung cancer is having to give up smoking,' Savory replied.

Suddenly Jack leaned over to him and grunted: '... in every woman there's a bitch raving to get out, and Nature's provided a couple of right frontal holes for just this, one topside, one below ...'

He certainly had it in for Jill tonight—but why?

'You can't be certain,' a man's voice said close above.

'You certainly can't,' another replied.

Suddenly Savory was on his feet, his shaggy length quivering, black eyes dancing with anger under the wobbling forelock. He pointed at the print above him on the wall: 'It's taken one hour and forty minutes for that bloody hussar to get that bird out of the carriage and he hasn't done it yet. . . . Gentlemen, I have a proposal. Let us adjourn to a spot I know where romance is romance, and not a cook-up. Friend Buckett shall drive us thither.'

Lyle looked at Jack. 'What about Jill—I mean, Susan?'

Buckett looked vague: 'She can wait,' he shrugged.

'Where's this chap taking us?' Powsey said.

'Ah-ha!' Savory barked back at him, waving them out.

They all straggled into Buckett's expensive, uncomfortably low-slung motor.

Lyle said to Powsey: 'At least you don't have to worry about getting back to *your* missus.'

Powsey gave a high toothy laugh. Then, with polite concern: 'I say, but how about your own lady-wife?'

My God, the man had forgotten! And then a second

later Lyle thought, My God, I'd almost forgotten too!
Is it possible?

And a few minutes later, as through the lamplit hush
of grey streets Savory told Buckett where to drive, he
was wondering, 'A place of romance? What could Savory
mean? A place with girls . . .?'

They came to a stop outside an old-fashioned underground railway station.

'Here we are!' Savory shouted. 'Just a tick while I nip
in here.'

He disappeared into a bright-lit off-licence next door,
returned with a bottle, beckoned them in through the
grimed Byzantine brick of the station portal, and bought
four tickets to the next station up the line.

On the way down the echoing stone steps, he explained: 'They get suspicious of platform tickets. Now—'
and he opened his arms wide as they reached a wide
platform open to the night air, 'isn't it magnificent?'

Beyond the old fretted wooden eaves acres of rails
extended to either side, fields of wet-looking steel about
which groups of trucks stood like cows. Here and there
the squat bull figure of a shunting engine blew cigar-
rings vertically upwards. Delicate tinkles came from
loving buffers. A junction of some sorts? Where were the
girls?

'No Man's Land where British Rail and London
Transport meet ! A sacred grove,' Savory recited as he
led them to a worn wooden bench. 'Iron Arcady! It's
not quite the same since the Diesels—but nonetheless be
seated, gentlemen.' He screwed off the top of the bottle
and passed whisky around.

'There,' he said pointing to a closed glassy door over
which stood the faded word *Refreshments*, 'was where we
used to sit and watch the iron horse go by. As feared, it's

closed. Tempora, mores. But look!' he shouted as a thundering down the line grew greater, 'here's a fine fat fellow coming up! All alive-oh from the merry Midlands!'

A sudden burst of darkness and light and fiery smoke as the monstrous train debauched from a far tunnel. But then, with an efficient smooth clanking, a long serpent of red slid in from the opposite direction and stopped at their platform, cancelling out the passing train.

'Croqueted!' yelled Savory. 'One up to Transport!' he roared with maniacal laughter.

A single youth alighted from the tube-train and glanced at them with sullen disinterest. The train wheezed its rubbery doors and left, and then, right in the middle of the sliding black web of rails, a fully lighted express came speeding by. 'Avanti!' Savory hissed with bated breath. 'The Master Butler hell-bound for the Dukeries!'

Trains then came and went, a few people got on and off, the whisky bottle passed to and fro. Nobody came to disturb their small symposium, it was a deserted platform in the centre of a fairly busy conjunction of rails. A few mid-evening travellers bound on lonely-looking errands; a linesman or two plodding by with lantern and hammer; and once a woman in a flowered hat, looking like part of a wedding, who crashed into one of the iron canopy pillars, hiccuped and apologized. Sometimes the spidery slim young ambled by, looking as though they had never eaten in their lives, murderous, shoulders hunched, hands deep in pockets weighed down with bicycle chains. A few negroes passed with faces like pieces of the night.

A portly gentleman stepped down from a carriage just as Savory let forth one of his wild bursts of laughter. He was dressed in a black overcoat, a black homburg perched squarely on his head. He marched over and peered at Savory through heavy horn rimmed glasses. 'It's not nice at all to laugh at another man's tribulations,' he said angrily, 'it's not decent. It's not done. You might be in the same boat yourself.'

Savory stopped astounded: 'Laugh?' he said. 'What boat?'

'I refer to my bump.'

'Bump?'

'My tumour,' he said. And in confirmation raised his hat to show the shining dome of a bald head with a big pink bump jutting up like an extra cupola. Replacing hat on bump, he moved off.

A second's silence as they tried to work this one out. But to Lyle, in his general confusion, the man's action fell into line with those chance phrases overheard in the pub—the more meaningless, then the heavier with strange, isolated significance. Why? And then he went on to consider glumly that Zoë's present action, though on the face of it equally erratic, held no such significance . . . it was only hard and unbelievable. Savory, who had started cackling again, noticed his gloom and whispered at him savagely:

'Having yourself a little weep? Why don't you do something, why don't you go home and give her a piece of a proper man's mind? Why don't you hit her like a man?'

He was plainly a quarrelsome kind of drunk. Lyle said quietly: 'How can you hit against nothing? She's given me nothing to—'

'Then do some bloody shadow-boxing. Go home and throw things at her—'

'I have.'

'What?' Savory spat at him.

'Chicken jelly.'

Savory's jaw fell open. 'You're certain?' he said. 'Chicken?'

Lyle giggled. An endless goods train idled musically by. He felt newly exhilarated: the sharp tone had been welcome, somebody had told him to *do* something. He could no more hit Zoë than fly—but being told to do so was in some way effective. He livened up. He even prodded Buckett in the ribs of his up-to-the-minute overcoat and asked him why *he* was so quiet tonight?

Buckett's black button eyes were lowered. 'It's damn funny old man,' he said, 'but you're about the only person in the world I can't tell.'

'But why on earth—?'

They were interrupted by Savory. 'Come on,' he said, flapping big sleeves at them, 'the bottle's drying and we haven't seen old Carew's place yet.'

Still wondering, Lyle was taken up the platform to where a glazed brick out-building stood wedged like a lavatory between sprouting iron pillars. The maroon-painted door was open, a weak light shone down on a wooden table. Oil-lamps stood about on the floor, there was a little bottom-high fire grate, rough coats on pegs, white and blue enamel tea-mugs, a big brown kettle. All the hard and weathered railway past lay here, last outpost on the brink of the dangerous sea of sliding steel rails.

'Old Carew's lair,' Savory intoned like a lecturer, with the others peering and swaying round him, 'from where he kept his station shipshape. A wintry fire in the grate, and old Carew trimming his lamps over a mug of char dark as boot polish. Or in summer—tending his lupins through the long June evenings! No man ever grew a lupin like old Carew. One year there was even talk of a floral clock.'

GOODBYE

The room smelled of oil and the past. A cosy kind of cottage, manly, for one man alone, Lyle thought: and envied it, yet at the same time trembled at the conception of hours passing, the slow tick, the weak yellow light. A vision of liberty and loneliness.

'Where's he now?' he asked. 'Where's Carew?'

Savory's voice lowered: 'Cut down in his prime by a 4-4-2. Lost him both legs, laid him six feet below. So no floral clock. It was the luck of the sidings: third accident in a group—they go like that, infectious, like plane crashes, like suicide.' And in a surprising soft baritone, he began to sing:

> '*Farewell, my love, farewell,*
> *The golden days are dying fast*
> *Summer and love are past*'

while the others stood uneasily round the little lighted empty room and glanced sometimes at the dark night stretching chill as iron beyond.

Savory sang on. Perhaps he was carried away by inner emotion, and felt himself to be a romantic figure—but he looked no more than a tall, tousled medical student tolling out a beery ballad. Yet the sound soaked into them and they stood moved in the weak light of Carew's illuminated shrine.

''Allo' 'allo? What's all this in aid of?' a deep voice barked.

'Another gallant railwayman!' Savory intoned. 'Heir to Carew!'

A rough figure pushed past them into the sanctuary.

'Gallant ballocks,' the man grunted from a hard, lined face. 'Get aht of it!'

Savory blew him a courteous kiss. Powsey waved.

'Not to worry, my good man! Our ways alas must part.'

'Bleedin' carols in September, unauthorized bleedin' persons—where's my tea?'

They left him mumbling on. 'Don't want to get on the wrong side of them,' Savory muttered. 'They're a lonely lot, and the puff-puffs are very sexy, you can't keep a good symbol down.'

They swung laughing up the steps, four middle-aged men with overcoats flapping open, Buckett in his little new hat and the others with their remaining hairs tousled by the wind—and Lyle thought: This isn't half bad! Nights out with the boys! Where to now?

Savory handed the tickets to a surprised inspector. 'My friend here'—indicating a now swaying Powsey— 'got taken with his weeping hernia,' and they were through and out.

'Where now?' Lyle asked expectantly.

But Savory flicked out his watch.

'In my case, to meet the redoubtable Liz.'

And Powsey said; 'Patsy'll be back soon. I'd better get home too.'

Buckett yawned. 'Check,' he said. 'Jump in and I'll drop you all off.'

And there it was, ten o'clock, and the evening collapsed.

Lyle sat quiet in the car, the others now spoke little. Games were over, the work of dealing with others lay ahead over the housetops, round the corners of lamplit tarmac, through voiceless front-doors.

Once, as they stopped and the red traffic light stared at them, two passing girls glanced down, paused, passed on. Lonely on the pavement, their two-togetherness homeward bound suggested possibilities of pleasure, delights impossible to arrange, an evening discarded. Lyle remembered an earlier disappointment—when he had thought Savory's invitaton to romance might have been to some place with women about.

So when Savory was dropped off at a terrace house which contained his Liz, Lyle managed to whisper to him through the goodbyes: 'You said about getting a girl. Where?'

Savory replied like a computer, while he was still shaking hands with Buckett: 'Paddington. Norbert Club, Norbert Street. Ring upper bell.'

Lyle was so surprised he remembered this address as if it were card-punched onto his forehead.

They drove on to let Powsey down. An upper window shone out bright, curtains undrawn.

'A-ha!' Powsey said, swaying out of the car.

'She's back then? You're not too early?'

He stood for a moment large and tall above the low-slung car. 'I must hurry upstairs and hear all about it!' he said, and his glasses caught the lamplight and glittered urgently.

Then, as he said goodnight, his voice seemed suddenly to sob. The drink? The sudden urgency? And Lyle could have sworn that something else glittered in the lamplight, something like sweat or a tear rolling down his cheek.

As Buckett drove off he said: 'It's not raining, is it?'

'No. Why?'

'Nothing. Yes. You know, I think I'll get out and walk a bit.'

Buckett said: 'Look here—I'm sorry I couldn't do more about your business. But that's—well, that's all Susan said. I think you'll just have to face up to things.'

'Yes.'

'These things happen.'

'Yes.'

'Here?'

'Yes.'

He got out and muttered thanks for all the trouble. Buckett seemed to be in a hurry, and as people do, looked for something more to say, not to appear discourteous. 'Send our love to Tom, by the way, next time you're writing.'

As the car coughed off and its low back winked lighted messages of corners and brakings, Lyle felt terror rising as he thought: Childless, oh, to have been childless and bound so close together like that Jack and his Jill. Tom! If only that bloody boy had never been! If only he'd drown . . . even now, if only he'd drown! And bit hard on his teeth to grind down his mind. Shook his head violently. Walked fast away from that spot.

Not home. Anywhere but home.

And seeing the lights of a pub: Why not finish it off? Why not make the alcohol do its full work?

Loathing himself, despising the banality of the bottle, he went in and ordered two large whiskies. He poured one glass into another, took a cigarette packet from his pocket, and wrote down Norbert Club, Norbert Street, Upper Bell.

Tonight? Not tonight. Drink tiring. He sat there thinking how he had set out for company and consolation, and each one of his consolers had finally emerged with a problem of their own. Powsey's strangled sob and tear. Buckett's withdrawn look, and this secret matter he could not mention to Lyle alone in the world. And Savory suddenly turning on him, savage ringmaster.

He ordered more whisky, began to get properly

fuddled. It was a different pub, but very similar to the other one, though nothing, when you looked hard, was the same. Thus again a carpet, again pictures, mixed wallpapers. No gilt here, but lots of bright blue paint: no hussars portrayed, but photographs of grinning band-leaders and singers: no plastic flowers, but great bowlfuls of the real thing nowadays never in public to be trusted—he only found this out, and was most un-nerved, when a petal fell.

And was this all the pub manager's choice? The real flowers his doing? How little one knew. And where did all these people come from? Once or twice he tried to talk with other men at the bar. They answered affably, but soon turned away to their own companions. In sudden anger, feeling immensely sober and purposeful, he left.

The night air hit him, he staggered again. He would go home? No—to the Norbert Club. No. But definitely to the Norbert tomorrow. For the moment, more sensible to go home and enjoy a quiet nightcap 'among my own things'. And half of them gone, he added.

But when he had let himself in very quietly, not liking to appear drunk in front of Zoë, and had checked her light on upstairs, and had poured a drink in the sitting-room to drink it by the light of one shaded lamp, he looked round at his 'things' which were all still there and wished them heartily gone. Scarcely an object, colour, piece of furniture but reminded him of their life together: not where it was bought, or by whom given—but in terms of time, always how long it had been together with them.

In the shadowed and silent room things stared and, in his own ears, whirred at him. He shook his head at them, laughed at them to put them in their proper place.

But then stopped. Suppose Zoë came down and found him grimacing to himself all alone?

He sat on rigidly still in his own armchair. Unable to move. Unable to stay out. Unable to move from room to room, unable to mount the stairs. Unable.

V

Hangover day.

He awoke at the usual time from an unusually lovely dream: woke up happy—before memory and the room hit him, his head hit him, and he turned over and grasped back at the lovely dream, to fall back into it, to dream and sleep his head off.

For once, marvellously, the dream did come back. It was about Tom, in the garden, and a rambler rose in full flower. Tom was dressed in a sailor suit of the time of Lyle's own childhood, and he and Tom were using the long green briars of the rambler as a field telephone, each using a full-blown pink rose as a speaker. 'Dot,' said Tom. 'Dash', Lyle replied, and the shade shone with sunlight far above.

But now in this regained dream, which began again quite as blissfully, Savory's voice came through on an extension line, a long green briar like a rope, booming horribly: 'I do hope nothing's happened?' And again, boom of doom: 'I-do-hope-nothing's-happened?'

He found himself shrieking back: 'How could *nothing* happen? It's absurd!'

'You should know,' boomed the voice and Tom grew an old salt's beard, his boy's face wizened and turned into a baked apple from which a stream of wasps flew like real electric cord winding about the green strands of briar.

He was wide awake. The day had to be faced—and now with a good dream turned bad, which would continue ominous for several hours, as well as a hangover. He listened for Zoë. Clatter from the kitchen. He went

135

quietly into the bathroom. Better not be seen like this, bloodshot eyes, shaky. Zoë and he had a long-standing difference on drinking habits.

Neither of them drank much regularly. But when he took too much he liked it to be in the open, a Bacchic burst, as permitted from old patriarchal days long gone. She was the opposite: she hid little bottles, and watered the bigger ones, for the idea of drink was still a guilty one, as handed down to women also from the manly old days. Once he had found that she watered her own private and hidden bottle: she even deceived herself, unable to face the accusation of the lowering level. There was also the economical trouble, drink was a great expense nowadays. So they went about stealthily on the matter: he only showing guilt in her presence, she hiding her guilt in his. The habit of guilt persisted with him even that morning. Even with the grey hangover shadow peppering round him, seeing the world through the binocular bone of skull-sockets, with a brain behind bedded in warm wirewool.

Cold water helped. And a good rinse of toothpaste to clear the mouth. But then he forgot to replace his false teeth before he looked in the shaving-glass, and found an elderly gumless grinning baby facing him—uneasy confirmation of the coming of second childhood.

He poised the razor and an awful thing happened—his face disappeared, he vanished. For a long second he stared at nothing, his heart bumped—but a long reaction told him that the little mirror had simply swung back on its plinth.

Yet the disappearance of identity had momentarily been complete. He knew now that it would be 'one of those mornings'. A hand would grasp at his tooth-mug: only seconds later would he know it to be his own hand.

Fingernails would break on cellophane, a passing jet-liner would be mistaken for thunder, newspaper head-lines would read unintelligibly, the jittery world would be shot with nameless fears. Once, on such a morning, he had put his face close down to a cat, playfully: the cat's upstretched and loving claw had got hooked into one of his nostrils. There had been a terrible tug-of-war. Better look out.

The front door banged, windows shook. Zoë off to the shops. How many times had he told her to close that door quietly? The house would collapse all around them . . . but only then, as the door slammed, did he fully see what shafts of sunlight had been arrowing at him all this time—for the sky had cleared, the wind dropped, it was a golden early autumn day.

Downstairs a note from Zoë: Back for Lunch. How calmly communicative they were now! In its essentials the home ran on like an efficient office—and at eleven he took a step through the French windows into the air.

Gold sunlight everywhere, bringing a rich patch of red from Virginia creeper which yesterday had looked only a dull sog of green, livening the patchwork rose and chestnut of bricks, lighting up a chrysanthemum, gilding each angled green leaf and living brown of bark. Now, no wind to move a thing. The whole green-red-brown garden had become a still tapestry, a weaving in detail of quietly burning colours wished up by some Late Victorian mediaevalist.

Then he saw that nature had responded instantly to the sun. A single rose had opened since dawn. Zazzing down to a dropped pear, a wasp. His dream leapt back at him. Prevision? How could this be? Sun through the curtains on to his eyelids asleep in bed? He shook his head, and went inside for beer.

GOODBYE

Bubbling cold beer alone would set his head right. No amount of ice-bags or aspirins would work such quick wonders. But bubbling cold beer must be watched. Beer led to gin. Beer was good and beer was bad. He poured two bottles of lager into a big tankard and took it outside. He sat on the blueing garden bench and took a deep draught: 'Bloody fool for last night.' he told the tankard. But then sense and the sunlight echoed back: 'What else could I do?'

The air was dancing with lightly coloured flies of many kinds. More wasps had joined the first. A fat female spider had spun a wide new web, and now sat waiting in the middle like a forty-stone acrobat on an enormous trapeze. Everywhere a million insects were at their jungle warfare in the grasses and among the steaming leaves. His mind went back to all the other days when he had sat and wondered at this green macrocosm. Before the day was out, a thin male spider would smell out that fat acrobat, and time and again would try to ascend the web. She would dart at him, bite, toss him back, and he would spin himself laboriously up to her again and it all would happen again and again until she was fertilized and his stomach perhaps eaten, leaving the lifeless legs stuck hanging like bones.

I suppose I'm better off than that, he told his tankard. But am I? At least what the spider's doing's natural? This with Zoë's an aberration—a lower-middle-aged mother sparrow leaving the nest?

How many late Julys had seen the ants rise, the air for a day full of wings, the window-panes splotched, the huge exodus lamed with casualty yet finally, somewhere, efficient. How many Augusts had seen the purple buddleia alive with butterflies, Red Admirals, and the cats come over the wall to get them? And what month was it the starlings would descend, all in a blue-black pack, pecking all over the lawn with their thin beaks and plump bodies, a manna-storm of miniature kiwis. Zoë loved to clap and see them rise, all at once, chittering a flashing black-jet life up into the trees.

Zoë had loved.

Zoë and he had sat here and loved doing and seeing things, those that brought you close, small matters growing large to make the bad large things grow small. The play of many coloured pigeons in the brilliant red maytree, as tropical a sight as you could devise. The myths they made up of previous owners of this house— of strange wooings in the now rotted summerhouse, of a mad Miss Evangeline in an upstairs room, of the good Major Pinkerton who spread sweetness and light everywhere he walked and covered the walls with assegais. Of the black-dressed Draper and his herb garden; of the first ones in crinoline and stove-pipe hats playing croquet at eventide, a candle on each hoop against the lawn-sweet darkness; and of that great question-mark, who had planted the Bluebottle Tree?

But the Bluebottle Tree was a reality. A castor-tree whose late autumn flowers, white balls on pins like atomic constructions, attracted the late and lay-about bluebottle. Hundreds of bluebottles would be found honey-drinking, or simply sunning themselves on those white pin-balls on a warm November day. And if it rained, there would still be clinging a few late drenched flies, like the last men of the season in a Belgian café, macked and bottled and game to the last. And of course round this Bluebottle Tree (which now he glanced at, thinking, too early, too early for the blue darlings) they had agreed the myth that picked policemen, naked but for their helmets, came to ring-dance, crying Down-a-bottle, Up-a-bottle, on the warmer November dawns.

All of which added up to time passing in beloved company, with the hoeing and weeding and knitting and mowing which went with it, and seemed to have no co-existence at all with the rows; which after all, he thought, had neither been so many nor so unusual.

'It's good to have someone to kick around,' she had said once. And going in for more lager it occurred to him that often the protraction of a tiff into a row was the result of a fear to be alone: you would not leave the house and calm down because you had to have company, that very minute, and so you stayed and because both were courageous or obsessed you battled it out to its black end. To have the courage to fight your convictions . . . he stood still for a moment, tankard in hand, and saw that since he and Zoë had been virtually separated, there had never been the breath of a row of the old broiling, brow-beating kind.

He drank deep—much better now, the head—and watched the garden reflected in the dark television screen. Coloured telly indeed, and a much better programme than usual. Indeed, how magical the garden looked, removed one step from reality. All beauty invites a remove—the pang of beauty is of something happening not exactly now but reflecting the image of something very like it long ago. Which does not mean that the beautiful moment did in fact happen long ago—but rather that long ago, in days of hope, you hoped it would happen; and it is really the hope you remember with so poignant a depth. Like the myth of golden youth cut down in its prime, he pottered on, being a magical back-look at the youth we all once dreamed of having but never did have, because we were from minute to minute always real, tied to our snot, our daily duties.

Like lovers, who do not love each other for their faults—which they simply excuse as easy parents excuse a child's faults—but faults which after a time they cannot do without, as one cannot do without a familiar disease: no, like lovers who love each other for the few hints which realize a dream of how they have always wanted someone to be, an old dream never to be relinquished, again the relic of times of hope.

But, whatever love was, the great friendliness of their times together. . . .

He sighed and looked round the beautiful, withering garden . . . no more, he thought, and went in for more beer, bringing a couple of bottles out to stand like company, two shining bobbin-chaps, at his feet.

When in spring the rosebeds flamed red with the first young leaves . . . and together they had considered her darkish skin, and traced on the map her genes coming from India across Egypt, dancing for a century in Roman Cadiz, then much later taking sherry-ship for Bristol . . . or the decisive moment when her great-great-etc-grandmother, Queen of the Cornish May, had been raped in her own cove by a Moorish pirate . . . in fact, their enquiries into each other; which had no end, for who finds out anything much about the other, God be praised? Though scratching the surface could be a perennial pleasure he supposed, he supposed—when the doorbell rang.

Who in hell's name now? Man selling brushes? German with a carful of hock? Zoë forgotten her key?

GOODBYE

It was Jenks. Jenks with his curly hair and red face, all flat cheekbones and boxer's brow and dimples even to the chin, Jenks in his white overalls and big tattoed bare arms strong as a lion. And his little old man, pale and bald and grey, standing by his side.

'You said to call,' Jenks said.

'Why, Jenks—yes.'

Lyle motioned him in. The man should have come in the afternoon. But then they never came at an appointed time, free men all, and better not to mention it. Now what the devil could he give him to do? The point of summoning him had been really to compensate for Zoë's political error with alternative work. But he had forgotten to think about it in detail.

Quickly he remembered a broken sashcord, a trellis blown down, a swollen door to be planed. Jenks and the old assistant went round with him. Jenks was not pleased. He agreed, he grunted: fiddling little jobs, his eyes said, and shone with the disciplined cold scorn of a corporal for a lieutenant. He wanted to build his bicycle shed.

The broken trellis was near the bench where Lyle had been drinking beer. He did not like to be found taking his ease with bottles by workmen on the job. The only thing to do was get a couple of glasses and pour a protective libation. This, the golden weather, and the underlying necessity to keep Jenks at any cost attached to the house, gave him a sudden and erratic idea. 'Sorry the bicycle idea had to fall through,' he said, 'but why not let's make it into a sort of toolshed-summerhouse at the end there?'

Jenks was not letting him off so lightly. He grunted approval, but added: 'Concrete floor and all?'

Lyle quickly nodded.

142

'Then I'd better nip back in the van and get a level and things for measuring up.'

Beefy and spring-heeled he had already started off. Lyle had to follow him to say: 'But do you need to start today?'

Jenks stopped and gave him a straight look: 'Well you do want to have it, do you?'

'Of course.'

'Only—' and for once Jenks hesitated—'I did hear you were leaving the district.'

'What?'

'Sort of—leaving the missus, I heard.'

Lyle caught his breath in anger. Surely Zoë had given no such news?

'Who told you?' he snapped.

'Oh, well—'

Jenks had crumpled. His strong blue eyes were glancing everywhere. 'Just talk, you know,' he muttered at his boots.

'It's utter nonsense.'

'Sorry, then. Beg pardon, sir, I'm sure.'

Sir! A 'sir' from Jenks! It almost cancelled out the new horror of the bush telegraph, with its whispering, its visions of hundreds discussing him over cups of tea, bacon counters, in and out the dry cleaners, over pub carpets. Pub carpets—that must be it, they had been overheard, misoverheard, last night.

'I'll leave my mate here, if I may,' Jenks said. 'Tim— take a look round at the site.'

'Right you are,' the old man said glumly, not moving, taking a slow sip at his beer.

As Jenks went, so Mange came plodding up. The old man looked at him distastefully.

'I see you got a dog,' he said.

'Yes,' Lyle nodded. 'Do you like dogs?'

'No. I 'ates 'em.'

'Oh?'

The old man shook his head. 'All shapes and sizes,' he grumbled, 'all colours. Can't abide 'em. You might say, like us, like the 'uman race. But dogs is more so.' He looked up sharply. 'Why can't they be the same?'

Lyle patiently nodded. The old man's words spangled the air like liver spots, the sun glazed his eyes. What next, this golden beery morning? And suddenly his confusion grew so strong he gave in to it. Calm came across him, he let himself see himself as discussing the time of day with a fine old gaffer over a pint of ale, and began to expatiate on the garden, the seasons:

'It's like being in the country here,' he said, waving a hand out at the tired trees, the lawn. 'Almost. Take a day in May, with the hawthorn heavy on the air, the green leaves massing, brilliant young green against a slate sky, the birds tweeting away fit to burst before the rain! Ah!'

He blew out a deep breath. The old man was looking at him in astonishment. 'Or early spring, the buds yellow like a dizzy screen after winter's black trellis, the crocuses so bright you need dark glasses, the early bumble bee tumbling about like a teeny-weeny teddy-bear—'

'Oh no,' the old man said shaking his head. It was plainly too much for him.

'Or even in winter,' Lyle went on, 'and snow all over, and the cat's paws making little holes which get bigger and bigger in the thaw so you'd think an abominable snow-man had crossed your lawn!'

'You can keep your gardens,' the old man said, 'I 'ad a window box once.'

'Yes? Yes?'

'Which I planted careful with petoonias like. Forked

round 'em. Squirted 'em. Looked after 'em like a mother I did. Fed 'em good. And what did they do?'

'I don't know.'

'Turned their bleedin' backs on me. Soon as the sun come out they turn their backs on me. All they think of's the ruddy sun. And there am I like a right charley sittin' in my chair and starin' at a lot of petoonia backs.'

'Rotten luck.'

'It'd be worse if you 'ad a garden full. Take your daffs, now. One side of your plot comes out all yellow in the sun, and what does the other do? Sits there waiting. Oh yes, they'll take their time, they'll all just wait easy like till them first ones is finished and then out they'll come. Never two sides alike. My missus 'ad a rose-tree once. She often talked of that tree in the old days. Fed it and watered it and cut off its suckers and dead wood, like a nurse she was. And what does 'is Nibs Mister Rose-tree do?'

'What?'

'Sticks 'is bloody great thorn in 'er thumb and it's up the 'ospital with 'er!'

'Ah well. They don't know, you know. Been married long?'

'Long as I can remember.'

'Real old Darby and Joan, eh?'

'Dunno. We got a nice little flat.'

'But you get on well, don't you?'

'Better than most, I reckon. 'Aven't spoken for twenty years.'

'What?'

'Not one bleedin' word.'

'Good God!'

'Saves a lot of argy-bargy,' the old man said.

'Felt a bit funny at first,' he added. 'You know,

bangin' into each other in the passage. You soon get used to it. Learn to swerve like a fish. Soon get used to anything.'

Lyle retreated inside. While the old man wandered down to the garden-end, he stood in his sitting-room pouring out more beer and gently giggling. Should he propose this solution? A lifetime together swerving like fishes?

Though the half of him was empty as ever with the ache of sadness and self-pity, the other half was filling with beer. He was not drunk, but the beer had overcome the hangover, a great mildness filled him. He remembered from his father's day how quiet and reasonable that man became after a night out, when he was at rest with a glass of wine: all attack gone, non-desirous and accepting. He looked through the window to where the old man was pottering: the bald head shone like bone, his soiled grey clothes took no glint of light. As if neither sun nor wind had ever weathered him, the old man walked about like a piece of white shadow. Then it struck him that the beer inside had not only eased his headache but eased by its bulk his stomach too. He wanted to call out to the old man this valid fact of life, as one wise gaffer to another: 'It's the great gassy bulk that strokes your inside, man! We're all wanting to scratch our insides. Look how we inhale cigarettes, scratch, scratch! Look how we like pepper, paprika, pimento—scratch, scratch! Think of the fiery throat-scratch of raw spirit! No wonder the exiled Londoner longs for a lungful of pea-souper!'

And while this near-joy of golden day and wisdom elated him—and while a dark sector was also saying that a lifetime's love cannot be interrupted, for it is like painting a house three-quarter's way through, you cannot leave it, alter it, or start all over again—the brief thought of raw spirits said to him: 'A drop of gin? Why not?'

But just then somebody who knew why not turned her key in the door, and came straight into the sitting-room where he stood, tankard at hand.

'Lunch'll be ready in about ten minutes,' Zoë said. 'I got us chops. I thought you'd better have a good hot meal.'

His instant reaction was fury. How many times had she spoiled this particular pleasure! How many times played the comic-paper wife standing between husband and bottle! And worse was that the back of his mind knew her to be right.

'I must hurry and get them on,' she said evenly. 'Will you lay? I shouldn't have any more of that, if I were you.'

His mind began to shout: 'You're *not* me!' when the great mildness overcame him again, and indeed a thought abruptly brimming with hope: 'She bought chops. She cares.'

She capped this with an enquiry. 'Who were you with last night?' going out with her string bag full of chops.

Interest in him!

'Chap next door. That tall advertising chap, you know, bit of an eccentric in his ordinary way. And Powsey the house-agent'—and he chuckled slightly—'ordinary chap in his eccentric way. Full of psephology and cybernetics and stuff.'

She shook her head. 'I don't know what you're talking about, or is the beer talking? Where were you?'

'We had a drink on a railway station.'

'All boys together?'

'If you like.'

'Wasn't Jack with you, I thought?'

'Then why do you ask?'

'Did he say anything?'

This made him angry again. Coldly he said: 'Only what I've heard before. Why do *you* ask?'

She started to go: 'Oh, nothing—nothing that can't wait—I must get these on.'

His brain leapt at the idea that at last she had changed her mind—that she probably wanted to cancel Jack's message of confirmation? He looked at his watch. Not one o'clock yet! There was just time!

He rushed out of the front-door, his whole frame singing and suddenly agile, even meeting Jenks on his way, not stopping for Jenks, just calling 'back in ten minutes' at Jenks—and after puffing round two corners found himself opposite the antique shop full of clocks and vases.

There it was still—an old but not ancient Greek silver arm-band, a bicep-bangle he knew she would like, she had admired a new one brought back by a friend from Greece. Before, he had hesitated to buy it. Mean, he now thought. Mean. Mean. And went in, and found himself lucky enough to have the money on him to take it away. And some over to load his arm with flowers from the flower-shop.

He went into the pub and had a quick large gin, slily getting one over her, before hurrying back to go quietly round the side of the house to get and fill vases at an outside tap and set white chrysanthemums out all round the sitting-room. 'There! That looks a bit more like home!'

He coughed and made stamping noises to show he was in.

Zoë came straight in. 'Where've you *been*? It's ready on the table. My God, what's this—a funeral parlour?'

He spread his arms, the gin rising facetious to announce: 'All my own work! Looks a bit more like home, doesn't it?'

She looked at him hard: 'Come on,' she said.

'Coming quietly,' he laughed.

He would dearly have liked another gin, and considered even popping back to the sitting-room, but knew by now she would be after him, so instead bit with a will into a chop. After a few mouthfuls the playful spirit subsided, he felt again comfortable and expansive. He was reminded that though these new omens were good, he had to play carefully.

'Time of year always reminds me of coming back from summer holidays,' he said. 'Not quite autumn, but summer finished. And so much cooler than abroad. We've had some good times away, haven't we?'

She ate fast and neatly. Her dark eyes looked far out of the window. 'Yes. Of course.'

A table for two in a restaurant is an excitement, festive, intimate, filled. But a dining-room for two is the opposite, empty, impermanent as a waiting-room, polished spaces doing nothing, a lack of silver and wine, empty chairs making a meagreness. A table, whatever is eaten, suggestive of cold mutton and silence.

'Which was the best, do you think?' he asked gaily. 'Best holiday of all?'

Ingenuous and intimate, like the very young discussing anything. Something must always be best. But then what followed? That best was unfair to something else.

'Oh, I don't know.' She looked at him sharply then

returned to the window. 'Bits and pieces of each, I suppose,' she said vaguely. 'Budva? Port Cros? Derwentwater?'

'St Tropez before the Trop set in?' he joined genially. 'Oh dear me, the places we've been, the balconies, bedrooms—the chandelier always hanging off its socket, the mysterious thin cupboards, no coat-hangers, no wastepaper basket, the salami-shops: I don't know,' he wagged his head reminiscently.

'What don't you know?'

'Which pill was which.'

'What?'

'Sorry—wandering—thinking about the pills that got away, the ones you find in an empty suitcase when you get back, you don't know which they are.'

He pulled himself back to what he really wanted to say: 'Look, Zoë—we haven't been away for the last couple of years. Would you like a holiday? Go right far away somewhere? I could manage it.'

'I'll bring the pudding in.'

She put a big plate of marmalade roll in front of him. He knew this was an after-drink confection for 'soaking it up': he also knew his offer had not been accepted.

'I meant I could manage the money. For you. By yourself,' he said. 'You know I've been damn careful to save some reserves after the landslip.'

'All the more reason to keep them.'

He thought for a moment. 'You know—if you wanted a real blow, I could get you half way round the world. How about that? Have a real good breather?'

It had not occurred to him before. He swelled magnanimously, his hand went to his pocket where the bracelet lay. He gripped it ready.

'Why not *all* the way round the world?' she said.

His hand left the bracelet. Yet there was still a familiar last hope:

'But you haven't even yet given a *reason* for all this. Have I *done* something? Have I *said* something?'

She stared out of the window, then got up to collect the plates. 'Eat your pudding,' she said. 'No, you've neither done nor said anything.'

'Then *why?*'

'I can't tell you,' she said. And thoughtfully, 'I really can't.

'You must.'

'I can tell you what it's *not*. It's not a man. It's not something you've said or done. It's no physical change in me. It's not Tom. It's not the house or anything specific, it's not,' and she looked at him a moment curiously, 'it's not even you.'

Anger tickled up: 'You having a slow brainstorm or something? Are you just fed up or what?'

She said evenly: 'Fed up? Yes.'

'But don't you see you're doing what thousands of people from time to time would like to do? Only they don't.'

'Oh yes. I see that.'

'You're just giving in, being weak.'

'No. I'm doing it. They don't. I should have thought that was strength.'

She put a hand to her forehead, remembering something she had forgotten.

'But of course!' she said. 'I should have asked for a divorce, shouldn't I? Right at the beginning. That's what they do, don't they? They come all glassy-eyed at you saying, "I want a divorce." Would that have made it clear?'

'Tone doesn't suit you,' he muttered. 'Do you want a divorce?'

'I haven't thought,' she said. 'Anyway—it could come later?'

Absurd hope rose again. But he said bitterly: 'And what am I supposed to do while you take a year off making up your delicate mind?'

'It won't be for only a year,' she said. 'Don't you *see?*' And then snapped suddenly matter-of-fact: 'Look, there *are* a lot of practical things to consider. There's furniture, for instance. We'll have to do that by letter. I'll need some things. I don't know yet. And there's Mange, I'll take him, he's always been really my dog. O God, it's not so easy, is it?'

'Like to take a couple of chimney pots while you're at it? A slice off the old wainscot? There's a tasty dado in the—'

She left the room.

So she was even taking his dog from him! And Mange's white old jowl, which he despised so, came dearly to heart. The long walks from lamp-post to lamp-post no more. . . .

He got up, and saw Jenks and the old man busy at the end of the garden. One thing he detested was a new creosoted hut at the end of a garden. It would have a bright green roof too, trust bloody Jenks. But could he now rescind his new order? And lose Jenks? Did he ever really want Jenks or the house any more? Would he go on living there? Christ, but everything was in a mess . . . at least they couldn't put concrete down today, he'd speak to him later, the thing now was to go upstairs and have a really good go at Zoë, she'd not given any concrete explanation yet . . . concrete my God . . . he went upstairs and found Zoë sitting on the bed sewing.

He sat down by her writing-desk, put his feet up on a trunk, and started in.

Round and round they argued, talked, discussed for an hour or more, round and round as these things go, where no decision could be made nor solution found. Like people discussing the future of a neurotic friend, all impatient for a cure, all knowing it must go on and no way out.

Zoë sewed. To one side she had a pile of unmended clothes, to the other side the neatly coiled and folded mended things. All through their talk her two hands sewed on voraciously and without pausing, like silk-worms munching through a great pile of leaves and leaving behind them an orderly and compact faeces.

He tried to analyse her daily life, to find out what was wanting. What did she do? Well—the house. That was a good half-day. Was it so very boring? In some ways, of course: but in others, quite creative, satisfying to see it all arranged and done afterwards. And the rest of the time? Nothing that sounded very particular—meeting people and talking, shopping and window-shopping, sometimes a film or a picture exhibition. 'And I do read books', she said. 'And I walk, I like to watch people. Altogether not very much more than life in an enormous village—a day made up of human contacts, news and a few artificial stimulations. What does anyone else do?'

'Keep rabbits', he said, 'learn fencing. Everybody needs a hobby'. 'Really?' she wondered, 'and how many have one? In point of fact I have a nervous leaning towards early Latin-American architecture. Will that do? And you can throw in the odd *fado*'. He said quietly, 'We do like our trips out to the country'. 'Yes', she said, 'we do like them, don't we?' And went on sewing.

Whenever he touched on her future, or the reasons for her going, he met the same blank wall. Only when he digressed, did she become interested in spite of herself. In a way, what with the sewing and the bedroom afternoon light, it was a little like talking to a nanny who would amiably let the child ramble on, but pursed her lips close at any mention of naughtiness. However, Zoë responded more than a nanny. When he chanced to mention the Change, and how fearful an idea it was to contemplate a woman judge, she flared up with a fearful comparison of a lonely old male judiciary full of port and the belly-ache, prostate trouble and wig-itch.

Married love, he ventured, was a prison without bars, where each invites his gaoler to share a cell: but since they invite, they are their own gaolers. And later you find you cannot do without your gaoler. 'But who', she replied, 'is to distinguish between prisoner and gaoler? Each one is each—but always between two people one of them rides into the ascendant.' 'The ultimate motive being power?' he asked. She thought: The motive being to have an effect, to make your mark on someone else. 'That's a rather male attitude', he complained. 'Hah', said Nanny, biting cotton thread with fierce teeth.

Her interest seemed to rise at any problem of love relationship. As when he talked of the closeness of two living together—identifying oneself with the other, so that when she, Zoë, had sometimes in the past got ready to go out alone, he had found himself half-doing the same, pottering about after his key-chain, looking for a clean handkerchief, filling absent-mindedly a cigarette case . . . or as when he mentioned 'family' stories, which could only exist between two, how their repetition was both ugly and beautiful according to mood—you sat back sometimes lovingly, as if a consolatory pipe were being smoked out of the wife's mouth, yet at other times in a fury at such reiteration you picked a hang-nail under the dining-table until it bled.

'Oh?' she said. 'For my part, I've often stopped myself. I get so embarrassed and I don't even remember, from time to time, whether I've told you of something or not, whether or not, and so I just don't talk. That is one of the reasons for married silence.' He looked at her amazed. That this closure could go on at the same time as the ever-open mouth speaking the thoughts of the mind-thing above?

'But sometimes', she said, 'I've wondered whether you love me, *me*—or whether you just love your love of me?'

'Put that in Metro-Pan-a-Color', he nearly said. But being a man, spoke back about sex, and sex being nothing to do with marriage, an entirely different function. Marriage was living and loving, sex was a right good and sometimes complicated and distinguished meal.

Sex was an elevated eating, he said, and like other organic functions sieved through the human brain it had many forms—just like everything else, he said—so you could have farmyard sex or gourmet's sex or troubador's non-sex, or prisoner's hunger-bread-sex, or curiosity-killed-the-keyhole sex, or climb-Everest sex and so on. Nanny's interest lessened at this, she stitched on with an unblown sigh. 'Yes', she said vaguely, 'like anything else there's lots of kinds of it. But a woman likes to lose herself', she said. 'Farmyard?' he asked. 'Celestially', she breathed. 'Cow schmow,' he smirked, 'celestial-bestial.' She shut up.

'It's a pity,' she said, 'that you haven't got more friends round here. I mean, real friends.'

'They go, in any case, when you're married.'

'Well—even close acquaintances.'

'You're my closest acquaintance.'

'Toothbrush style.'

'No. You're my best friend.'

'And I'm taking your dog, I suppose?' she now sighed.

But she was then suddenly sympathetic. 'I can't say how much I sympathize with you,' she said softly, 'it would sound odiously conceited. After all, who am I?'

'After all?' he said dry.

'Who am I?' she repeated humbly.

He let a pause come. And then said quietly: 'All I've got.'

Her lip curled quite cruelly at this.

Her diary lay open by his elbow on the writing-desk. It was blank on both open pages. He was astonished to notice the date. A month ago! And not written on yet? Zoë kept a fairly constant diary. 'Notes of a few happenings,' she always said, 'from which I can often recall whole days.' Those blank pages were thus an unusual interruption, as if life had then abruptly stopped. He asked her when she had made up her mind to leave. 'Oh, about a month ago.'

Sewing, sewing, implacably going. He looked round hopelessly at the suitcases. Several were already locked. One had its lid open, and he saw embedded in clothes a large medicine bottle: it was filled with pills, he recognized them as her 'sleepers', but these were a mixed aggregate from several half-empty boxes, all colours, and looking like bright little assorted sweets. 'Hundreds of thousands,' he thought, 'and hundreds of holidays they came back from. Funny, when I said that at lunch.'

When he mentioned middle age, her fingers moved more quickly, as if scampering away from the question. 'If and when you go,' he said, 'it's no good thinking that time will hang heavier on the hands. It's speeded up for-ever now. Things keep coming round, keep coming round—the weekly journal, the cutting of the nails, the milkman's bill, the haircut. Very soon, it almost seems, I shall be cutting my nails every day. But as time speeds up the body slows down. What middle age, the upper middle age that's soon coming to us, means is that the failing body needs the close companionship of another, for it must discuss itself, compare itself, compete also with another close to it. Not just a friend in the park, but someone to creak about the stairs with, groan on the john with. What we think of as boring talk about illness is no joke, it's the very meat of living.'

She nodded, and smiled as at a bad taste: 'A few years to go yet. Though what I do look forward to when I'm old is Tom. When he's stronger and perhaps wiser than I'll be. A mother becomes a kind of daughter to her son.'

When she said anything like that, or anything—which was not much—about the future, he could still summon up a little hatred. He could look at her sewing there, and think: What a friend. What a rotten nurse she is when you're sick. That's when the self-centred really show themselves up. It's almost worth being ill to watch it.'

He tried again and again to sound her further, to get some sort of explanation. The sun went shadowing round the garden. Inside the room, it projected brilliant tree-devices on the wallpaper, luminous ink-washes breathless to watch. As he tried again and again to worm out of her where she was going, how her life would be; and again and again what reason there was for it? But she never answered, only bent her head more firmly to her sewing.

Though once, as again he tried to draw her sympathy with talk of the past, she evaded him with generalizations about all hankering for the past. For me, she said, it is not the historic past, not the melancholy-sweet vague wish for this period or that. That's just romantic golden-ageing. No—I want one exact period, and that is the period when my parents were married and about to have me. Sometime then. For whatever we think later of our parents, and whatever better or worse we might do ourselves, we want dearly to satisfy our very earliest childhood ambitions and become some kind of a replica of those particular 'grown-ups'. To grow up and to take the *exact* place of our parents.

'But when we do grow up there's no exact place to take, the world has changed. Too often we get it given us the wrong way round, we do in fact assume their personality, inbred in us and flowering in middle age: but there's no place to take, it's gone. Some people cling to old houses and never change the furniture: it goes some way towards satisfying this want, which is as fully unsatisfiable as any other.'

He thought: So it's Hampshire she's after, after all. She's let the cat out of her big bad bag at last!

'It's not Lessingham,' she said, 'if you're on to that one. Lessingham's changed, Lessingham's quite gone. More's the pity,' she added, 'though, as Jack Buckett probably told you, I'm getting a spot of help from someone near by.'

'Still—that's where you're going.'

She shook her head. 'No.'

'Who is it?'

'Nobody you know. A family down there—I've talked about them in the past. You never listened.'

GOODBYE

'I've tried a million times to explain to you that you can't digest people you're just told about. Just names and no incident. Anyway, it seems these old nameless names, or your early years, are abducting you.'

She shook her head again. 'No. Just an introduction from them. To somewhere else. And I'm not saying what or where.'

She closed her lips firmly.

He felt tired out. Earlier he had thought: I shall give her a brain-washing, hard one moment, soft the next. I shall wash it out of her. But now he found his own brain washed out, he was un-nerved and tired and the morning's beer was telling and his relapse from effort brought on a dull headache. The late sunlight glared straight into his eyes: 'I think I'll go and lie down,' he said.

She sewed on. Not until he had opened the door did she say absently: 'You do. Jill's coming in for half an hour soon.'

He stopped. But then at the thought of Jill felt even more tired. 'Why? You two—I suppose she's relishing this.'

'No. I don't think so.'

'Whenever that woman does any one thing she natters about it before and natters about it afterwards. She does everything in fact three times. Must make for an exciting life.'

'Not at the moment.'

'Why?'

'Oh, something. I don't think you'd better know about it.'

'My God, can't I know anything?'

'Just better go on thinking she's making mountains out of molehills.'

He felt like bursting.

159

'The bloody opposite to what you do!' he shouted and slammed the door.

Just what he had not wanted to do. Again she'd made him lose his temper. Again emasculated him, put him in her female position of having a last word and flinging out.

He went into his bedroom, darkened it, lay down. The blood throbbed as frustration boiled up in the darkness. His pillow grew hot, he thrashed it over. He could not get quiet, turned, put his legs in different positions. Got up, took aspirins. And then slowly sleep came. The doorbell rang, and he dropped off.

When he woke up the sun was gone.

Voices downstairs. Female voices thin and continuous, like a muffled sound of music. He washed and went down.

Jill got up as soon as he entered the room. She did not look at him, but said to Zoë in what was plainly a confected tone: 'It's late. We're dining out. Suppose I'd better get dressed and go as little me.'

Zoë said: 'Must you go?' not meaning it.

He said: 'Evening, Susan.'

Jill made no reply but busied herself with her bag and pulling her dress straight. 'I'll be ringing you,' she said to Zoë.

'What exactly is the mystery?' he asked. He stood purposely in the way of the door.

Jill spun her big flowery form round at him: 'If you want to know, Jack's leaving me. And it's all your fault.'

'Jack? My fault?'

She took out a little handkerchief and began to dab

at her mouth, then one eye and then the other, but very carefully. 'You and Zoë. It's infectious. It set him thinking. Your fault for telling—'

'But dammit, *I'm* not leaving Zoë.'

'You *told* him. It's your fault for telling. And your fault for being so—wet. Wet and weak, why can't you *do* something?'

Zoë said clearly over her: 'Susan came here because she thought there was something between Jack and me.'

She saw then that his eyes had grown wide and his mouth had opened as if to bite on this.

'No, no,' and her foot gave a little stamp, 'don't *you* start thinking—she was only putting two and two together, that is one and one. . . .' She began to laugh weakly, and then covered it, but not before Jill snapped: 'I'm going!'

He found he could only say: 'But why—why's Jack—? I'm so sorry . . .'

But she had left and Zoë followed to see her into her car. Lyle was left standing astounded and sorry, but also furious that his own unhappiness had been swept aside, rejected even by this Jill.

When Zoë came back he said: 'What's at the bottom of it? Jack seemed oddly angry with her last night. Wouldn't say why.'

'Felt guilty. Shifting the blame, I should think.'

'Why is it, then?'

'I think,' she said, 'it's because he wants a child. At least, that's what he told her.'

'Heavens, that's pretty rotten—'

'It is, isn't it?'

She shrugged her shoulders, smiled sadly.

'But Zoë—after all this time? And why did she pick on you?'

She stood there thinking. 'Not only putting one and one together. Instinct. There's a lot in what she said—it's infectious. That's the damnable thing. He's probably nursed this thing about a child—and, well, it was us who brought it out.'

'Us?'

'I'm sorry. Oh God, I'm sorry. I mean, me.' She suddenly sat down and broke into tears.

'Zoë . . . Zoë . . . sweet—'

He went over and put his hand on her shoulder. It was shaking up and down with her tears. It took one big heave up.

'Oh, shit off!' she shouted.

Her upturned face, ugly with tears. He turned away and left. Went upstairs, put on a suit, came down again and left the house. He shut the front door quietly. He knew it had been a moment when he should have accepted anything she said, and should simply have tried to help her in her distress. But he could not. Closing the front door quietly was as much of a concession as he could manage.

VI

DISORDER. A man now of fixed habit, this exit from the house had been too quick. No money in his pocket. But the local wine-shop was open, he went in and cashed a cheque. Then looked down and saw his shirt was unchanged. He reversed the cuffs and took a tube to the West End.

To get right away, have a stroll around the West, take a look at things! End of a perfect day indeed. But no more drinking, no more of that. Just a lonely old walk around—there would be more of it in the future.

An hour later he was sitting more shaken than ever in a brassy old-fashioned bar which had remained reasonably unchanged since the turn of the century. How much his old West End had changed! Landmark after landmark had gone. Rock-like old restaurants made of mahogany and marble and golden cupids had vanished without trace, old brown pubs had been gutted and refurbished with undrinkable textures. The shops offered intemperate new eye-levels of plate-glass filled with coloured commodities whose nature he could hardly recognize: lamp-posts were painted new colours, the overall lighting had become hard and strange, the shape and colours of the passing crowd was unlike anything he had suspected.

And the amount of young people about! He knew about all this from his daily papers. But the live impact was considerably different, no grey-and-white comment. Spending his time largely between the still-male City and his quiet inner suburb, he had not properly walked about here for a half-dozen years. Going to an occasional theatre glassed away in a taxi had no parallel with this walking and mixing in with the crowd: occasional visits to shops away towards St James's had been absorbed errands. What he found now was that he was afraid.

He tried to tell himself that this was a result of momentarily jittered nerves. But was it? It was not general fear. It was a particular fear of incapability: of not knowing what something might be if he were asked, of not replying in the right up-to-date language if he got into a passing argument, of not even recognizing roads or bus routes or anything at all about this new old place. In a foreign city he would feel protected by his status as a foreigner, all excused: but here he would be expected to know.

He felt dated and done. He had even seen a shop labelled MENSWEAR and his reaction had been 'of course they do and why not', before the intended meaning clicked. Grey parkometres lined the pavements where prostitutes had once stood. Hardly as colourful, but cheaper. Wandering along, head in air, he bruised his chest on a couple of them: but just as hard, he told himself.

So he sat with his lime-juice and tried to get a proper balance on things. He tried to think of Jack Buckett, and whether it could really be true Jack had been affected by Zoë's leaving? And to give such a reason to Jill! Then he called to mind Jack asking after Tom with more meaning than before, even as if he had really meant it, the previous night. And Zoë had wept ... she must then be more moved by all this than he had thought? Yet hitherto she had shown little emotion—in fact, the opposite, a fearful efficient calm. Had she been steeling herself?

He thought not. When throughout that afternoon she had talked and sewed, a sort of vague contentment had emanated from her sitting figure, as if, yes, she were sitting on an egg and pleased to be doing so. He was forced to conclude that in his company she remained unmoved, but was very capable of being sympathetic with the troubles of others.

He sipped at his lime-juice and looked round at this old bar he knew so well. Something was wrong about it. Yet it seemed to be unchanged, the cut glass still glittered, the brass electrolier nymphs still held aloft their light-bulbs as if searching for Edison, the great mahogany horseshoe of the bar and the dairy-like faience pillars and the brown nicotined ceiling and everything else seemed as stable and weathered as ever. Then, of course, he realized it was the people. They were very different, all in their dress different from old days only five or ten years ago. There were many more and much weirder women about. He said aloud: 'Women!' and a man sitting beside him said, 'Ah!'

This man seemed to have a very stiff neck, his whole upper torso and face was turned to Lyle, so there was no possibility of avoiding a polite acknowledgement.

'Another bloody bloodless revolution,' the man said. 'They got us good and proper.'

He was elderly, with white hair yellowed by pomade, dead grey eyes, and an amiable smile in a fleshy pink fish-face. He looked like a mullet.

'I meant no disrespect,' Lyle smiled.

'You got to watch your mouth these days. A man can't holler out a decent oath these days.'

A big stiff mullet, in a stiff white collar, stiff as a stiff pink fish on a slab. Lyle took to him. Simply because he was sitting there? Simply because he had to communicate? Or—more simply—because here was a man whose generation he could manage?

'My wife,' Lyle said, 'likes an oath. Doesn't do it often. But now and then out it comes—and when it does, a navvy isn't in it. Comes from an upper-class family, you see.'

'Ah,' the man said.

He was a stranger. Lyle could unburden himself freely. 'As a matter of fact, I'm falling in love with my wife all over again. She's going away on holiday, you see. And suddenly knowing I won't have her there I see all her ways I love, and, well, it's like ten years knocked away, my heart beats at the sight of her.'

The man nodded. 'What you've got you don't want. Excuse turning away. Got a broken neck.'

'Yes?' Lyle said. 'You see, I've got to get a hold of myself, remember all the times we haven't got on, get it into perspective. Just now, it's easier to remember the best. Know what I mean?'

'I buried mine a twelve-month past. You like to think back on the good times before.'

Zoë dead? How would he feel? How much of his present distress was vanity? He found himself pleasantly sad to think of her dead. But even then, was he really thinking of her, or just dramatizing himself as a lonely widower by a little grave, flowers and memories?

So he just tried to think of Zoë dead. He looked into his green lime-juice and saw her absence in death. The little soda bubbles rising showed up the green stillness. Dead. It seemed right.

'That cat of mine,' the mullet was saying, 'is almost human. You should see her looking up at a doorknob waiting for it to turn. She knows, she knows. . . .'

His compensatory companion, the cat. But a wife dead? Zoë? Was it possible to wish dead someone whom he now seemed to want more than anything else in the world?

It seemed too romantic a thought—like plunging a dagger into your girl-bride. But don't I want to be romantic? Isn't it the lack of romance that's made such a repressed, decent, soundless, blind, dumb nothingness of all this?

'You should see her dig her little hole. Lookin' round everywhere, nobody's going to see *me* do my business—you'd think tigers was coming at her right and left. And when all this cover-me-tracks digging's done, up she sits and pees away innocent as the day, with a look as to say, 'Me? I'm doin' nothing. . . .'

Why should his dead missus have dug holes in this way? . . . of course—the cat. No, there's another feeling about death, not so bloody romantic, more like tidying up a room. 'There, *that's* over.' But it left his own particular room, with Zoë's calmly laid-out body, somehow still untidy—something or someone was missing. Who? What? He looked harder at the glass, a prescience of something else there un-nerved him, he drank it all up.

'Something attempted, something done,' the man said of his cat, with satisfaction.

The words seemed to echo whatever unknown element had lain among the soda bubbles in the glass. Lyle shivered. How had all this started? By saying that Zoë sometimes swore. And that took him back to Menswear. Things were echoing, things were clicking. This was bad. A well-known symptom. Tangled nerves jump for a coincidence, forgetting all the rest that does not co-incide, relishing only a new mysterious meaning in a world difficult to assemble. He got up.

'Fancied a tasty plate of semolina,' the man was saying.

Wife or cat? Lyle looked down at the pink fish head and thought, In the end that cat'll gobble you all up. As your wife would have done, had she lived. A happy release.

'Goodbye,' he said, 'I must be going.'

'It's been nice to chat.'

'Yes. Good evening.'

'Look before you leap. See you around.'

Not on your life, he would not. And, prising himself out through the frosted swing door, never again in a hurry shall I grip this old and dear brass handle, tarnished as it is with too personal a kind of time. What with Jenk's mate I seem to have spent the lonely day communicating with old men. Is there nobody else? But men of my middle age are all involved in the great marriage migration. You seldom see one out alone after sundown. Must remember to lunch out more often.

Once outside he felt better. The street was less frightening, the effect of the pub had been counter-irritant. You get used to anything, he thought: and what's the use of getting used to anything?

He clenched his teeth to strengthen his jaw. For God's sake stop being morose and remember you're a decisive and efficient foreign bond and exchange dealer who knocks up thousands a day for your firm, the kind of chap in the prime forties who'd think nothing of risking a hundred thousand forward guilder, even a packet of blocked zloty on occasions, and you're fittish, and in the glass quite a brushed up picture from time to time. Only respond! Here's London after a good golden day, an echo of the summer past, and these people on the streets dawdling about with the blowsy warmish London-Italian look that no real Italian would have time for.

All the pretty girls out and about. All the fat men—who usually seem to disappear for the winter—now abruptly on view again: collars unbuttoned, acres of moist hairy flesh, and the girls primping soft with skin and silk. He stood in Piccadilly Circus and even smiled: A land fit for Eros and no mistake.

'I must eat, I'll dive dauntless into one of these new-looking dives. A place of mottled stone and planked wood and glass and playbox tile—a coffee-musak, where I can see a bit of movement and eat a bit of something without sitting alone at some slow and lifeless restaurant tablecloth. 'I'll even go in among the young.'

He walked on a bit past a bewildering assortment of strip and clip joints (intriguing, but I'm not going to be taken for a sucker in my thus early dotage) and finally turned through a door made of glass with a coloured freize of safe-looking, almost traditional lobsters and guitars.

Inside it was dark and young. As far as he could see in the rich brownish half-light, it was packed; though when he found a small space and wedged himself down and looked around he noticed it was really more sprawled over than packed. Shoulders hunched, arms flung out backwards and round something, legs shot straight and wide under tables—it seemed that all their bodies were longing to get out of themselves,but were too tired to do so. Sometimes they spoke to one another. There was a sour laugh or two. Music played and the glum faces listened, or perhaps just let the rhythm run through from ear to ear.

He could not understand much of what was written on the menu, even with his glasses, but spied goulash. A scratch of paprika would liven up the old tum? An expressionless figure in a dark sweater and trousers, a young man or woman, came up and stood by his table. He pointed at the goulash on the menu. The figure left him without a sign. But in a very few minutes a plate arrived with tepid lumps of meat stewed in tomato sauce.

'I asked for goulash,' he said smiling.

The face above the sweater nodded, its finger pointed at his plate, it went again.

He decided to tuck into this Italian-tasting mess and forget. And then an absolute woman-woman, with breasts and long hair, rushed at him from the dusk with a pair of whitely boiled potatoes: 'You're right,' she said in the hoarse deep voice of a child, 'they forgot your boiled!' And stared straight into his eyes and opened her mouth in a big mischievous personal smile as if this were the beginning of a never-to-be-ended conspiracy between them.

It worked wonders with him. Her lids had been lowered, too. So he was not too old to be chosen? He took a big mouthful of food, and in doing so nudged with his elbow somebody to his right: 'Sorry,' he said.

A young man turned and grunted affably enough, 'S'all right, Dad.' Not so good. But then he quickly remembered, they used Dad between themselves, a form of jazz-address. He hoped it was still so.

Meanwhile, where had the waitress gone? Impossible to see. Besides, what was he doing bucking with sudden sex in this dismal cavern of youth and innocence?

But there was certainly a sexish feeling about, among lowered lights and music, though an oddly wistful one, like adolescence waking up to something never yet tasted. These young people were mostly twenty or over, yet they looked so young and weightless and tender-limbed: even the girls, with all their paint and hair on, looked incapable of getting down to real bedrock. Though of course they would be at it like anyone else, many a bedsitter rocked half-way through the ceiling. But of course, he thought sadly, I can only look at such matters through the weight and spread of middle age.

Yet a sad thought? Not quite right. There's not much envy. Having grown into a bigger meaty me, I can't envy *them*: nor can I envy what they do, eat, see, how they dance and dress and otherwise behave, it's nothing to do with *me*. It's all too different. Yet . . . how would it be if I were transported to a familiar place among young people as I knew them in my own youth? And uncomfortably his mind went to a wedding not much more than a year ago, where in a traditional church and a traditional hotel-room the wedding and its breakfast had collected many of the young in fairly formal dress, indistinguishable in fact among the gladioli and champagne from the bright-eyed, stiff-collared, flush-faced eager ones he had once known in his own young days. Standing with marzipan in his teeth, he had envied the young men's gaiety with one another, their preposterous energy, their shine. And their girls who would dance till the milk came home. On that day, he had been called 'sir' by men who looked almost thirty!

He looked again round the dark coffee-room: Thank God they're like this, a foreign tribe. They're my armour in which I sit protected against myself.

And still wondering vaguely where that waitress was —while a still small voice from his rolled-gold past informed him that it would be just his sort of luck if she'd gone off duty—he listened to what the tribal young to his right were saying. Glumly examining the fetishes of their extraordinary clothes, they discussed musicians and actors. It was all 'do you like the Hamstrings?' or 'what do you think of Murdoch Inglis?' and the answers in contemporary clichés for yes or no. It was the old human leaning to affirmation and the right thing to do.

Expressing revolution in every antic and visual attitude, here they were simply yessing a new establishment. Lyle remembered that he must once have done the same. In what way did life not repeat itself? Like your wife running away from you. Other wives had run, were running. And yet—to be personally involved did indeed seem most unique. The difference between theory and experience, between idea and realization lay as far apart as ever: as with these young people who were having their say for the first time: it didn't matter a damn whether it had all been done before.

He reached for his bill and stood up. They were playing a tune from his own early dancing days. Once he had felt a time-nostalgia for such music—as if he himself had really had a golden age, which was surely, on consideration, not right. But now he was even sick of feeling nostalgic, you could not go on and on with that for ever: such nostalgia was simply another experience done with, a further satiated but unsatisfied step into age.

He went stumbling past the dark tables. But how did they slip in and out of their tight jeans to make love? It must be quite a business. And a real facer to get them on again in a hurry, say at the sound of a father's tread on the stairs. And with the girls—were such difficult skin-tight trousers a kind of thigh-size contraceptive?

Hello . . . the waitress! Waiting all the time behind the cash till! Old devils galvanized him. The exact small change in his fist fell back into his pocket, he reached for his wallet to get a note for change and thus for time to talk, and in his mind's mirror his face took on its good-looking look.

GOODBYE

He bounced forward with a winning smile. The waitress looked back at him blankly. She took the money, rang out the change, thanked him without a smile, and turned to yell to someone along the counter: 'I couldn't fail to disagree with you less. . . .'

The triple negative or whatever it was rang in his ears like yet another form of contraception of a mental kind. Not even recognized! She had never in fact even noticed him in the first place, he was no more than a potato-less goulash. Thoughtfully he slid out through the glass lobsters and guitars into the street.

Youth, he thought. That's that. Vast acres of the town were henceforth out of bounds to him. There was a new army of occupation, citizens of his age must put up their shutters. But there were surely compensations, didn't middle age still hold most of the dough, and wasn't woman eternal? Restaurants had only been going for two hundred years, there was an older profession than that. He hailed a taxi, and made for Norbert Street, Paddington.

It was a gesture of both disgust and revolt. But the possibility had already been at the back of his mind for some hours. He had kept it as a reserve temptation which he could easily resist, but liked to have there as a security: much like the second string a woman might keep handy in case of trouble with her true love.

Moreover, the word Norbert had an extra element of reliability, he had heard it from Savory's lips, and Savory was a man of his own age: with his love of locomotives and drainpipes he was unlikely to have sought out any unnervingly modern atmosphere.

Even so, thoughts of escape occurred to him on the way: Ought I to go and call on Jack Buckett? Jack came to me in my trouble, shouldn't I go to Jack in his? Ridiculous! Behaving like a bloody tennis ball! Still, shouldn't I perhaps just ring him?

He stopped the cab by a telephone box. In the box he found he had not got the right coin. Rather than go looking for change, or asking the driver to search through his deep pockets, the excuse came that Jill might answer and what would he say then? So he did not telephone. This bare excuse was soon reinforced by the brilliant notion: In any case, I should think Jack's real reason is because he's only been married once. He feels he's out of touch, out of line with the other smarties.

Norbert Street was dark, lit here and there with tall day-blue lights which seemed to have no real business with the crumbling grey plaster all around. A few shops, a yellow-lit pub. And a lot of solitary groups of men just standing about.

Fear returned—but this time it was physical. A man of his age was always fair game: it's the older ones that are supposed to carry the cash. He saw a policeman walk by at the end of the street and felt much relieved. He would have embraced even a traffic warden, a bus conductor, anyone in a peaked cap.

Why am I doing this anyway? he asked himself. Because she's emasculated me? Or is it a kind of hooliganism, breaking loose on the side because I can't face the real trouble? Am I ripe for ripping up railway seats? He was well on the way to analysing himself out of it when a tall, burly figure lurched slowly at him from the shadows. It must have been leaning against the area railings. It wore a long striped jacket, no collar or tie: its heavy yellowish negro face said to him: 'You lookin' for somethin'?'

This was it. He got a little on his toes to run or dodge, braced his chest muscles, took his hands from his pockets. No time to think, say the first thing in your head . . . and put an American-Cockney accent to the words: 'Yeah. Norbert Club. Know it?'

The big negro smiled affably: 'Sure, man. Right along—see the li'l yellah light?'

'Thanks. Thanks very much.'

'Anytime.' And the man turned and walked slowly, at peace, away.

Bloody fool I am, Lyle mumbled to himself, where's the worry? He walked briskly along to the yellow lantern showing poorly painted red words: Norbert Club. An ordinary house, with music coming from curtained street-level windows. A row of bells by the chocolate-painted door. Not much cash spent on this, he thought, pressing the lowest bell marked Club. While he waited he read the cards on the other bells: one name had 'Masseuse' after the name, another 'French Lessons'. Health and education. The district was eager to improve itself.

The Club door opened slightly. A man with a ginger moustache up to his ears asked him what he wanted. Members only, he was told. Past the moustache he saw several men drinking beer against a background of slot-machines. The bar had a man behind it. Not a woman in sight. He did not know what to say. He started to say: 'A young lady told me . . .'

'You after a bit of grumble?'

'There must be some mis—' But the man, reassured by Lyle's non-assurance, interrupted him: 'Next bell up. Second floor too,' and shut the door.

Masseuse. Of course. Well, he had expected from the

word 'club' some sort of dancing-hostess: but if this were to be a straight, or even bent, call-girl affair, then in for a penny in for a few pounds, it was getting later and the evening had been eventless and why was he here anyway? He gave the bell a long decisive ring.

A window above opened. A woman's head poked out its mop of black hair. 'Where's the fire?'

'Excuse me, but—'

'I'm busy.'

'Oh—er—I was told—'

Again his lack of assurance proved him, and the woman said more quietly: 'Can you wait?'

Her voice fell soft on the street like a voice in fog.

'Where?'

'Come up then.'

She turned to shout to someone inside: 'You done, Maureen?' The front door clicked and swung with a troubled buzz, as if it had been opened by a huge dark bee.

He went up surprising clean stairs, freshly carpeted and painted. It might have been a small Swiss hotel. On the first landing he passed a man coming downstairs with an absent look, like a man coming from a phone booth still considering his conversation. And then the black-haired woman poked her head round a door and said: 'Go straight up,' and called, 'Maureen!' He saw she looked tired and tousled, like a housewife in the middle of a dozen daily chores, too busy to smile.

But when the upper door opened, a much younger woman, a grown-up girl with a dressed-up mound of copper hair and a wan pretty face, greeted him, and indeed smiled.

'Parlez vous français?' she giggled as she showed him in. 'Short time?'

He stood in a bed-sitting-room newly furnished on

some modern plan principle, exact, neat, everything matching, featureless: it might have been a shop window representing a room. 'How'd you know we was here?' the girl asked. 'The advert?'

'No. A friend. Mr—' but stopped himself, adding, 'Jones.'

'I wouldn't know no names,' the girl said. 'I'll take my present first if you don't mind, dear.'

He glanced quickly round the room as he gave her what she asked for, wondering at the freshness, the strip lighting, the lack of anything personal, no magazine, no bottle or tea-cup, no flowers, nothing—but of course, it was a new set-up, she'd been installed by her owner on the never-never. He was in banking circles again.

'We haven't been here long,' the girl said, slipping off her dress. 'You put your clothes over there.'

He got his coat and trousers off, then sat down in shirt and pants. He could go no further. He could not even look at her.

She was naked except for her shoes and stockings, and already leaning back on the bed squatted and open, like someone in a gym class waiting for the next order. Her face and hair, human and dressed-up, had nothing to do with the body. Below was the invitation; the face did not even bother to associate itself but looked upwards a bit at a corner of the door, as if thinking: 'I must get a hook put on *that*.'

But the lips soon spoke: 'Come on, soldier, what's keeping you? And mind my hair, won't you?'

Slowly and quietly he told her that it was impossible, he couldn't do it, and she asked him whether he was married and when he said yes told him don't worry most of my customers are married, it's simply they like a change. And he asked her, could we have the light out?

Not on your life, not alone in the dark, I don't *know* you, she was very quick to say. But would you like my vibro, my vibro works wonders, wait while I plug it in. No, no, he said, I'm sorry, it's no go. And she got up from that clinical gym-spread and began to walk about the room. He relaxed a little. She was really very pretty: far too pretty and too young for the routine of this job, which her youth invested with a kind of innocence—as if, although her body was doing it, she herself had no connection whatsoever.

He sat there for some minutes more talking, making excuses about tiredness and drink, above all stopping himself from asking her about herself and how she came to be doing this—not *that* old one, which he'd heard every Tom and Dick did, and which seemed anyway an insolence—and never thinking because of her youth to speak about his own troubles, which seemed of a very sinful and grown-up order.

Among the little pale-wood matching drawers, on the grey fitted carpet she just walked around, settling this and that—her face and hair in the round rimless mirror, a touch to the coverlet whose tailored neatness covered used sheets, and once a glance at her watch, as if it were a taximeter, and her client had in all fairness so and so much time left. Once or twice she looked at him with a sudden personal curiosity, a long look of her grey eyes framed, as with minature spectacle-frames, by black mascara. Why? Had he thrown in some sort of compliment? Perhaps in passing he had called her or the furniture pretty?

He spoke to his feet in their socks or to her face, avoiding her body. All the time the body was walking about, and from between a lacing of girdle-straps her bottom stuck out with separate impertinence, as if conducting the whole operation. It was somehow more

shameless than the rest of her. Perhaps because it stuck
out so, perhaps because it was on the opposite side to her
face? 'Why can't she be ashamed?' his mind shouted
between his quiet words: and then he would again look
into the pale, thinly oval face, and once he felt it was like
a young schoolteacher's face, and doing very much the
same thing, being attentive and kind because it was
necessary to get something out of you.

The grey colourless light shone on, the room breathed
its new-furniture non-smell. It was all the more impersonal against these personal-looking things going on—
there was the awful neutrality of a modern hotel-room,
unweathered as yet, unbattered by people and time. He
found himself saying how much he loved youth and
somehow mixing her with Tom, at any rate bringing her
in—his nerves were so muddled, high and low at the
same time, he might have been drunk—when suddenly
she went across and switched the main light off.

'There,' she said, 'that's better, isn't it? Come on
now, I've—I've—'

She stopped speaking and for the first time came to
him. She put her hands on his cheeks.

'I've kind of taken to you,' she said, looking at him
and very carefully.

More technique? It was the worst yet. He stood up,
her body was too near his eyes.

She must have thought he had stood up to go over to
the bed. She went there immediately, but this time only
sat on it, waiting and looking at him with what seemed
real meaning:

'Come on, darling. I've took—taken to you. Really.
Us girls do, you know. It sounds silly, but then why not?
We're all human. I know you're twice my age, but I like
that. I got a daddy-fix or something.'

He looked away. He believed her. He began to mumble, 'I'm afraid I can't. I'm sorry. I don't—'

'Oh, come on,' she said. 'It won't cost you no more. Look, I'll pack it in for the night.'

'I don't think I—'

She suddenly laughed, lay down full length and patted the bed: 'Give a girl a busman's holiday!' She was quite sure of herself.

It was a hundred times more dangerous than before. He struggled into his trousers. Did she feel rejected? Did they have a professional pride or something? No. Normally she'd be jolly glad to be rid of him. She must really and honestly mean it. So he did a dishonest thing. He said: 'Look, not tonight. I'm worn out. I've got troubles. But give me your telephone number. I'll ring and come again.'

She sat up. 'I don't believe you.'

'I will, really.'

'I don't think your a pansy. I think you just don't like me.' She shrugged her shoulders coldly. 'All right, go. I can leave it like I can take it.'

He got his other clothes on while she sat silent.

'I do mean it, you know,' she said, when he was ready. She got up and put her dress on very quickly. 'Here,' she said, 'here's your money. I don't want to take your money.

'Please. You need it.'

'Need it? I've made twenty times this today.'

'Please—'

'Look, take it and give it me back—like a real present —next time you come. Buy me something with it. Here's my card.'

His hand went out and took the money and card. It seemed the only way. He took her face in his hands and kissed her cheek. 'Mind my hair,' she said. But her eyes were closed. 'Goodbye, you bloody bastard,' she said softly.

On the way downstairs he heard her voice calling from above: 'Doris?'

And as a voice answered, calling again: 'I'm free if.'

He walked fast, no more fear of the night and loiterers, only desperate to get away from that house and its embarrassment. A mixture of pity, disgust and delight shivered through him. But the disgust part receded with the house. And by the time he had got right away and into a taxi home pity had changed to a starry-eyed vision of youth. What an extremely nice, personable young girl! He had been unfair to judge young people by a few layabouts in a café. In any case even they were hardly to be blamed, their rampart of music and clothes was only part of a castle to keep dull old tradition out; with these things around them they felt safer from the fud-dud voice of age always trying to keep them back in line. And individually? Well, look for instance at this sweet and tender young Maureen, welcoming him!

And a radiance of amazed self-congratulation flooded through: 'I'm attractive, I'm wanted!' He conveniently forgot about the 'daddy-fix', and as the taxi shuddered through the lamp-washed streets he re-affirmed himself to himself. He felt better and stronger and bigger than for any of the bad days past. He felt like storming a trench, climbing a cliff, having a ball.

What he did when he got home was to go straight and

have a bath, a big hot bath, in which much was shed. Nor did he go quietly about it. Although Zoë's light was on, he made no attempt to efface his footstep on the stair. He let the taps sound through an open door, and in the bath he made what splashing noises he wished.

VII

UP early and out to breakfast. Renewed and different. Breakfast out was different too, facing a kipper and hot strong tea in an easy workman's café in that little village of shops round which his residential neighbourhood spawned. The sun shone again. But why, he wondered, did bluebottles, or at least large black flies, keep bursting from under the white skin of the waitress's bare arm as it hung by the tea-urn?

These flies seemed to pullulate beneath the skin, pushing or wriggling themselves hungrily out—as might dark little moths from a white chrysalis—then to stretch their wings, shake off the wet, and buzz away. She must be absolutely full of flies, he thought. The girl was otherwise quite healthy-looking. He was not upset.

And he felt much, much better. The question of Zoë still occupied his main thoughts, but somehow today he was able at least to isolate it, prevent it from swarming everywhere—much as a general, though set upon from all sides, may see at a certain academic remove the encircling enemy. Zoë would probably win, he could see that: but were there no rearguard actions which might yet turn the scales?

Plainly that girl last night had had a liberating effect on him. He had no intention of seeing her again: but to have been accepted, even desired, was revitalizing. It might have been the same, he thought, if a group of any young people had asked him in to a party, or something like that. Because one thing the girl had put paid to was any idea of a future sex-life. Paradox indeed—but now he knew that any such action, in such circumstances, was quite beyond him. Perhaps some thoughtful widow, in merrier surroundings, might one day come his way: but these are not found under the next bushel.

Sex was out. Added to this, he was obviously henceforth cut off from a good three-quarters of the West End occupied by youth. He would have to join an older kind of club—but these bored him—or take on a new leisure occupation, go shooting at Bisley, crayfish-netting in the near fields of Kent. Did any one still rub brasses? What about a little sailing-boat? None of these ideas cheered him.

But the morning sunlight did. And the easy chatter of the workmen taking their tea-and-a-slice around him, and the fresh morning bustle about the huddle of shops. People looked different out before nine, less of a crowd, isolated like groups in holiday sunshine: and the shopkeepers opening up and setting out fish, fruit, newspapers. People at this time of day paused, and stretched easily as they did it. Even the pub doors were wide open —presumably for an airing: the glint of bottles and a bar inside suggested an open continental café, mornings abroad . . . and the early morning air was fresh yet.

Suppose he should go abroad? Vistas of the Mediterranean rose, the easy bustle of small ports in the cool morning sun. But Varley and the Bank would never allow that. Unless he pleaded a proper nervous breakdown? Yesterday he had indeed felt quite close to a breakdown. But today? His nerves felt resilient and fine. There were flickerings: perhaps he was over-nerved, over-charged?

But really, that waitress . . . he put on his glasses and took a closer look. The flies stopped wriggling out. Through the magnifiers he saw they were no more than numberless dark freckles and moles; tired eyes and steam from the urn set them coming and going. The urn even buzzed. He shook his head. Then his glasses reminded him he might get a paper and read a bit over another cup of tea. He went out and returned with a weekly journal—the ordinary daily headlines of national disaster would be sickeningly ordinary and too far removed from his own.

But when he opened the weekly at a competition page, which involved parodies of contemporary ballad-mongers, he read the following:

> *'Misty mild Octember weather*
> *Golden on a redbrick home:*
> *Standing with his washing leather*
> *Car agleam and hands afoam*
>
> *Henry Alister is soaping*
> *Muddy mudguards, as of sin:*
> *While his love-life packs its baggage*
> *Up above—she's leaving him.'*

'Christ alive,' he muttered and read on.

> *'Twenty years of married murder,*
> *Twenty years of so-called bliss,*
> *Giving, taking, loving, loathing,*
> *Ending with a thump like this.'*

'Well my God!' he said.

> *'Thump of trunks upon the floorboards,*
> *Air-raid noises from afar,*
> *Clitter-clatter flak of heel-taps*
> *Echo to the sunny car.'*

He banged the weekly down on the table. Workmen looked round startled. 'It's about Chalcott-Bentinck, not me,' he said aloud. One of the workmen tapped his forehead with his forefinger. But they did not laugh. They were embarrassed by his being there, in classy cardigan, with classy voice and gesture.

God-damned coincidence, he thought—forgetting all he must have read or glanced at in the last days which had no bearing whatever on his predicament. 'And I've got a car, sitting in its garage, waiting for weekends. Ought I to go and wash it? Would that put a magic spell into action?' He looked quickly through the rest of the poem, and saw it ended with the wife jumping in the now-cleaned car, thanking him, and driving off for ever and ever: leaving the man with both wives gone.

Along the chromium base of a deep-freeze machine a mouse ran, and then another. He drew in his feet, looked harder: they were reflections of people passing in the street. It did not worry him. Nor did the poem. Keep your grip, he vaguely thought. Such things are always happening. And worse could come—like the day with the watering can, when instead of a refreshing jet of cool water the pink drowned tip of a whiskered mouse's nose had poured out, a poor little thing with its eyes closed right up, wistful sight indeed.

'I'll write that bugger a poem back,' he muttered and picked from the floor a fallen daily picture paper. All grimed round the white edges, but a nice space of white on the big bikinied belly of a late-summering belle. On this, avoiding the navel, he wrote:

'The last day of the year.'

'Not what it is,' he said to himself, 'but it feels like it . . . it's feeling that counts.' And sucked his pencil stub and wrote on:

GOODBYE

'The last day of the year
But where is the end?
Leaves have fallen,
Love is gone,
But here am I,
I go on.'

He stopped. Put back his head, and surveyed it from a distance. But it was rather good! Leave it, don't add a word.

He read it again, and it made him feel sad; but pleasantly sad, with a well-filled melancholy. He tore the sheet off, folded it, pocketed it, and got up to pay. And there, coming through the door, was Hodgson the invaluable plumber!

He nodded to him.

Hodgson met his eye, and looked away.

'Morning,' Lyle said, to make sure.

Hodgson pressed his lips thinly together and made no reply. But spoke up loud to a builder at the next table:

'Till death do us part,' he said, 'I don't think. Barnyard behaviour.'

'Eh?' the builder said, puzzled.

'Playing ducks and drakes with the word of our Lord,' the plumber insisted. 'Tea and tart,' he said to the waitress, and echoing his own words added, 'that's about it, tea and a tart.'

Lyle sat astounded. So the word had got round? But what word? It inferred that he was to blame. Gossip as usual up the wrong end of the pole. He pretended to read his paper. Unfair, unfair, the paper yelled, and you've lost a plumber into the bargain.

He saw himself standing up again and having it out with Hodgson, voices raised among the overalls, shame and unhappiness pouring out in his unhappily educated voice all over the sauce-bottles and boots and muscles—and thought better of it. But to lose a plumber? Could it be true? A man at the next table caught his eye, winked, made a praying gesture with his hands, mumbled sanctimonious mouth movements. Hodgson was a Tabernacle man.

He left. But as in a war, on a spirited day, this reverse enlivened him. His steeled-up nerves rose higher, he strode more than walked.

Zoë was dressed to go out but giving a last duster's flip round the sitting-room. She looked him over with habitual possessiveness, unable to check this. Her eyes said, '*You're* up bright and early!'—but she stopped her mouth from saying anything. He found himself answering her unspoken words, though with no habitual tale:

'Quite a night last night,' he said brightly casual. 'Found myself down in Chelsea, and d'you know, a crowd of young people called to me from a window—you know, I was just passing—and beckoned me in. Quite a little party going on. Short of men, they said. My, we had a rare old time—these young girls, my God! Which reminds me, I managed to mend their car too. Broke down going out to a roadhouse. Fast little job. Luckily I was able to find the trouble in a jiffy.'

'Roadhouse?' Zoë asked quietly. 'I didn't think they had them any more.'

'Don't they?' he asked, surprised. Then: 'They jolly well do,' he said emphatically, and bounced away upstairs.

He nipped into her bedroom, lipsticked the handkerchief in his pocket, and laid it on his dressing-table to use later.

She called upstairs: 'I'm going out now.'

He bounced on to the landing and down to her: 'Where you off to?' he asked brightly.

She was standing in the hall, smart, detached, an absolute adult, a cool figure about to step into a Rolls-Royce in a smooth advertisement. How different, he thought suddenly, from someone like the big blonde sausage Jill, who looked all flesh beneath her clothes, as if she were full of holes, as if things might fall out from underneath her. Zoë hadn't a hole to her name.

'A million things to do,' she said. 'You'll have to lunch out, or out of a tin. Sorry, but I must see Jill among other things. She's going through hell.'

'Thoughtful of you.'

'One must help one's friends.'

'And the charity that begins at home?'

'You know that's different. As a matter of fact, I am doing something to help you as well. I'm going to call in at the police.'

'Eh?'

'No one knows where I'm going. *Woman disappears.* It'd be unpleasant for you if they came round digging up the garden, wouldn't it?'

'Digging up my garden?'

'You know what I mean. I thought I'd just let them know. Goodbye,' she said.

'Very considerate of you. Goodbye too.'

Sod her, he thought as she closed the front door: but quickly went to the hall-window and watched her figure as it crossed the street. Already she looked a stranger. Mine, he thought frantically. Today and tomorrow only?

Never again? The lonely left-out feeling rolled back, he
followed with love the figure on the street, he made it into
all his past love for her, girl and young woman and
mother . . . then cursed it and went out into the garden.

There was that damned pile of dead mickies still facing
him at the end. But no Jenks? Now where was the man
. . .? Probably upset because he had not shown much
interest yesterday afternoon. They were so touchy,
these big fellows. He went over to the tool-shed and found
a can of paraffin.

He walked down past the blue-bottle tree—deadly
still green leaves flying like a dancer's skirts, but no
bottles yet—and past the stout geraniums, the shrinking
hydrangea heads, to the bonfire. He emptied the can over
it and struck a match.

'Up she goes!' And stood well back as the pile broke
into crackling life and a dirty smoke rose to drift over
gardens elsewhere. It looked good and active. Why on
earth hadn't he done so before?

He caught sight of his robin, perched very still and re-
garding with affront the equally hungry flames. 'Roasted
worms today,' he called over to it, 'toasted weevils.'

The bird flew off.

A pigeon thrashed in a tree above. Another pigeon
called out: 'That God-damned cuckoo,' over and over
again. A false spring, he said to the sunlight. The bonfire
settled down after its first crackling, old damp sent out a
thick column of grey-white smoke which cast cloud-
shadow on the garden and wreathed off over the wall.

He had nothing to do. 'This damned old garden,' he
thought. 'Year after year, season after season. Think of
the spring—wearing dark glasses against the daffs, the
searing purple and yellow crocus. Fresh green set off by
so much black about, leafless rain-blackened tree-trunks

lit up for once by low sunlight and all the haze of buds about them. Wet black earth lit up by fresh green grass. Blackbirds about. It all happens again and again, year after year, how can I stand it? Coming in with green-fly-squash all over the fingers, under the nails—but in future nobody to tell me off? And summer? The long July days under grey skies and all that dishcloth light, a sou'wester blowing the chill evenings along—it's been a great year for cow-parsley.

'Pip-pippety-pip,' went the wall. 'Over!'

'What is it?' he said back, not wanting to play.

'Pip! Why the smoke-screen? Best day of the golden year, and you have to behave like a frightened frigate. But listen—I've got news for you!' And then came a clear baritone humming: 'Da-da-dee-da. Da-*da*-de-da.' That Wedding March.

'Bit of a change from Farewell,' Lyle called, and suddenly his heart leapt—wedding-plus-news must equal Zoë? Had she called on Savory, emptying whatever she had in her heart?

'Come over and have a drink,' Savory shouted, and hummed louder.

Lyle was at his front door in under a minute.

Savory had the bigger, fuller look of a man who is indeed bursting with something to say. He grabbed Lyle by the arm and led him inside.

'It's early yet, but I thought you'd better know—'

'Well, what *is* it?'

'Let's have this drink first. Scotch? Beer? Madeira? No seed-cake, I'm afraid. There's Swiss Roll.'

GOODBYE

Lyle looked round at the bachelor's room again—dated thirtyish functional furniture, folk-weave curtains. Only four nights before had he sat here. It seemed weeks ago.

'Scotch. Why aren't you at work?'

Savory frowned joyfully at him, pulling his big hairy eyebrows together in excruciating fun: 'I just couldn't go in. I don't have to, you know. Exalted figure, Copy Chief! Here's to hookey!'

'Well now, what *is* up?'

'Ah-ha!'

Lyle's eye caught a new gold frame, with a mount of purple velvet, and in the centre a simple plastic cuff-button. 'Good God,' he pointed, 'that's . . . that's . . .'

'Yes,' Savory said proudly, 'it's called Smilin' Thru.'

Again Lyle thought, only four nights ago. 'Now what is all this—' he began again.

But Savory's mind had flicked on to something else. 'I saw that extraordinary Powsey of yours today. With his missus. They were having a real old one-two right out there on the pavement. Shouting at the tops of their voices, umbrellas waving, red in the face, white in the gills, the whole shoot—I think she won, she went off strutting like a Stanley Crane and left him, as they say, quivering. Wonder what's up?'

'For God's sake tell me *your* news,' Lyle said firm.

Savory glanced down at his hairy trousers, his big weather-proof shoes. He smiled big and sly. He was being casual in the over-coy way big men have. He screwed his eyes up at the sunshine coming low through the window: 'Two have decided to make peace and face the future in Holy matrimony.'

'No!' Lyle's heart jumped. The whole room blazed with sunlight.

'Liz and I are to be married.'

The room still flooded with sun, but a kind of smoke, like the thin after-smoke of his bonfire, took all the fire out of it. A slight grey, grey like washday doom, occluded everything.

'Ha,' he sneered. 'That's the bloody limit.'

'It's certainly mine,' Savory said and looked at him surprised.

Lyle leaned forward.

'Don't you realize what I'm going through?' he said slowly and carefully. 'Don't you see I thought the news was for *me*?'

'Why?'

'You haven't even asked me how things are.'

'Of course. I suppose I should've. But it's all decided, I thought?'

'It could change.'

'I thought—thought it best to keep off it. Delicate matter.' He put on an amiable tone, seeing that Lyle was hurt. 'You want to get your mind off it, surely? And you know, I'm overexcited, can't help it, giving in at last to this great masterly bear of a girl—did you know bears suck blood, never eat flesh, just kill to suck, like honey, red honey, and hence your vampire stories—'

'The other evening I thought *you* rather masterly,' Lyle began slowly.

Savory laughed. 'Nonsense. In fact, come to think of it, I owe a lot to your good self. You and Zoë splitting made me think, really always before I've been the one to make the split before getting properly involved, you might say I've been in a state of constant split, so I said to myself, Why not *do* the thing this time and then see what's really what—'

Lyle stood up. 'Masterly? You're just a very ordinary

egotistical mess. Thanks for letting me help you. Thanks for the drink. Goodbye.'

Savory followed him out to the hall: 'Look, I *am* sorry—I really am—I didn't mean—'

At the front door Lyle turned. 'I went to your Norbert Club. Top Bell. You're mixing things up a bit, aren't you?'

'Maureen? That's different.' Savory gave a sudden high laugh. 'Hard little bitch.'

'Hard?' Lyle said, and went out.

Back in the house, he rang Buckett in his office. His nerves were racing. He even got Buckett's secretary to call him out of a meeting.

'Jack—can you tell me exactly when it was you decided to leave Jill?'

'Now look, Tony, I'm very busy—'

'Just think and tell me exactly when.'

Because Buckett had no time to talk he told the truth.

'On Monday night, after I left you.'

'Why exactly then?'

It boiled out.

'There's cause and occasion. This was the occasion.'

'Because of me?'

'Well—'

'You mean yes.'

'I suppose—perhaps.'

Buckett lowered his voice and spoke quickly as if against time on the line: 'But if so, old man, there the similarity ends. She won't stop getting after me. She won't stop talking. She's talked at me morning and night. She says the same thing over and over again. She goes on and on and on till my ears are breaking, she's not reasonable, Tony, she's even been up here at the office, I've had to warn reception, I daren't go home, I'll have to move out to my club, she goes on and on. My God, you've had a light time with Zoë. . . .'

'You mean Zoë's had a light time with *me*, you crass idiot,' and he banged the phone down.

'It's catching,' he said to the quiet hallway. 'Get me a leper-bell.'

A hard ice of anger froze him. Outside on the street a woman passed. She wore a high pink hat, and walked dedicated as a priestess. He suddenly knew, absolutely and for certain, that if he went through the door and up to her and kissed her, a thin tube of forked tongue would flicker out from her open lips, dart and flicker all over his mouth like a little lizard. He went into the kitchen and got the breadknife.

Upstairs he opened her wardrobe. A single dress hung there. He slashed it up and down, up and down. Then he saw the heavy iron door-stopper and took this up and smashed in the lock of one of the two closed trunks.

This won't do, he thought, this isn't clever, this is simply anger, and won't do anything to retain her. Might even do the opposite.

He took the dress from the wardrobe and folded it and put it in a lower drawer under some bed-linen. He looked at the bashed-in lock and shrugged. She would only learn about it at the other end.

The bedroom now looked terribly neat. She had done most things, it already looked uninhabited. He shivered and went downstairs.

On the mat lay a letter. Far-East postmark of some sort. Macao? Hong Kong? Tom. He opened the letter, got his glasses and calmly read it through. As he did so, Mange plodded in and flung himself down on one shoe as if in family sympathy.

Tom was well, Tom was off to Australia, New Zealand and across the Pacific and Atlantic back, he hoped in time for Christmas. Though you never knew. You got diverted, and ate flaming Christmas Pud in the Antipodes. He had met a nice girl in Hong Kong. They had agreed to go steady. But he was in a silly sort of job for that, didn't they half think?

So Tom's well, no help from that end, he thought vaguely, no yellow fever.

Glad he's fine, he thought, I might be able to help him a bit in the future. The way things are, he dully thought, there'll be more cash in the bank.

He put the letter down and saw his hand huge in the magnifying lenses. He made it into a big strong fist and held it there. It looked most statuesque and powerful, emblem of strength and will. But the fist began to shake. A pretty shaky strength. I must be more het up than I feel, he thought. And beneath the dithering fist he saw Mange, bigger too, size of a small pony—emphasized, as if especially to be brought to his master's notice.

And Mange started a new train of thought. He considered Mange slyly as he walked into the kitchen and cut himself a sandwich. Slowly munched it as associations coincided, his thought in the café earlier of washing the car as a means of magic; and now the consideration of Tom fit and well—but here was this Mange a member of the family much closer at hand, a shaggy scapegoat. Dogs get run over. With a wounded dog on her hands she could never go. He looked at the breadknife and wondered. Could you cut him about and make it look like wheel-wounds?

And with this shaking hand? Anyway, too messy. But poison? He looked down at the dog with affection, man's best friend indeed and about to prove it. He looked down even with admiration, as a sacrificial priest might admire the trained and chosen youth laid on the altar. But I don't know about poison, he thought, and anyway their sense of smell and taste is acute—except perhaps for those sleeping pills, those hundreds-and-thousands in that bottle up in the open trunk? Suppose I mashed them all up?

But at that point the thoughts 'car' and 'run-over' returned and suddenly clicked—the car was poison itself, CO, excellent! Without pausing he walked out into the garden to look for a piece of severed hose-pipe coiled up in the toolshed. He had often wondered why he kept it. Mange trotted after him.

'Good boy,' he said. 'Now where was it?'

He slung the hose over his arm, got some twine to fix it with, and called to Mange: 'Walkies.'

For some reason, perhaps of unconscious delicacy, he did not take the lead.

They walked out and round a couple of corners to a mews where the garage stood. He reflected that the mews was half-derelict, soon in fact to be pulled down, and there would be nobody about. Unless boys? They used the place for throwing bricks about.

No boys. It was a deserted forlorn place of drab brown brick and slate-blue roofs, little cottages where ostlers and coachmen had once lived. Now, later garage doors hung open, leaning off their hinges. A few coloured cans of oil about. Grass and willow-herb in the cobbles. It looked quietly desolate, a place where old motor-cars came to die.

He walked to the end where his own lock-up was.

GOODBYE

Once upon a time this much inhabited place had sparkled in the sun with water and ginger horse-drop, a place of movement and glossy hides, harness, buckets, and the population of coachmen and their families. All gone, he thought. He opened the garage door.

The hose was rubber and had lost its flexibility in the weather. But it would do. Twine, he saw, was ridiculous. Better to stuff the hose right up into the exhaust pipe and block it round with paper. Easy enough, plenty of newspaper blowing about.

When he had done this, he went forward and started the engine. It ran pretty smoothly. It was an old car, an open tourer they both loved, but now he thought the engine was coughing a bit and listened closer. It was not the engine. It was a grrr-ing from the back where the exhaust was. In fact, Mange growling with the hose-pipe in his mouth, pulled right out again, and now dragging it proudly to his master.

'Down!' he said quietly. 'Drop!'

Mange did. But stood there panting expectant, alert as a big old puppy. Such moments overcome even aged animals at least once a day, after sleep or before meals: a brief return of playfulness, when for a few maverick moments old dogs race round after unseen balls, when aged cats canter like bridled cavalry, tails erect as lances.

Lyle pulled the hose away. Mange made a waggish pounce forward, hanging his tongue over one side of his smiling teeth like a leg over an armchair. Lyle curbed the dog with a sharp word and went back to stuff the hose in again. The air was dirtying with blue smoke. He coughed, and flung the garage doors wide.

Now the exhaust came through correctly. He wondered how long he should leave the dog inside the car? Near to death but not dead must be the plan. With the hood up and windows shut, he could watch for the right moment from outside.

A shadow fell across the garage doorway—he looked up, it was a woman. He stepped back and turned his face away. Should she kiss him, that tongue would flick out forked and spitting. They were full of flies, too, he remembered. 'What do you want?' he called sideways to her, hand over face, ready to jump back. Better that they were all put down, squashed dead with the tongues and flies in them.

'Is it,' a voice intoned, the kind of voice that commands in buses and shops everywhere, 'is it a dead end?'

'Not yet,' he said. Calm, calm.

'Not yet?' she said. 'What you mean?'

'Well—you might say it is.'

Mange gave a high little growl. These two were talking, he could play again. He pounced back at the hose and worried it. His moment of virility was by no means exhausted.

Instantly the woman cried: 'Is he a biter? I think—', she nervously laughed, '—I'll leave you.'

'Good dog,' he said, saved.

The woman walked away. He wiped his hand across his mouth, thinking of that tongue. But now Mange was getting the pipe-end free again. He stuffed it quickly back and carried both hose and dog to the car. He shut them in, letting the hose fall over the top of one window.

He went and closed the doors, and came back to watch.

For a moment Mange sat still. The inside was already filling with blue fog. He began to worry that he would not be able to see the dog if it got thick. Did it get thick, this thin blue?

But Mange was staring at him, adding up carfeel and master—what could they all be off to but a drive in the country where the rabbits lived? The thing was to show excitement and jump all over the seats ... but he was fat and old, the slippery leather seats were precipitous and difficult, so instead he gave a few sharp and joyful barks, rose on his hind legs to paw the window and then near his eye saw the hose again, gripped it hard in his mouth and tugged with all his weight. Then fell back coughing.

He had pulled it out of the exhaust pipe again. Lyle went back and stuffed it in. Then jammed the car-window firmly up on the rubber. And again settled down to watch. After a while, he saw Mange's nose down by the offside door, where there was a draught. He felt weary. God, what next?

The engine stalled.

He opened the car-door and turned the ignition off, called Mange out, and left the garage. Mange followed dragging the hose-pipe with him, growling with triumph.

Lyle smiled: 'Bring then,' he said, and together, Mange dragging the dead snake all the way, they walked home.

He gave the dog a plate of milk and biscuits. He thought fondly, what an old fool I am, playing about with dogs in a garage! How mad can you get? We'll have to be a lot cleverer than that. And he went upstairs to tear buttons, one here, one there, from a couple of suits.

He took another suit out, and looked for something to dirty it with. Nothing about. He stuck his finger down his throat to bring up a mouthful of vomit—then remembered Zoë's room, full of unguents and varnish. He got red varnish and a brown cream and carefully dropped spots of these here and there. He put his finger in the cream and tasted it. Nasty.

A brilliant idea occurred to him. He had always objected to the nervous human habit of popping this or that into the mouth throughout the day—cigarettes, tea, coffee, drinks, food, sweets—why not put this cream into everything, and then you wouldn't want things? But— he thought a split second later—you'd just go out and buy others, wouldn't you? No matter. He would think up other things. He was really very clever. There was lots to do. For instance, he must really ring Varley.

'And how are we?' Varley's voice cooed its ten year's seniority.

'Don't know about you, Mr Varley, but I'm feeling fine!' A slight pause.

'Then we'll be seeing you shortly?'

'We-ell,' Lyle went quickly sly, 'the actual circumstances haven't changed. My wife's little trouble—'

Varley's tone dropped: 'Look Lyle, don't go into it now. We're an understanding bank. Take it easy. When you're my age you'll see things in perspective. There's more time to pass—but oddly enough, it passes quicker. I don't know why. Perhaps being set in our ways, it's lack of choice. Young people are always choosing between one or two, even three things. Choice extends time. Look at it that way.'

'My heavens, you're right. I've no choice. My wife Maureen—'

'Maureen? Zoë, I thought?'

'My wife's sister Maureen—'

'Let it go, old man.'

'Well, your advice has really been most helpful, Mr Varley. Let's see, it's Wednesday today—I'll certainly be in on Monday.'

'Look after yourself then.'

He put the receiver down deft between finger and thumb, exact as a conjuring trick, and whistled out his breath like a schoolboy. My God, but I skated that one close! Clever as tell your Mum! But funny how that Maureen had crept in—very psychological indeed. He wagged his head knowingly. Now isn't it funny, he thought, that I haven't given a thought to that dear girl all day? Tom's age. A bit more perhaps.

Tenderness rose at the memory of her, and with it the well-being of being wanted—but a big shadow came as well, vague presences of a pink tea-urn like a hat, tongues, flies—and he quickly reached for the telephone and asked for old Peter's number in Banff, all the way up in Scotland. My, but he'd got round old Varley double-quick! Warmth spread in him. But really, Varley was very good, people are nice. Maureen was nice. Old Peter'll be nice.

And when old Peter came through, he was nice. Offered his spare room immediately. Any time. Next week? Monday? Why, certainly! Do with a bang at a bird or two, get my own back on that blasted robin. What robin? And Lyle told old Peter about his robin, while old Peter laughed and told him all about his arthritis. Zoë faded away. He arranged to travel to Banff overnight on Sunday.

He went and got himself a long whisky, carefully very weak. In mid-afternoon—naughty! He felt remarkably free. Stop corseting your mind with habit, he told himself, think straight and true and you'll outwit them all. He looked down and saw Mange had come squirming up at the tinkle of glass. It was a custom the dog had adopted ever since they had happened to feed him from an old glass bowl that was hanging about. Now whenever he heard glass, he was there. An alcoholic, they had all laughed. Now he tried to sit up and beg, but, too fat, failed, and just went on going up and down like an old crane. Lyle looked at him and thought, Messing about with dogs in garages, I must be off my nut, why not burn the whole blasted house down?

Why not indeed? Her trunks would go up with it, the disorder would delay, they might go away together! And the insurance money too! The past wiped out in a single gesture! No tell-tale petrol cans, start it naturally from the kitchen, arrange draughts to take it through the house and up. No smelly oils, get some plastic stuff, plastic flares up to nothing, tons of white plastic straw left over from Christmas in the box-cupboard—he stopped slyly, no, it's too big a job. But then: Why ever not? It would be a simple decision.

He reached, reached hard at decision, and very nearly got it—as at critical points phlegmatic men at last rise to decisions and thereafter stick the harder to them—when the telephone rang. He crossed to it quick with excitement.

It was Jill.

'What exactly do you mean by insulting Jack?'

'What's that?'

'You called him a crass idiot.'

'*I* did?'

'He says he hasn't a friend left in the whole world. I think it's absolutely rotten of you!'

Her voice, in spite of the words, went up and down, moulded in the music of the usual coo. Lyle listened to it with expert interest. My God, that's it—women are conditioned by children, cooing to children, getting the habit, cooing to each other, *it's fundamental*, women's mags covered with a coo of exclamation marks, womanly shrieks of laughter to affirm whatever is said, women broadcasters cooing cosily down, all other radio announcers getting the bug with half their audiences women, my God I'd give my best striped bags to hear a Woman Cooing Judge. . . .

While Jill cooed on passionately about poor Jack.

'Brilliant!' he said aloud about himself.

'Brilliant what?' she said sharp as a real judge.

'Brilliant tactics of mine. Well known that if you slosh a husband sloshing his wife she sloshes you.'

Glory be to God, what skating! He danced a little dance on his toes, quiet soft-shoe shuffle.

'You can keep your brilliance to yourself. You've done quite enough already. *You* started all this. Now I can't get a word through to the poor man, he's down.'

'Just go on talking to him. Never let up, darling. What's that air in your big tits for?'

'I beg your pardon?'

'Come up and slosh *me* some time,' he cooed, 'and bring back my Zoë to me . . .' he sang. Then as suddenly stopped. For this was indeed a diabolically good clever idea. Now—quickly—how to get sloshed in front of Zoë? Tell Jill she looks like a great fat suet-bag. Tell her such redolent mounds of roly-poly would send a whole starving gaggle of choristers raving mad! Tell her the bags beneath her eyes are the talk of porters from Waterloo to Penge West! 'And your big fat arse, Mrs B? The old two-decker? It would look far, far better for a tail. But careful you don't get the window-boxers after you with their spades and brushes, Mrs B—it's that shire-horse stance, that big flaired skirt, gives them the idea. . . .'

He mouthed the words like a man in a mac and a phone-box, breathing them heavy, trying them quietly over. And meanwhile Jill was cooing on:

'. . . *you've* had children, you don't understand, do you now, no—you—do—not—'

No, it would frighten her off, he thought. Better try something else.

'Jack,' he said suddenly over the flow, 'told me a thing or two about you Monday night.'

'What's that? What's Jack been saying?'

'I wouldn't like to say over the telephone.'

Her voice became cautious: 'What do you mean?'

'Not for the ears of innocent operators. Really, Susan—I'd never have thought a woman of *your* kind could ever have—still, we live and learn.'

'It's lies! I'm coming over and you'll jolly well *have* to tell me.'

'Why not? It'll be all over town soon, the way your gaffer's holding forth. A disappointed man.'

'Disappointed my Aunt Dolly. Will you be there in a hour?'

He danced for silent joy. She'd risen like a thorough-bred. But better make sure Zoë'd be in. 'No go. Make it eight this evening. Love to be of help.' And then he could resist it no longer: 'By the way, Susie, how's that sweet little rosebud mouth of yours?'

'What?'

'Little old pursed up kisser like a monkey's fundament right there under your nose?'

'What? I didn't get it. What*ever* has Jack been saying? I'll be round. Goodbye.'

And when she comes, he said to the marvellous tele-phone as it went down to rest, I'll simply stand here and smile, 'Madam, you remind me of last year's Siamese and your hemline's out by a six-month. How do you get the New-Town Poodle Look? Oh, you passé old bag—acquired in Majorca two seasons past by the size of you.'

And wham goes the real bag about my ears just as Zoë steps into the room (I'll have sent her out to the kitchen for ice, know that timing to a tee)—and then see the sparks fly! It's a natural.

Afterwards, my bleeding head cupped on Zoë's lap, my darling'll softly say: 'And all the time I never knew! It takes a bit of a war to open your eyes, your heart, too—doesn't it?' 'British to your gippo core,' I'll give her and we'll go muddling through till the cows come home. All this after taking Mrs Big-Arse Buckett off to hospital, of course.

He suddenly retched. He went into the lavatory and was sick. Excitement, he said to himself. And came out feeling clear and twice as nimble. He looked at the telephone and felt that here he was at the hub of a great web, power pouring in at him, forgetting that he had made two of the calls.

Now—what now? And what the devil had he been thinking of before the phone rang? It had been good, very good—whatever it was. Memory awful. It'll come back later. Meanwhile keep a hold, don't get too big. Every card a gimlet from now on.

He went into the sitting-room to pour himself another whisky. But found—by mistake? on purpose?—the lime-juice bottle in his hand. Funny. Still, better that way. Play it safe, safe and cool. But lime-juice? Where lime-juice recently? Pub, widows . . . a pink mullet-face swam up and flicked a quick little black tongue into his mouth.

He shuddered away—but then for a moment stood

back still thinking he was on the edge, the very edge of something of the deepest importance of all.

Widening his eyes to clear his mind, he looked out and up to the sky. But there saw a wide cumulous cloud gathering slate-grey and fleecy with thunder, doom to the good weather massing across the whole sky, mounting and now dowsing the last hope of remembering whatever revelation his troubled mind so nearly offered.

He looked again at the monster rolling motionless within itself, yet also moving up and over towards the house, its great depth of ink raying out long silver shafts of hidden sunlight like the Saviour's crown. Marvellous! And he loved a storm. How long before it should come? Now a deadly pause, death of bird-song, not a leaf rustling—he was back in summer, critical cricket-days, will rain stop play? Or better, those momentous matches when not only are they batting an eleventh-man stand to edge up the last few runs to win, but batting against the storm, too, sloshing with sudden carefree grace inspired sixes as the first heavy black raindrops spatter a hat here, a hand there.

The light dimmed, all went ominously violet, then dark as doom: he shut the French windows, and hurried to the front of the house, where he knew from the sky-scape a better view might be had. And was startled to see through the hall-window Eric Powsey strolling by, in fact halting and peering into the house.

Summing up the chances of a let, he thought. Damned jackal. He took up a macintosh, caped it, and strode out. He was mouthing nastily, it made his mouth thin and his breath look bad.

'Afternoon. Want anything?'

Powsey looked quickly to right and left. He said, 'No,' then stared straight into Lyle's eyes with a pained, shameful look. 'Yes,' he whispered. And pointed up-stairs: 'The Missus in?'

'Yes,' Lyle said. 'And so am I and you can keep your thieving hands off this house for good and all.'

He looked at Powsey more closely. 'The Missus? Eric! You're not hanging around after—'

'No, no—it's you I wanted to speak to.'

He broke off and looked round at the trees. He tried to smile. 'It makes you think of all the green things, a time like this, doesn't it? All so thirsty. All knowing it's coming. They're like animals. That'll be the day—when mankind discovers all these green things feel pain. As I'm sure they do. *That'll* be the day.'

Lyle looked at him curiously. 'Hitting each ear of corn with a humane killer? Painlessly gassing the gladioli—'

He stopped, amazed. A single big tear had welled out of Powsey's eye and now rolled jerkily down his cheek.

Surely the man could not feel that deeply about it? He took a quick breath of relief as Eric's tongue came out and caught the tear at the last moment. Then a sudden sob, just as the first big drops began to fall: 'I've got to speak to you, I've got to. It was you I spoke to once, I can't bear it, I can't bear any of it any more.'

Another big tear rolled down from one eye, then another, as the raindrops quickened. 'I've been living a lie,' he sobbed, and his voice gulped high, his jaw fought against it, 'I can't stand her doing it, I pretended I could, I thought it was p—p—progressive but it's not, it's low and beastly and I can't bear it, my own Patsy doing it there with other men—'

'Here, hold on!'

'I won't hold on!' Powsey shouted, his face now streaming with tears. 'I've been holding on long enough! This morning I'd had it, I burst—we had words—I h-hit her with my umbrella—and she laughed, she just *laughed* at me, and went off as usual. What am I to do? What?'

Lyle felt excited but kept himself cold. He watched Powsey closely. Here was a man breaking up. And now you didn't know which was tears and which was rain, his face was streaming like a window.

'You're speaking to a man in much the same boat, you know,' he said carefully.

Powsey's face howled with rage: 'It's your bloody boat's set me off,' he yelled. 'You got me worried she'll go. Yours is going but you've got a faithful wife! Faithful! Not a bloody whore like mine what's staying. Nothing's wrong for you, nothing's wrong—things'll all right themselves. You can talk! I *hate* you.'

'D'you really think so? Here, have my mac,' Lyle said.

'Do I *think* so?' Powsey cried.

'That things'll right themselves between Zoë and me?' Carefully draping the macintosh round Powsey's shoulders.

Powsey stamped his feet with rage, knees high up and down, yelling: 'There you go, thinking about your blinking self, only about your blinking self, and what have I got to think about?'

He stopped, and suddenly giggled to himself. His glasses glinted, he whispered confidentially; 'I've got to think of a big long rubber-dubber duck-wuck . . .' Stopped again, and stood there with his teeth out foolishly grinning.

Saliva and rain drooled down over blubbery lips. 'I used to let her tell me all about it, I liked to listen, I *had* to hear, you see, but I liked it and I loathed it, I listened and it's all my fault, *all my fault*,' he shouted and beat his wet chest, 'like those filthy mags I used to look at, I had to,

I hadn't a girl, it wasn't so wrong, was it?' he asked humbly.

His eyes gazed wide as a child's in their odd three-cornered appeal, the ends of his eyebrows rose agonized for help.

'Of course not,' Lyle murmured patting his shoulder.

'I couldn't do anything else, could I? I never had no way with girls.'

'Of course not.'

'And then *she* comes and gets hold of me. My first. Easy for her, anyone would do for her. Even me.'

Lyle was walking him gently away from the house.

'Ah—but why did she marry you, then?' he asked.

'She was broke. She played straight with me for a year. But now—' his voice wailed high again—'now she won't let me touch her. She's turned herself into one of those bloody magazines. I just have to lie there and listen to her tell me all about what the other fellers do to her. I'm back where I started.'

'There now, now you go straight along to that pub and have a good stiff drink. You'll feel better among other people. You'll pull yourself together.'

'Do you think so? Do you really?' He spoke like a child, led, pushed.

'And thank you for cheering me up about my own little affair,' Lyle said amiably.

'I'll kill her,' Powsey said under his breath.

'Keep the mac.'

'I broke my brolly. I hit her with it. I love her so.'

'Now off you go and don't do anything silly. Pull yourself together, man. Action's what you've got to take. Stand up to her—tell her who's the boss, make it dead clear and no nonsense . . .off you go!'

He gave Powsey's back the gentlest push. It was like

easing off an empty row-boat, that gentle push seemed to send his slow footsteps drifting all the way down the street.

Lyle watched him for a bit and turned back.

'Not letting them do that to me,' he muttered, 'oh dear no.' And said it over and over again as he went upstairs. He was drenched. It would have been difficult to say whether the wet or words were chattering his teeth with such obsessed excitement. Poor fellow, he thought, and went in to turn on a hot bath. He thought of Powsey's words, 'I'll kill her.' Hope he doesn't do anything desperate. Suppose I ought to have asked him in—but then, I've got things to do.

He had nothing to do. He lay in the bath thinking. The things people do, he thought up at the ceiling, behind what looks a dull old terraced life of houses—that mouse of a woman, face like a shopping-bag, and him pounding round all day letting leaseholds. And showing people up to the bedrooms—'the bed should fit nicely here, side to the light'—and seeing his Missus in the bed thrashing about with an electrical worker.

What was that awful case about a door-to-door salesman? Young fellow, sound as a bell, married, kids, sold kitchen oddments, including those red rubber what-d'you-call'ems they stick on taps to jet the water. But never showed one of these to the housewife. Waited for her to ask what they were like. Got coy. Simpered. 'Well really they're just like this, Madam,' and exposed himself.

It takes all sorts, he thought. Perhaps Eric *would* do her in? What with? Pound her to pulp with a SOLD board —Henbole, Gutteridge, Powsey and Powsey, SOLD? There must come a breaking point. Pretty odd behaviour this afternoon, come to think of it.

He looked down from the ceiling and saw a big brown boat sinking upended over by the taps. Toy boat? Tom? But it was one of his own shoes . . . he had got into the bath fully dressed! Well, well, well-a-day, he laughed. Must have got pretty wet out there.

He played about for a little while, flapping his sleeves and watching the long submerged trousers—then thought: What if I tried it on Zoë? Stay here and pop my head under when she comes in? Suicide! Might pull her up. We'd have a laugh afterwards—but it might plant the idea? Tomorrow I could seriously pretend I intend doing myself in—it would be a picture in her mind?

No, we've got to be cleverer than that. He got out of the bath and undressed. What the hell to do with the clothes? He took them out and hung them to drip over the landing banisters. Fits in nicely, he thought—poor fellow's helpless, can't look after himself, pathetic. He chuckled as he thought of the line he had already planted with his smeared, buttonless suits.

Slowly he dressed. The rain hammered harder on the window. A low grey cloud centre was passing. Lightning started. A violet thundercrack rocked the air close overhead. The house seemed to crouch, gathering into itself like an animal. It became full of little sounds, creakings, drips. Small pockets of silence held their breath. Everything inside waited while everything outside moved. Then the cloud burst, played its booming game of blind man's buff, and lightning again blinked an enormous eye. The tops of trees thrashed about like the heads of feathered dancers. Inside, among darkly smiling mirrors, Lyle quietly dressed.

Later he went downstairs, had a look round. He went from room to room like an officer inspecting the ship—everything in order, he nodded to himself. He still felt steely strong, calmly excited. His head was full of little plans: Lipstick, buttons, Jill coming to assault him. He was drawn to the kitchen, but again could not remember why. Puzzled, he put a potato into a saucepan, lit the gas and left it. The potato began to char, making a big burning smell that filled the kitchen and smoked out into the hall. Curious, he thought—anyway, it fits in with male incompetence, big pathos. He turned the gas off.

He was upstairs when Zoë came in. 'Let her settle in for a bit.' Sounds of umbrella shaking, clicking heels heavier as she came upstairs and went into her bedroom. After five minutes he went in. She was sitting on the bed reading the letter from Tom.

'Hello.'

'Letter from Tom. Seems to be all right. Silly about the girl.'

'Now, Mother!'

'He's far too young. Lucky she's in the wrong place.'

He took out his handkerchief and carefully wiped his mouth. He laughed:

'Better there than here in London. Pretty hot stuff here these days.'

'Tony! What's all that blood?'

He looked at her coldly. Damned fool woman. 'What blood?' he said.

'On your—why, it's lipstick!'

'Lipstick?'

Now very casually; 'Oh, perhaps something to do with last night. Quite a party.'

She got up and took the handkerchief from him. He looked down at it as she opened it out. It was like a bloodbath. The end of the lipstick had broken off. 'But that's *mine*!' she said. 'I wondered how it got messed up.'

She flicked the handkerchief back at him, smiling to herself, sparing him.

'So you're dressing yourself up in drag now?' she only said. 'And I never suspected.'

But his mind flashed quick:

'I'll soon have to,' he said. 'Hardly a suit to my back.' He hurried out and came back with the buttonless jackets and smeared trousers. 'Look at these,' he said, putting on a forlorn look.

'Oh God,' she said, taking them. 'And what the hell are those wet things doing dripping all over the banisters?'

'I got drenched.' He shivered. 'Think I've caught a chill.'

She was looking at the suits. Suddenly she bent down to sniff them.

'My Lapège lotion,' she said. She looked quickly at the jackets. 'And that amount of buttons doesn't come off all at once.'

She turned and looked at him steadily. 'You're forgetting to shiver,' she said and handed him back the suits. 'You can send all this cleverly arranged nonsense to the cleaners. And another thing, try not to burn the house down with unpeeled potatoes. You're well known to be a careful man about the house. It doesn't suit you.'

A big smile lit his face. Thank you, Zoë! Burn the house down! He had quite forgotten. He washed out the smile and said lamely: 'I'm sorry. I'm a bit upset.'

She looked at him closely: 'You do look a bit odd.'

'Odd? How?' Preposterous.

'I don't know. Something—about the eyes.'

'Eyes?'

'And come to think of it—what on earth have you been saying to Jill? I had the hell of a job stopping her coming round here.'

'You *stopped* her coming?'

'Why not?'

'Oh—nothing.'

'You haven't any news for her, have you?'

'No.'

'Well. She thought you had.'

He took his suits back to his room and sat down. Bloody woman, he thought, have to go more carefully. He sat and jingled the change in his pocket and thought. His brain felt as if it were wildly planning, though no plans came. Outside, the rain fell steadily.

She burst into his room.

'Come in here!' she shouted.

He saw her face set and fierce with anger. From his sitting position she looked suddenly huge, her hair half-brushed shooting out wild.

'Now it's you that looks very, very odd,' he said slyly. 'What's up?'

'Just you come in here!' she said quietly.

He followed her into the bedroom. She walked high on her heels, arms swinging, hair massed and sprouting everywhere, snaky.

'Look at that!' she shouted.

On the bed was the dress he had slashed.

She pointed to a chair.

'Sit down,' she shouted.

'Don't shout,' he said.

He watched her carefully. It was very interesting.

'I can just about stand all your ridiculous play-acting, but this kind of thing I can't! It's loutish.

215

'Now, my little psychopath, you'd better listen to *me*. You've asked for it the hard way and you're going to get it. You wanted to know why I'm leaving you and I'm going to tell you and it's going to hurt you a lot more than it hurts me.'

He sat up keen. At last he'd got her to it! At last there was going to be something to bite on, something definite to fight! And like a marshal in the field measuring up a worthy opponent, he stared at her with admiration.

From his chair, looking up at her, she looked again taller than usual, like a figure seen through magnifying glasses. Fury invested her broad-shouldered slim figure with the plinthed presence of a moving statue, yet she hardly moved, she stood with arms hung straight down like a singer reserving all force for chest and throat and mouth. Her pale plain dress and brownish skin cut clean against the patterned chintzes and dark wallpaper behind, her hair was still half-fanning out in coils. A real Medusa glittering those dark eyes all over him, he thought. She needs a lightning flash or two.

But the storm had passed, only the rain fell hard and dull and drumming outside. She went on:

'I haven't told you before because I didn't want to be insolent. I stupidly thought I could manage this without hurting you too much. And I stupidly hung about here instead of getting clear away, as I see I should have done.

'You ask your big Why. Well—phrases like "I've fallen out of love with you" hardly suit our time of life. The truth is I've fallen out of any interest in you whatsoever.

'To me you're nothing, absolutely nothing.

'I don't hate you, I don't even dislike you. I just don't feel anything about you. And who in God's reasonable name wants to go on living side by side with a nothing? It's no company.

'I'm lonely with you.

'It takes you to make me lonely. When I'm alone, I'm not lonely. But when you're about the house there still seems to be some slight and messy thread which spoils the solitude one might expect if you were really nothing, just air. A word or two between us, a need to eat together or answer a telephone for you or something, trivial matters, but enough to spoil the free air, like sharing a house with some meaningless janitor, who nevertheless has a human right to some sort of consideration.

'I know that somewhere on paper you're a fairly decent kind of man. And that you earn goodish money and have probably been a goodish kind of husband. And that we've brought up a child together. I know we've had our past—but it feels no more now to me than a book of old photographs, facts recorded but quite inconceivable, as if two other persons were involved. There's no identification. No, there's this much identification! Without you I might grow to respect and love that past, wishfulfil it into a pleasant dream. But with you about? Oh no.'

She strode over to the window and looked out through silver rain running down the black glass. He sat quite still and looked round at the coloured trunk-labels bright against faded carpet, battered baggage: at old streaks of red on the white skirting board marked by an idiotic red-painted brush years ago: at the ring-marks on a polished table top, at the fuzz of dullness where salts-bubbles had danced out of glass after glass after glass—was there nothing he could say to her? His calm was collapsing. He was uneasy because this was not like her usual rowing, she was not repeating herself, she was not slamming out of the room only to burst in again. It was like looking at a loved one acting a part incompatible with her true nature.

He broke the silence, unsurely: 'Is there—is there nothing . . . ?'

She turned round and started again, vehement as before as if she had been boiling up whatever poison was inside her.

'Nothing? Do you know what I mean by nothing? I mean among much else that—when you come into the room I don't flinch. When you leave a room, I don't sigh with relief. You don't even irritate me any more!

'Once there were things which used to grate. At least they made you into something, you only mind about those things when you care for somebody. Your greenfly fingers, green under your nails—I don't give a damn now. Your old disastrous way of trying to appear unbored when you're listening to what bores you, and looking twice as bored, with your eyes popping like a doll's with galloping thyroid—I can remember it driving me mad, but now, now nothing, I couldn't feel a thing . . .

'Of course, if ever you lie or boast, if you behave in any obviously shoddy way, I'm momentarily upset, just as if anybody had done so . . . but it passes very quickly . . . it's the lie, the action that's upsetting, not the fact that you're the one . . . I don't even feel like opening my mouth at you—and you'll admit that's pretty far gone for a woman. . . .

'Even now I'm raising my voice not against you but against a situation, I'm spitting at an ugly unkind situation, I'm shouting to make myself clear, clear, *clear*, and my way out from here *clear*!

'Everyone wants a motive for everything. For this, I can't find one. I don't know why it's happened. Perhaps it's the erosion of too many small rows—though one hears that these should be compensated by so many little bouts of extra love? Maybe I'm not good enough to bear what's supposed to be Life with all its little Crosses everyone's so intent on facing. Maybe its something deeper I don't even know about. But what I do know is that I find it absurd to sit about with a nothing, cooking for a nothing, talking to a nothing and occasionally sharing a nothing's bed.

'Life's too short. There must be *something* more to it. And I suspect I'm pretty ordinary in thinking this. It's the reason why people provide the kind of reason you're looking for—like taking to the bottle or somebody else's bed. Well—not me, I'm nipping it in its overblown bud.

'My God, I need to take action! About the only active thing you do to me is make me dislike myself. For having to talk like this—but generally for failing: for not being able to manufacture something out of life with you—we're back at those grimfaced pat-on-the-back Crosses—as other people are supposed to grin and make do. For not being able to suck some kind of human sustenance out of you.

'I know this is selfish. I know that I'm supposed to bear the responsibility of two people's lives, not only my own. But if my own goes dead, where's the two?

'So I'm taking the jump.

'I'm thirty-eight. Attractive enough still. Anything can happen. Though I'm not after much happening just yet—this isn't one of those see-the-world-before-you-die rushes of blood to the head, and I haven't any particular man in view. Later I expect so, absurd not to. But just now it's a little peace and change I want and I think it's even safe to tell you what I'm going to do.

'You'll laugh. I'm going to do what is certainly not unusual for a woman on her pensioned uppers to do, I'm going to run a tea-shop in a small country town. So there you are. The absolute hideout. You could spend a lifetime searching for me through the copper pans and spinning wheels of olde England, the endless poker-work forest....

'That's it. And above all, it's not your fault. It's nothing to do with you.'

'You've done nothing. You can do nothing. You are nothing.

'Nothing. Nothing. *Nothing.*'

She stopped. She stood there only breathing hard.

He was still sitting forward in the chair, but now with his head in his hands, his body sunk, it seemed the consequential movement, both of body and mind, to go forward from the chair on to his knees. He swayed there a moment, then just let himself sprawl forward. It was no abasement, more an absolute weariness, his keyed-up nerves had let him down and a disgust at it all laid him on the floor.

For a minute perhaps he lay covering his eyes. Once he made a little moaning sound. He was not expecting her to pity him, he felt perhaps she was still up there holding herself in against saying some consoling word, but now he scarcely cared.

And then, amazingly, he felt a kiss on the side of his cheek. A wetness of lips, she had kissed him, she was sorry. . . .

'Get up,' her voice came coldly from far above, 'you're upsetting the dog.'

He got up slowly. Mange backed away. 'Quite right,' he said, 'quite right'.

Then, standing slack, muttered aloud to himself:

'And I'm supposed to be a man. And I can do nothing.'

Suddenly she broke into tears. 'Oh, I'm sorry, I'm sorry,' she sobbed. 'Oh, I didn't mean to speak like that. Only I had to make myself clear, I had to—'

She was shaking her head, holding it as if it might fall off, as she ran from the room.

GOODBYE

He heard the bathroom door slam. She had, of course, been acting, he thought. She had made herself say all that. She'd been repressing too much, as a woman she had to speak sometime, and what she had said must have been a truth, if not all the truth.

He saw the big bottle of many-coloured sleeping-pills in the one still-open trunk. He picked it up, and took it to his room—then went downstairs to get himself a drink.

He stood in the empty sitting-room sipping whisky. The curtains were not drawn, he looked at the darkly streaming panes of glass and listened to the rain. It all looked cold and hopeless, a room out of use. 'She's upstairs crying in the bathroom,' he said aloud, and suddenly welled with love for her. 'Poor girl, poor little girl.'

He looked round the room—there was nothing to do. Nothing to do about anything. It was only half-past eight. He took his glass of whisky upstairs, shook three of the pills out of the bottle, put the bottle away in his bedside cupboard, undressed, got into bed.

He took the pills, washed them down with the last of his drink. 'If I'm a nothing, I might as well drop off into good deep nothingness.' Within a quarter hour he was deep and sound asleep.

VIII

H^E woke up late and went downstairs in his dressing-
gown still half asleep, stumbling as if on some kind
of night errand. Coffee from Zoë's breakfast was cold:
he filled a cup and drank it to clean his mouth for a cigarette.

He lit the wrong end of the cigarette, the filter burned
with a papery smell: like the smell of newspaper and fire-
wood in a grate, the housemaid smell of early mornings
long ago—funny that Tom, so much of his flesh but so
little of his experience, would never know that particular
smell and all it evoked. Would Tom's elderly days be
comforted by the remembered whine of a vacuum cleaner,
the perfumed scent of latter-day lavatory purifiers?

He shook his head. Sleepiness muzzed him as grey
and heavy as the sky weighing on the trees outside the
kitchen window. But—he must have been half mad
yesterday? His deep-slept mind dully saw now how
nerved up he must have been: forked tongues flickering,
flies out of flesh, dog, garage and—of course, Zoë's
remarkable outburst? That had been as peculiar, in its
way, as his own behaviour?

Yet on consideration it was all too reasonable—two
people so close had bottled up too much over the past few
days. It must have been particularly difficult, damn her,
for Zoë. A woman needs to talk.

'Hello,' she said. He turned and there she was standing
with a hat on and a string bag in her hand. Going out
again.

'Good morning,' his old wool dressing-gown muffled
at her, 'and goodbye?'

She came to the kitchen and stood facing him, feet together, hands clasped in front, the string bag hanging down like a little sporran; a stance of some humility, of recitation. She looked at him straight, a concern pursing the sides of her eyes, as if she could not quite see him clear or close enough.

'An apology,' she said, 'for last night. I suppose I'd been bottling up too much.'

'You'd had one or two all right,' he said absently. 'Often wondered where you keep the stuff. However, nothing to do with me now, nothing—'

Her face darkened, a cloud of impatience. She controlled it. 'No I don't mean that. I've been bottling—suppressing too many emotions. The whole thing's my fault—obvious—but nevertheless I've just had to be cold. It's not natural, Tony. I said too much last night. And too little—I left out all the good times, Tony.'

'All right. Leave it.'

'I'm off tomorrow. Couldn't we sort of—well, have dinner together tonight? Part friends?'

He looked at her with curiosity. Compassion for him? No. For her own comfort. Wanted it her way all the way.

'The last supper,' he said.

She looked away. 'I suppose I deserve it. But Tony, couldn't we? I mean, it seems rotten after all these years—'

'It is rotten.'

'Well, if you won't, then . . .'

'Look, I can't possibly envisage sitting down at the end of a table with a tie on and passing you a dish of vegetables. But I see what you mean. Why not just let's have a drink or two?'

She could not stop herself: 'Now Tony!'

Then swallowed it.

223

'Yes, all right,' she said. But had to add: 'There'll be some cold food about.'

'As you say.'

'About seven, then?'

'Or half-past, or eight,' he said. 'We know each other well enough?'

She took it again, and turned to go. 'Till later then, Tony. I'll be in about seven.'

When she had gone, he wandered into the hall and once more watched her through the street window, wife walking away into an isolated woman figure. Would I be attracted by that woman? A slight welling of self-pity pushed behind his eyes as he nodded: I would.

He watched closely, looking for mannerisms: but there were none: she walks well, he thought, you could put a pot on her head.

A husband seldom sees his wife dressed up and walking away: nearly never. Perhaps abroad on holiday, in cities: and his mind vaguely wandered back again to their times away together, unreal periods photographed in the mind as moments of greater reality. They had divided Europe not into north or south, nor trans or cisalpine, but either above or below the hygiene belt: above you broke your nails on dwarf lumps of paper-wrapped sugar, below you had a spoon and a bowl of the good granulated stuff. The poorer the country, the more the sugar. Now why was that? The high cost of wrapping little lumps up to be unwrapped? His mind wandered on, he decided to stay in his dressing-gown all day. No point in dressing. And if the bell rang, he would look like an invalid and so could the more easily excuse himself.

The bell rang. Jenk's old man stood there. Pale eyed, grey-white, as if he had stepped from some dark cupboard where he lived among tea-pots, pudding-moulds,

cheese. But of course he had a nice little flat, with a win-
dow-box and a wife.

'Mr Jenks 'as gone off,' the old man said. 'I thought I'd
come to tell you.'

'Gone off?'

'So he won't be building no shed for you. Least, it
don't look like it.'

'Gone off?'

'Gone off up north. Left a note for his missus. She's
in a state all right.'

'You mean he's left his wife flat?'

'Done a bunk.'

Good God up High in Heaven, but this couldn't be
true too? Surely this was a way-out ricochet? But they'd
been talking in the caffs and pubs, Lyle knew, about him
and Zoë . . . and now he does a bunk? To set himself up in
some northern city, Hartlepool, the first step towards
bigamy. No divorcing, no paper and courts and costs for
Jenks. He had the builder's way of never communicating,
never putting pencil to paper, nor pence to telephone . . .
he preferred to 'turn up', very free, Jenks.

But the old man was saying something. His old eyes
were eager, his strong little chin jutted proudly.

'I'd build you a little shed,' he said, 'I'd *like* to. Course
I'm not saying you couldn't get yourself an off-the-peg
Spacemaster, jig-built and that, but I'd put you up a real
quality job, I would honest.'

'But, you know—I'm not sure —'

The old man's eyes appealed, he chewed with his
mouth swallowing disappointment:

'Shame. No lie, I'd have truthfully liked to put you up
a little shed. Still . . .'

Lyle looked up at the grey sky, the shrinking green
leaves. A drift of the first yellow lime-leaves blew down,

showering gold against the green. Where would he be living? In a hotel? But the kind of hotel he could afford, with a shared bathroom full of other people's bits of soap, with discreet water softeners, bowls of sweet peas the colour of bath-salts? Stained oak and whispers? *The management will not be responsible for articles left in the bedroom.*

'All right,' he said to the old man. 'You build it for me. Mind you, I must have a proper estimate first.'

'You mean I can? Really?'

The old man's eyes were sparkling. He took a deep breath. 'I'll make you a proper job. Only timberized wood—rot-resistant cedar. Solid red-wood if you like? Down to your last glazing sprig—I can see a nice green roof down there.'

'I'm afraid not a green—'

'Not a green roof?'

Already the matter had risen from contract to pure creation, no longer an affair for master and man, but for man the masterful artisan. There would be arguments all along over this.

'No green roof,' Lyle said firmly. 'And seeing it's a Victorian house, I'm not sure it wouldn't be best to have chalet eaves, and dark wood.' He thought: I can always grow Russian Vine over the blasted thing.

'Chalet?' the old man said emptily.

'Swiss-style. You know?'

'Oh.' And pursed his lips.

'Go down the garden and have a mooch round,' Lyle said, trying to brighten things. 'Measure up, and we'll talk later. I told Jenks—what?—eight by five? That'll do.'

The old man raised a finger to his capless head. 'Very good, guvnor.'

'I'm sorry, I'm a bit seedy today,' Lyle said, holding

out his dressing-gown skirts. 'Call round Saturday with your figures.'

The old man nodded and grinned happily. Turned away, then turned back. 'I don't know what he done it for. I'd never leave my old Dutch, Lord alive no.'

Lyle smiled. 'But you don't even talk,' he said. 'What's the difference?'

'The company, I'd miss the company,' the old man said and went off round the side to the back garden, small, grey, content.

Lyle thought: Jenks too? After Powsey, Savory, Jack B.? I don't need a leper-bell, I need a bloody fog-horn. And suddenly he hurried out on to the pavement and looked along for Chalcott-Bentinck's motor-car. It was still there. At least one relationship continued un-swayed by this weird—but, alas, so reasonable—infection. But what about Chalcott-Bentinck's future? Probably some appalling development like what Powsey would call 'an integral garage'; the dear one housed in a concrete basement ex-kitchen, no more polishing and the less love.

South-west wind still, warm enough in the day to dawdle around outside in a dressing-gown—he walked back and through into the kitchen and looked at the coffee-pot. Better boil a pot of strong fresh black coffee, get himself properly awake. But then stood just looking at it, and looking out at the withering green and grey like a weary man with a glucose tablet, who knows this will give him immediate energy, but lacks the energy to reach for it.

Trees all around, leaves now about to fall. Year after year they grew again, the tree was renewed. Perhaps next year he would renew himself too? The long sleep of a bad winter first—then new life?

Well, he'd already started to build the future—a new garden shed, eight by five. The thought cheered him— but then he remembered that for all the years since Tom was born he had meant to do just this, construct a quiet place for himself where at weekends or summer evenings he could study or develop photographs or do this and that away from the family din—for there had been mother's helps and a daily woman in those days. And now the family was finally gone, the house was empty— and he was at last getting a shed. Ridiculous! . . . still, he'd have the old man on his side from now on. Benevolence paid off.

Disgusted, he went upstairs and to bed again. Without bothering to draw the curtains across, he fell into a deep sleep and did not wake until the late afternoon.

Before he woke up, he had a good dream. It was a dream of that infrequent kind which kept almost exactly to real life.

He was back with his landslip. The whole event flashed photographically true. One day the lawn outside the French windows, the next day a great earthy hole. And a big crack up the back wall of the house.

At first, horror! Then gradually wonder—as the reason was given, an ancient subterranean water-course. The agent said that once near by, in this area riddled with springs, a lorry had disappeared in the very middle of the road, sunk to its roof.

And then Zoë and he had quietly rejoiced, for this meant an insurance claim and a chance to put the whole place in order—the brickwork had needed re-pointing, the turf was tired. But the dream cut quickly to the next day when they found first that this particular Act of God or Mother Earth was not covered by their policy, and secondly that in the darkness of the fissure in the house wall were concealed timbers growing huge and moonlike fungi, shroud-white flowers alive with death.

Dry rot. Yards and yards of it. Years and years to save to pay off the cost. He saw the fungi expanding hugely, like round white exhibition buildings, and the garden-hole yawning like an immense and vertiginous opencast mine-work.

However—what did not expand, but simply retained its true warmth, was a new closeness which came to Zoë and him. They had to pare down all expenses. They stopped going out, they stopped buying clothes, furniture, anything much. And thus redeemed from the necessities of choice, and from the complication of a desirous life outside the home, and altogether kept from keeping up with anything—they had lived quietly and contentedly and close. Faced with a hurdle which would eventually be overcome, they were like people who pull in their belts during a war, and benefit from it—a time looked back on afterwards with wonder and regret: and they were like people travelling abroad who do not read the newspapers, and realize afterwards that they have really missed nothing: and most of all they were like people involved in the plot of a truly satisfying play or film, where life lives up to itself and effort wins heroically through against all odds. It had been, in retrospect, the happiest time of their lives. Without stating it, for it would then have sounded absurd, they had really known it at the time.

So he woke up feeling happy and exhilarated. The memory of the dream was so strong that realization of real life a few moments later did not depress him: the exhilaration had taken a deep hold, it seemed to be some sort of a proof that life was basically good, or could be so, or even had been so. Also, he was now well slept.

He looked at the time, four o'clock; and went and took a quick freshening bath, dressed himself and went downstairs. He felt athletically active: and on the way down reached up to put a picture straight, but jerked it so hard that it came away off the wall into his hands. At the last moment he saved it from falling, and lowered it to the stair-treads.

He went into the sitting-room and stood there for a few minutes quietening down. Zoë was going tomorrow. Tomorrow Zoë was leaving him. Tonight they were having a last drink together. Tomorrow she'd be gone. He repeated this over and over to himself. Well, he shrugged, so be it. He now felt able to face up to it quite clearly, as if he saw the fact clinically and in calm for the first time: and went over to the drink cupboard to check over the bottles for later on. He stood looking at them for some time. The bottle of lime-juice particularly held his eye.

Of course, he thought, what was patently wrong was that Zoë was going away to an elected new life while life for him held no future at all; as he had proved to himself in the last few days—neither friends nor love, neither acquaintanceship nor sexual pleasure. This was not fair, not fair at all.

It was then, staring at the lime-juice bottle, that once

more a pink mullet's head above a high stiff collar intruded—he saw a raised glass of green lime in his hand, and in the glass the bubbles rising, and pink lips saying that they had buried the wife a twelve-month past. And he had thought: Zoë?

Like a computer spawning up its dark digits, his mind brought up other subdued thoughts—a forgotten moment later on when he had thought: Set the house on fire!

This he had rejected—but another thought had hovered unthought behind . . . now it surfaced concisely and clearly, as if his mind had quietly been preparing it all the time, detail after detail clicking precisely into prearranged place.

It was really very simple. Zoë was going? Then Zoë must be made to be gone.

It was only fair. And he knew exactly how it should be managed. Without questioning it, he went immediately into action. His mind felt very clear after that second long sleep. Action was what he had needed all these days— and now the means of action had been cleverly revealed he followed it up with a kind of racing calm, absolute, dedicated.

He went upstairs and checked on the sleeping-pills. Still there in his bed-cupboard, dozens of them. He took a pair of scissors and went into her bedroom: but here stopped astonished—the trunks and heavier suitcases had all gone! She had returned while he was sleeping and, with somebody's help—moving men, railwaymen?—had had them carried quietly downstairs. He thought of the tip-toeing, the shhh-ing, and this above all seemed disloyal, underhand. He gripped the scissors viciously and went for the telephone wire.

But a second before cutting he stopped himself: Careful now—she might want to telephone someone when she came in, a cut wire might start up anything. And when the time to cut came, surely a rubber glove against shock? Now *careful* . . . two mistakes in the last minute—be calm, above all *calm*. The cleverest moments are the most dangerous: overclear mind, self-congratulation, all defences down, and the glaringly obvious factor overlooked.

In any case, he suddenly thought—people like me don't do this. Not really. He paused—and wondered who then did? Also, people like Zoë don't suddenly leave, do they? But Zoë did.

Interesting, he thought, and went down to the kitchen to fetch a rubber glove; also a pair of frosted green tumblers they used for picnics.

He put these tumblers and the whisky bottle on a tray and went upstairs to stand them on a table in her bedroom. It would be more fitting upstairs. Why? A bed-and-illness association? But anyway it fitted in more with her recent concentration on this room, and it was a picnic, and the picnic glasses fitted too. He hid the glove and the scissors under a chair by the telephone connection.

In his own room he took off his jacket and put on a light dressing-gown, it would help keep the upstairs look. He took a good handful of the pills, fifty or more, and spread them on paper on the little table. 'Well,' he smiled, looking at the little coloured sweets, 'she suggested it.'

He took a razor-blade and set to cutting open the plastic capsules and emptying out the powder. Each pill was like a little coloured chrysalis, he was back in his dissecting schooldays. After a while, he sifted the powder into a pile. Then laughed suddenly—he was cutting the capsules lengthways! Natural for their sausage shape—but difficult, they rolled away. From now on he stabbed them easily in half. Finally he made a chute of the paper and poured the powder into an envelope. He sealed it, placed it in his breast pocket, and screwed the coloured husks up into the newspaper and threw it away.

Now what—a note explaining that they were 'going away together'? Neat. And tidier. But to whom? To-Whom-It-May-Concern? And what about Tom? His brain slowed and clouded: he could find no excuse, there was no fitting Tom into this pattern—he simply told himself not to think about it. Tom was by now mostly a man, toughened in the sailor's hard school of life and as well equipped as anyone to face up to bad news. But he must remember to do something about Mange. Jack Buckett? A likely choice—the way that man got rid of his own dogs. Then . . . then . . . oh hell, somebody.

He was in no mood for objections. He wanted to concentrate, to go over this thing quite clearly in what felt to be a very clear mind. Now Buckett, for instance—and add Savory, Powsey, possibly Jenks—they had all been in some way affected by Zoë's decision to leave him. What had in fact happened? Each one in the past must have imagined the possibility of change and now, given an example so near to hand, had taken action. When he had gone for consolation to each of them, they had been kind enough to listen and sympathize, though in each case they had seemed to lose interest, or be seduced by some more material topic, pretty quickly. This was perhaps natural, since none of them could really have done anything about the matter? But what he had needed was not active help so much as a friendly baffle-board, to which round and round he could have talked. Had they all been women, this would have been easier. However, events had proved that these men had in fact thought a lot more about it than they had shown. Just as men would. And the thinking had worked just as infection does—a period of incubation, and then the active virus; and had acted, like other illnesses and poisons, both benevolently and maliciously according to degree.

And now this matter of suicide . . . this was also known to be infectious, like any other social decadence. From the moment Schuler's Farewell had first played, the idea might have germinated, heavily helped by such as Jack's suggestive 'You won't do anything silly?' after that dinner party. And so on . . . a fly's egg seizing, his conscious mind refusing it but the hot little fellow growing moth-huge in the warm and fertile dark.

And now it was out in the light—and with cool mind must be discussed. He went downstairs and out on to the verandah (must remember to write that note). Am I—he said to the old oracle of a garden—contemplating an act of suicide, or rather engaging upon it, out of cowardice? You might say that the last few days have proved to me that none of my alternative bachelor dreams are now valid: sex was a flop, a night out with the boys saw an early dispersal home, the accustomed pleasures of the old London Town are gone for good. Neutered by age, I'm a misfit. The blow to vanity could be absorbed: but not the much, much larger need for companionship.

Now—can the cancellation of an empty future be called cowardice? Would it not come into the same ambiguous bracket as 'escape'—a mauled word, for escape most often means 'sensible choice', as one might decide not to go out walking in the rain. The rain is, dear God, Reality. But so, dear God, is sitting dry in an armchair. This kind of simple choice goes on every minute of the day. Of course, to take one's life is frowned upon—but that frown is an old legacy of small communities where lives were of herd value. But switch to, say, Japan, or even to most military backgrounds, and one finds it is most honourable, it even retrieves dishonour. The sword in the stomach, the cashiered officer and the lonely revolver. It might further be argued that the taking of one's life is distinctive of man above the animal.

'SUTTEE FOR TWO. Mr Anthony Lyle, eminent banker and messer-about in gardens, took his life, and his wife's along with it . . .' While the balance of his mind was disturbed. Oh no, he was not going to stomach that one. The note must be coroner-proof. No good just writing. My mind feels as clear as a bell. Write instead to be read between the lines. 'Zoë has said she wishes to go, that life is no longer worth living with me. I apprehend that life is also not worth living without her, and opt also to go. It seems only fitting that we who both want to go, should go along together.' Something like that, but better.

It would have been too ironical to announce to the judiciary that the real reason for doing what he had decided could most truly be accounted for by an English obsession with justice. For injured justice was profoundly at the bottom of his mind. Like most other Englishmen of his kind, his whole life had been cast in a mould of justice—from a child with its repetitive summing up of 'fair' or 'unfair', onwards to more adult matters like the national consideration for animals, which largely exists because the animals have no fair chance to speak for themselves. He had also learned a loving adaptability to the queue, he had learned not to push himself forward anywhere, he had learned always to grant everyone a second chance. He had even learned to hang people who had killed others—it was only fair. Exceptions to this —anything to do with business and property: here a blind eye, rather than hypocritical logic, served well.

So it was unfair of Zoë, and unfairness must not be permitted.

He bent down and picked up a snail, two snails together. Calmly, thoughtfully, his fingers pulled them apart. He saw that each snail carried an erect penis, sculpted precisely like the white ivory minature of a human penis: and each snail was also supplied with a vaginal socket, the interlocking was interloving and complete. Dichotomiless snails! Fortunate, slimy, shell-backed hermaphrodites, never a hurry, never a worry—but what? Nothing? The heron's beak perhaps? Well, you could count the herons in this garden on your sawn off little finger.

He placed them down carefully close together under a wet leaf—give and take, give and take, he told them. And stood up and sighed, for the sun had come out, it was at its old trick of gilding everything, eaves, leaves, silk of September spiders' webs, and now a seasonal red house just making its winter appearance through dying leaves at the garden's end.

Doorbell.

He stood listening. Whoever it was rang with persistence. How empty it made the house seem! Scarcely worth answering? But then he hurried to the door—any persistent caller might return later! *Must* be more *careful*. But on the way stopped again. He saw the picture he had left on the stairs. It was the picture with a chip knocked off its gilding. For months he had been going to mend it. For the first time intimately and fully, he saw that there were many things like this that he would never, never now do.

Savory was on the doorstep.

'Sorry—but I heard you in the garden, I thought a really hard ring might bring you in.'

His rough boxer's face had a concerned look, a kindness grizzled the sides of his eyes: 'As a matter of fact I nearly pipped you, but something you were saying—well, it stopped me, and anyway what I wanted to say isn't so suited to garden walls.'

Lyle nodded. He felt sobered and grave. 'So I was speaking out loud again? Ah yes—give and take.' And then added: 'I can't ask you in.'

Savory looked down at his shoes. 'I deserve it,' he said. 'Look, what I wanted to say is I'm very sorry. Sorry about the other day. You were quite right to bawl me out. I've been pretty bloody unfeeling about this whole bad business of yours.'

'It's all right.'

'You get to be in my trade.'

'What?'

'Hard. Cynical's the big word. Most of us are manqué this and that, affluent misfits, misfired writers and painters become copywriters and layoutmen, our ever-dying lives devoted to the distortion of truth. Subliminal lusts, fears, treble-talk . . . there, listen!'

Lyle looked round alert.

'You heard! Talking about myself again! And what I came to do is apologize.'

Lyle smiled.

'Accepted. Did it hurt much?'

'Felt a bit odd,' Savory laughed. 'Odd world, come to think of it—you're a man if you're a hard hitter, yet you can be equally pronounced "man enough to apologize!" Even "man enough not to hit back"—I've heard that one. And old Abe Lincoln with his "man enough to change your mind".'

Lyle stared at him hard. 'What was that?' he said sharply.

'Man enough to change your mind. Lincoln said it.'

'Good God.'

'What's up?'

'Nothing.'

'Oh.'

Savory paused. Then: 'Is there anything practical I can do? How are things?'

'They're arranging themselves. Things are arranging themselves.'

'You look a lot better. More—sanguine, more sure of yourself.'

'Yes. I am.'

'Well now—look—what about the future? Are you staying on? What about the office? Will they let you get away for a bit?'

Lyle smiled. 'Yes. They'll let me get away.'

'So you are going?'

'Yes. I'm going.'

Savory grunted to himself, 'So much the better. Good thing.'

Lyle nodded. This must be what it feels like when your doctor gives you a month more to live. Meeting people all talking of the future—salesmen saying that this or that commodity will *last*, friends discussing the perpetual escape-routes of 'where to live' and 'where to go on holiday'. To all of which you must brightly nod, you must go to the grave with a lie on your tongue.

'Want that old dog looked after?' Savory suddenly said.

Lyle thought, Now that's decent of him. At last.

'I may be away for longer than you think,' he said.

'Liz loves dogs.'

'That's fine then. Very good of you.'

'We're—er, doing it next week. She'll be moving in here. Honeymoon later on.'

'I'll bring him round tomorrow—that is, could you come and get him tomorrow?'

'Sure. After the office?'

'Any time.' And he added with a precision that sickened him: 'Come round the back. I'll leave the back door open.'

'Not too sure of your movements?'

Lyle said firmly: 'Many thanks.'

'What does it eat?'

'Oh—oh—anything. Lights.'

'Tasty old Greek habit? So long!'

'Love to Lincoln—Liz, I mean.'

'Ha.'

The door shut. He breathed alone. The last man he would ever see? No, there'd surely be some tradesmen calling . . . but no again, it was Thursday. Early Closing Day. Well-chosen, good for a hollow laugh.

Suddenly he thought: But I'll never know about Powsey! Never! Perhaps he's shocked her to her senses? Perhaps he's even . . . but I'd better find out. And he hurried to the telephone and dialled the man's number. No answer. It rang and rang. And as it rang, the rhythmic buzz repeated 'never, never, never.' It seemed then appalling again that he would never know. Others would, but not he—and left out there in the cold the feeling came to him that nobody would ever know, *nobody* ever would know. It became a dreadful thought, too dreadful to dwell upon.

He gritted his teeth and went over to the writing bureau. No more loose ends. He took up his pen; 'My wife and I, after long consideration, have decided to die. We both agree we have enjoyed a good life, and we prefer to keep it so, to leave now rather than suffer the decline into old age. We deeply regret any inconvenience caused and would finally point out that this is the result of long and mature thought, and of mutual agreement.'

He looked it over: inserted 'as good a life as ever we expected', substituted for 'point out' the formidable word 'asseverate', made a fair copy of it and signed it Zoë and Anthony Lyle. Zoë's way of writing her name, with its odd vowel combination, he had experimented with unseriously before.

He placed it in an envelope and wrote in firm capital letters To Whom in May Concern. And nodded gravely: 'asseverate' was indeed good.

Then he wrote to Tom, telling him how happy they had been together and Tom mustn't mourn them, only remember the best days. And a more formal letter in the same style to Varley at the bank. A note to Savory thanking him about Mange. He added a word that Lincoln could go and stuff himself. Surges of levity kept bubbling up despite a sort of sad, racing calm.

Was this because he was creatively pleased? The plan was pretty simple, but nevertheless very cleverly watertight. The clouded green picnic glasses, enough barbiturates to see a platoon off the face of the earth, and a dose of whisky into the bargain. Telephone cut. And at some moment during the last aperitif hour, when her back was turned, the bedroom door locked. Could anything be simpler? (Better put Mange out.)

For a while he contemplated every detail. He wondered whether his or her constitution would give first. He was seven years older: but she was a woman, with perhaps a certain weakness after child-bearing? Who knew? He would like to see her go first—if only to be certain the affair was properly concluded, and with perhaps a trifling ironic satisfaction in watching her leave, for it had been her idea in the first place.

He even considered putting the timing forward to half-past six, there would be an aesthetic, almost musical pleasure in co-ordinating the matter with sunset, it should take fifteen to twenty minutes if all went normally —the darkness would close in sweetly, a last lullaby. Do we not always, his excitement told him, suffer a little death at twilight? Now, *careful*. . . . Do we not all, if we can, wash or change or have a drink, do something or other to swap the hairless day for the furry, tarsial night? *Careful*. . . . And later, when we go to sleep—another death? Every night we die. Or at least the deep, dreamless nights after drinking or other opiates—these were death, with the soul let out on a safe lead, the flimsy white thing.

Death itself did not worry him. Death the great rubber-out—but what was there left to rub out? In the last year or two he had begun to accept a falling away of all the old ambitions—like learning a new language, visiting far countries, writing a play, having every girl in the world. I must enter upon Miss Pamela Wong, 15 Nettingale Cottages, Bambers End, Suffolk. I must see Paraguay before I die. It mattered no more. No villa on the Tuscan Coast, no farm on the spur of a wild and breathing heath, no speech at a Fanmaker's Guild Dinner which would go far to changing the world. The great Greek Alexander had never got to Ceylon, why should yeomen-gardener Lyle worry? He didn't. He had no pressing reason to live.

But a second later his spirits dropped seeing the place where the garden shed would be built: where the white-frothed Russian Vine would stretch above that viridian roof, which, chalet-style or not, he felt the old man must ultimately provide. His erstwhile garden—but no erstwhile Lyle to see the brave new shed . . . but of course, the shed would never be built . . . for God's sake keep a hold. . . .

He wandered out into the garden again, and as soon as he was outside thought: The letters! They're lying about open on the bureau. Go back straight in to them!

But as usual the fat green growth of geraniums, tropical in their greed for life, stopped him: those plants were gardener's bliss, they thrived on ill-treatment, they were shockproof until the frost. But who this year would take them in . . .? He hesitated—it was still shortly after five o'clock—and then decided there was time yet to do something about these living creatures, and went for pots and a trowel. Why should brown Mange be the exceptoin?

Slowly and deftly he potted and carried them in to a sunny window-sill—giving them an overdose of water, for how long would it be before anyone retrieved them? He must add about the plants to Savory's note.

Then he glanced for the last time round this leafy place of mostly his personal manufacture, and saw it desolate in a year's time. How long would the estate take to sell? Or how soon could Tom properly attend to things? He wondered whether he had better dash off another letter to his solicitors asking them to arrange some sort of a trust and a quick sale for Tom. It was worth a try—and this reminded him again of those letters still lying in the open. For God's sake . . . Zoë might come in early? And then he wondered—Tom might want to keep the house on? For a few moments he stood sentimentalizing, dreaming of Tom alone in his place (or with that Hong-Kong girl? Both a pleasing and infuriating thought). But if Tom ever came back to take over, then the lawn would sprout saplings and briar, and young men off the streets would crash in chasing each other with bricks through the empty, rotting, deserted house . . . what tramps, what families of pigeons would live here next? It was almost worth taking a nearby room to find out . . . and momentarily he felt the pull of the strongest reason for living, curiosity and not being left out of things.

As he potted the plant he saw approaching his foot a long-legged leather-jacket balancing precariously on the grass-blades. This particular insect had always filled him with vertiginous fear: phobia rather than fear, uncontrollable. But today, although he still moved his foot away from the creature, he watched it calmly, without disgust, moving the foot quite slowly away. He wondered why he was so calm. Because a decision had been made? He took decisions and reasonable risks with other people's money every day—as one takes responsible but impersonal risks in war—but now at last here was a large and private and personal step taken. Self-appreciation boomeranged and he told himself again that this courted danger: the clearer you felt yourself thinking, the more likelihood there was for one perhaps very obvious mistake to be made—the journey fixed, intricately clever schedules arranged, money and introductions prepared, even the weather propitious but the passport out of date.

Then the telephone rang. He glanced at his watch and saw it was now well towards six and ran in with the pot. It was a wrong number.

In the sitting-room he saw with horror those letters still lying about—he added a quick word about the geraniums to Savory but had no time for a solicitor's letter, hurried out to the cloakroom to wash, remembered he had thrown the rough copy of the note into the waste-paper basket, rushed back to retrieve and burn it. He paused for a moment holding match and paper, hearing his breath come heavily, watching it blow the flame sideways, then blew it out and tossed the black rag into the fireplace. Back to the bureau to stow the letters temporarily out of sight.

Back to wash—and remembered soda-water. And ice. Twenty-past six! Everything must be upstairs. Food too —she might decide to go down to the kitchen at some critical moment. It became just like the last few minutes before giving a party, when all is prepared—but just before the guests arrive you notice a dozen things undone. Rush, effort—all smoothness rumpled, clothes in a sweat.

Lyle blundered to and fro unfreezing the ice tray and opening a pot of pâté and sawing bread and fetching soda-water. And got these upstairs just by half-past six. Panting, flurried—he faced his glass again to comb ruffled hair. It was all wrong. The supreme importance was composure.

Then he smelled burning. Glanced quickly at the windows—bonfire smoke? Windows shut! He raced downstairs and into the sitting-room to find it dancing with light, turned magically from a September into a late October room, a merry log fire blazing in the grate. That burnt rag of paper! For a brief swearing second he saw the coming winter, remembered past comforts, firelight shadows playing, ornaments winking, curtains drawn against the dark cold outside: before it came to him that this fire would plainly bring them both downstairs, it was marvellously cheerful.

He rushed into the kitchen for a bucket of water, dowsed the fire and watched the black water tide out over the hearth. Would she notice? The firelight had suggested guests; would she come in bringing guests? Now he plainly saw the Bucketts with her, and glanced up fearfully as a shadow came past the street-side window. A furniture van. She was not so tall as that. Nor, of course, would she bring guests—her mood had been personal and consolatory. But it could change? Indeed it could.

He puffed into the kitchen for a towel to wipe the black water up—twenty-five to seven. The fire was well out, the scrap of burnt paper disappeared for ever. He crossed his fingers. Nothing more must go wrong. Cursing himself to keep calm, he climbed the stairs slowly, and washed. But then for a moment, physically tired by such sudden effort, he felt the whole thing was absurd and not worth doing: in much the same manner as, when rain makes a taxi immediately unobtainable, the whole evening-out becomes a valueless bother.

But now he could at last relax and wait. He wandered into her bedroom to check for the last time on the trays of food and drink. He saw with astonishment that he had automatically brought up the electric toaster! A good sign indeed. As was also the appropriate red glow of a fine sunset gilding with sadness the upper friezes of the bedroom wall, bringing a dying glitter to glass. For a moment, as this light rinsed through the soda siphon, his heart jumped—it looked empty, had he brought up a used one?—but no, it was all right, only an effect of the light.

He listened for the key in the lock, and thought of her coming in and up, and her surprise at the dressing-gown and this upstairs tray . . . he saw a look of suspicion on her face, a knowing appraisal, and felt an old feeling of hate rise in him. So she thought he was going to make a grab at her? Bed her for the last time? . . . and he remembered moments of her coldness in the past, anguish of his own desire unreciprocated and the emasculating self-pity that followed: she had always been, he remembered, the kind of woman who would settle down to sleep 'playing spoons' one way but never the other, she always the outside spoon, as otherwise it might 'lead to trouble'. Though she was not predictably frigid. There were cycles of blatant heat: and this was confusing, they left him wondering who was really the man? And more than this—was man in any case what man is thought to be? Was man's situation not after all that of the vaunted hunter but more like that of a big old bog plant waiting to be picked? The peacock puffs himself and stamps about, not to attack but to be chosen? But then we're perverted, we're unnatural, we're like doggies, we're domestic, we want it all ways at once, we've got *minds*. . . .

He stood for some minutes more lost in thought, watching the red wintry-looking sunset. A burnt-out man and his burnt-out garden, at sunset, he thought, death of the day, death of the year, nothing more, nothing.

'Hello?' her voice called from downstairs, 'Tony?'

He hadn't even heard her come in!

He took a deep breath.

'Upstairs, love! Come on up!'

She brought the street-air in with her—the hat, the parcels—and stopped surprised by the tray.

A big smile. 'Well! That *is* nice! That's just what I dreamed of! My *feet!*' She slopped the parcels down and kicked off her shoes and went to the glass to take off her hat. 'What a *day!*' she said.

All the morning's apologetic mood had gone, it sounded like any other day out—and appallingly this suggested an infinity of similar days to come.

She must have felt this. She turned and said in a concerned voice: 'You've been all right?'

He smiled. 'Perfectly.'

She stared hard at him: 'But Tony, you don't look all right. You don't look well at all. Not at all, Tony.'

'I'm fine. Honest.'

She shook her head. 'Well—I don't know. Really?'

'Really, I'm fine. Look—I'll wait here while you have a wash—and then we'll have a drink? It's a quarter to seven.'

'I know I'm late. Just a moment, then'.

She had already slipped off her dress and put on a house-coat and now, leaving the dress slung on a chair, went out to the bathroom.

He suddenly thought: It's really all rather a pity. After all, she's made up her mind to do something, she's got a right to be free to follow it through.

He shrugged, and picked up the dress and folded it neatly. He put the two shoes together. There must be no disorder. The put-put of a lawnmower sounded far off through the window. A late-season lawnmower, the put-put of the last fishing-boat when all the deck-chairs are stacked, the beach blowing grey and cold.

> *My heart beholds*
> *Our summer island sink away*
> *Into a sea of grey.'*

And he looked out at a red brick house beginning to show through the trees. The dying sunset shadowed it to an ominous deep plum colour, sad as a school at evening prayers.

He turned to the drink table and poured a strong dose of whisky into each of the green glasses. He shook out the powder from his envelope, watched it mist the whisky, then spurted in a splash of soda. He watched it carefully. Very little floated to the top—it looked like a reasonable froth of soda bubbles.

'I heard you!' she shouted from the bathroom.

He started. Caught out, he automatically raised the glass and drank.

'Just coming!' she called cheerfully.

Of course—she'd heard no more than that, the convivial siphon sound! He noticed that the whisky tasted as usual: it was a good strong one.

She came in, freshly made up, and he signalled to her glass. And raised his for the toast.

'What shall it be?' he said. 'The future?'

She looked at him reproachfully, lowered the glass.

'No, Tony,' she shook her head. ' I think the point of this evening should be the past.'

She raised the glass again, and then quietly, looking at him quite humbly, said: 'So I'll say—to the past, the past we've shared together . . . darling . . .'

'The present,' he breathed to himself.

Then said aloud and cheerfully: 'Bottoms up!' and watched her tilt her glass high before he took nearly the whole of his.

She was making a blupping noise and shaking her head.

'That—that was a strong one!' she choked spluttering. And steadied the glass on the dressing-table.

'It's a strong moment,' he smiled.

'Moment?' she said. 'We've got more than a moment—damn, I've messed up all my lipstick, won't be a sec,' and went out to the bathroom again.

He sat down by the drink-tray. Did he feel different, he wondered? Nothing yet—only the normal drink feeling, a pretty good one.

Suddenly he remembered the telephone, got up quickly and quietly, put on the glove and cut the wire. He heard her coming back already, and slipped across to his seat again, staying bent purposefully over the tray as she came in. She had already crossed the room when he picked up the whisky bottle and held it out: 'More?' he casually asked.

She rolled her eyes up: 'Heavens, no! That last one was pretty strong!'

'Here it is when you want,' he said, pouring himself another. And had to add, as those bursts of levity would keep coming up, 'It won't kill you.'

She laughed. 'It darn near did,' and then said, 'Let's talk.'

She bent down to the floor, he supposed making her stockings more comfortable. While her head was down he strolled over to the door and locked it. The key dropped on to the carpet. The idea came to kick it under the door and into the passage, a neat consideration for others; then he thought, hell, and slurred it aside under a chair.

'Yes, let's talk,' he said.

They were comfortable and the drink glowed.

She looked at him carefully.

'Idiotic it sounds,' she said, 'but Tony, I do hate doing this. I know how unfair it is, I suppose I'm feeling rather, I don't know, regretful, sad about this house and all the things we've made here, the old times . . .'

'I know. But Zoë, you mustn't blame yourself. I mean, not only.'

He felt generous. 'You know this new thing of longevity—how there's a fair chance now of living to eighty or ninety . . .'

She laughed: 'I thought we were all dying young. Members of the fatty degeneration.'

'The starchfed new poorgeoisie?'

'Really, Tony!'

'No, I'm serious. There's this widely held theory that the real expectation of living to eighty gives a married couple of thirty to forty a new dangerous age. He or she

can't face the same length of the same life all over again.
Thus today's middle age becomes a springboard for
change. To exist, man has always needed a change-
stimulation . . . one has arrived, one wishes to travel
hopefully again . . . and now at last there's time to satisfy
this need . . . at forty you've got forty more years to
use . . .'

She looked at him astonished. 'But that's just it!' she
said. 'You understand! Oh, Tony!'

'Another drink?'

She shook her head. 'No.'

'So anthropology,' he said, 'now predicts a society of
accepted double-marriages. A young one, a middle aged
one. So no one's really to blame. There's neither hero—'

'—nor heroine.'

'Only Life the villain!' he declaimed loud and dramatic.
He was really rather enjoying this. They were talking
together again. 'I wrote to Tom,' he suddenly said.

'So did I!' she smiled.

'He was a bit of a villain,' Lyle said, 'growing up like
that. Taking over. Starting his dancing days so that ours
felt ended. His youth was about the only thing that made
me feel—' he began to yawn—'old. He was always about
the place. Had to watch my step. Setting an example
makes you one.'

'Jolly good thing too,' she laughed.

He yawned again. 'Now, now . . .' he said, and helped
himself to more whisky.

And suddenly sat bolt upright and looked at her.

She looked radiant. All he had always wanted and all
he was grateful and glad to have had.

'Zoë!' he cried, and it was a cry of dreadful realization.
The whisky was working. He felt marvellously on top
of the world.

He saw suddenly how good life was, he saw how, whatever she did, they would still really be friends!

Later on they would see each other and talk as they were talking now, knitted together in a way far beyond the solubility of simple leavings or stayings. Hope rose wonderfully!

The whisky whirred in his head, he felt terrific, marvellous! And life was marvellous . . . he wanted every minute of it, he'd use it wonderfully in future, he'd be friends with her, and he'd chat with that old man of Jenk's, with Jack and Savory and Powsey . . . what had happened with Powsey now?

Only then did he remember what he had taken. Only now when at last he felt life was really worth living again, when a little friendliness and a lot of alcohol showed him how very, very much he wanted to live. . . .

His stomach plummetted. He got to his feet—swayed, balanced himself: 'Zoë!' he cried, 'we can't . . . can't . . .'

'Can't what?' she smiled. 'What's up, darling?'

Ambulance! Still time? But no telephone—then the door? The key?'

She raised a glass to her lips.

It was a clear glass with yellow whisky in it. He saw it instantly. He saw the other green glass on the dressing-table. He lurched across. It was full. The glass in her hand was a bathroom tooth-mug.

'You didn't drink it!' he yelled. 'Thank God!'

'What on earth?' she laughed. 'Too strong for me—I got a mouthful, bubbled it back. It's all right—I had my own poison in the bathroom.'

'Christ!' he said.

'In the dirty clothes basket,' she giggled, 'I can tell you now. I had a nip as soon as I came in. It's the one safe place a hubby never looks.' She laughed outright.

'I'm pretty high already,' she laughed, 'though the old bottle was watered well enough to swig straight! Oh, Tony,' she laughed, 'it is nice to be able to say that straight to you, honest and—'

'Get an ambulance!'

'Eh?'

He was done. He had to sit down. 'Quick! The telephone's cut. By the door—key under the chair. Yell out into the street—'

'Telephone cut?'

'God's Pity, quick, Zoë! Under the chair—I'll tell you while you—'

She was over by the chair and looking underneath as he spoke again. His words came slower, everything seemed slower. 'I put—pills in drinks—lethal—overdose —get me to hospital—'

Silence.

He forced his head down towards her. 'Aren't you looking?'

She was kneeling upright, doing nothing, staring at him. And then she went down again, but it seemed slowly, making slow scrabbling movements with her hands.

'There's no key here,' she said. 'No key at all,' she said very distinctly.

He levered himself up again. The room was darker, pellets of dark rained in drunkenly, her figure alone stayed bright. Then he was down at her side pawing blindly with his hands.

'It's not there,' he said, 'where is it?'

She said nothing, only watched him and said nothing. She seemed to be holding her breath.

'Window,' he grunted.

He prised himself up on her shoulder, swayed over to the window and slammed up the sash with both hands.

He stood there and bawled out over the silence of the garden: 'Help! Help!'

But his garden, his place of peace and quiet, took the sound without echo.

'Help!'

The word died, soaked in the garden silence.

'Damn,' he sobbed. Yet muzzily he still felt marvellous, full of hope, as he turned back to her.

She was standing in the middle of the room quietly watching him.

He staggered, and fell.

The whole room lurched, and started to recede . . . she was going, going . . .

'Goodbye,' she said, and the room raced fast backwards into a dark funnel, as in a dream, with only her tiny figure standing brilliant at the end.

DATE DUE

1-26			
FEB 14 1968			
OCT 28 1971			
GAYLORD			PRINTED IN U.S.A.